Following a Prayer

Sundar Sarukkai

Following a Prayer

First published by Tranquebar, an imprint of Westland Books, a division of Nasadiya Technologies Private Limited, in 2023

No. 269/2B, First Floor, 'Irai Arul', Vimalraj Street, Nethaji Nagar, Alappakkam Main Road, Maduravoyal, Chennai 600095

Westland, the Westland logo, Tranquebar and the Tranquebar logo are the trademarks of Nasadiya Technologies Private Limited, or its affiliates.

ISBN: 978-93-95767-12-5

10 9 8 7 6 5 4 3 2 1

This is a work of fiction. Names, characters, organisations, places, events and incidents are either products of the author's imagination or used fictitiously

Typeset by Jojy Philip, New Delhi 110 015

Printed at Nutech Print Services-India

TWELVE-YEAR-OLD KALPANA WENT MISSING ON A MONDAY. That morning, in the peak of the monsoon, when the clouds played inside her mind, Kalpana left her home as usual. She was carrying her school bag and a small umbrella. The school was just ten minutes away, and all along the route, as part of her daily routine, she would greet the shopkeeper, wave out to the old mother of the tea-stall owner sitting forever outside the small tea shop, go towards the brown cow at the gate of the priest's house as if to pet its bony forehead. But on that Monday, she was preoccupied and did not perform these daily rituals. Very unlike *our* Kalpana, the old woman at the tea stall said, stressing on the 'our' after she heard that Kalpana had gone missing. That was the only consolation she could give to Kalpana's parents and her grandmother.

Kalpana's grandmother had reached the state where her status had become her name. Everybody referred to her as 'Ajji', and in this sense she was everybody's grandmother. Nobody really remembered her original name, not even her son. She was less than five feet on sunny days, and in the monsoon, she looked even more shrunken. She lived up to her name in that she was a quintessential grandmother, forever in a dialogue with the gods. Everybody agreed that it was she who seemed the most affected by the disappearance of Kalpana.

They only discovered that she was missing when she didn't come back home after school. Her teachers had presumed that she was not well. In the rainy season, students took turns falling sick. One of her classmates, who always ate the midday meal at school, remarked to her friend that it was 'good' that Kalpana had not eaten there that day. They had served yam, which Kalpana hated the most.

Her mother did not worry till after five, when three girls walked by her house. They were still in their school dress and as they passed by the house and saw her mother sitting out on the steps, they asked how Kalpana was. She thought that the girls were asking about the health of Kalpana's little sister, Deeksha, who was feeling unwell and had not gone to school that day. But when the girls said that they were in Kalpana's class and that she had not come to school, the world came crashing down around the mother.

Kalpana's father had gone to buy some groceries. He loved going to the cooperative shop with its smell of kerosene, jute bags and musty grains. Sometimes he would sit on the creaky plastic chair in a corner of the shop and look at everybody who came in with a proprietorial grin. That evening, he was standing and chatting with Bappa about the rains. Their conversation was often a mimicry of the weather reports in the TV news: were the rains ten per cent more this year or twenty per cent less? Neither of them had a clue, but they continued their discussion as if the very monsoon depended on their answer.

Kalpana's mother told one of the girls to call her husband from the shop. The girl ran to the shop and told Kalpana's father that his wife wanted him to go back home immediately. Kalpana's father turned to Bappa and said that he hoped something had not happened to his mother.

THE POLICE STATION WAS SOME DISTANCE AWAY, ON THE main road to the town. The 'station', often pronounced 'tation', was an old house with a new set of mud tiles. It was past six by the time Kalpana's father and Bappa reached the place, but nobody was there. The door was open, but the station was hesitantly dark. The rain had started again and the power had 'gone'. Even the dog that used to swat flies outside the door had vanished. The little hope that the two men had slowly ebbed away in the waiting silence.

Kalpana would have said, 'I told you so.' The policeman's daughter was in her class, and she was worse than her father. She came to school with a fancy bag that had come all the way from Mumbai. She had another girl carry this bag to the classroom. And a woman, the wife of a perennial troublemaker and drunkard in the village, would bring her lunch since, as the policeman's daughter, she would not eat the midday meal at school.

The growing darkness only made their hope fade faster. The rain would not stop, the power would not come, and neither would the policeman. Then they saw a small moped coming towards the station, and on top of it, a constable, wet and uncomfortable in tight-fitting khakis.

THEY WANTED TO SEARCH THE SURROUNDING FORESTS that night. They wondered if Kalpana had taken the path beyond the school and into the dense trees. They wanted to ask if anyone had seen her with a boy or a man, but these words dribbled into silence. They looked at the road that brought buses (and also took them away) from their village, hoping that she would—at any moment—step off one of them. Till eight at night, underneath a fading yellow lamp on the street, along with three sad dogs and two sleepy cows, they waited for the last bus through their village.

It came and went, and the dogs' ears drooped further.

IT WAS ONE OF KALPANA'S CLASSMATES WHO ASKED, IN THAT crowd of grieving parents and embarrassed adults, 'Did she run behind a butterfly like she always does, and lose her way?' And it was the policeman, the next morning, who spoke the words everybody else dreaded to use: Was she kidnapped, or raped, or perhaps even murdered? He looked almost sad as he looked around the room and asked this question.

There was nothing to do in the village except ask these questions. The school declared a holiday the day after. The school principal, a fifty-five-year-old mother of three girls, spoke to the policeman, who wanted to know if there were any boys 'behind' Kalpana. 'She is twelve,' the principal replied. She thought of the policeman's daughter, who would one day have many boys behind her. 'And our boys are not like that,' she stressed, *knowing* that the terrible crimes of sex had not reached her school.

The policeman knew what she was thinking. He wanted to provoke her and make her say what she would not. Brazenly, he said, 'You have heard of so many rape cases all over India, right? Why do you think such a thing will not happen here? What is so special about your girls or boys or men that rape'—he paused, and with an added emphasis continued—'... *rape* will not happen here?' She kept quiet and shook her head.

They stared at each other. She would not yield. Neither she nor any of the women in the village would utter the words 'rape' or 'sex'. When he left, he was quietly satisfied knowing that the virtue of his daughter was safe with this woman.

THE VILLAGERS ORGANISED DIFFERENT SEARCH PARTIES TO walk the many paths into the forest that so densely surrounded them. All of them feared the worst. No adult, let alone a girl, could survive a rainy night in the forest alone. It was scary to watch the rain in these parts, even with the protective cover of the daytime. In a sense, in a terrible sense, the best they could hope for was that the girl was lying dead somewhere in the forest. Anything else was too much for them to even consider.

An inspector from the neighbouring town was supposed to visit the village, but nobody knew when that would happen. Kalpana's mother was devastated, but made coffee for all the visitors to her house. Ajji was the main problem. She would not stop crying and talking to herself, murmuring prayers that almost sounded like shotgun curses.

Two days went by. There was no news of the girl. There was no news of the inspector either. Kalpana's case too would have ended like countless others like hers, but Ajji would not let go so easily.

ON THE MORNING OF THE SECOND DAY OF KALPANA'S disappearance, Ajji went to the bus stop. She was waiting for the first bus, which came at half past six, on its way to the town below the hills. A brown dog and her four pups came and stood next to her. It had rained hard the previous night and now the sky was empty of clouds. Ajji knew that it was just a matter of time before more ferocious clouds rolled in. As the bus stopped, the driver leaned out and asked, 'Ajji, any news?'

She got into the bus. 'Is Siddaiah here?' she asked. Siddaiah was her relative and also the conductor of the bus. He had come to their house on the day Kalpana had gone missing and had walked through the forest looking for her. Siddaiah came towards her from the back of the bus. Ajji held him by his elbow, took him to an empty seat in the back and sat with him.

She told him that she wanted his help. 'Nobody else can find her,' she said. And added, after a pause, 'I can't ask anybody else.' Siddaiah kept quiet, not wanting to tell her that perhaps it was all too late. Ajji sat in silence as the bus made its way down the narrow, winding roads. As a gesture of respect for Kalpana, the driver drove the bus slower than usual. He too had liked the bubbly little girl.

Ajji held on to Siddaiah's arm throughout. She refused to let him get up and give tickets to the few passengers who got into the bus in between. By the time they reached the town, the clouds had gathered and the bus was almost full. The passengers came to Siddaiah to buy their tickets and looked at Ajji with kindness. She held on to him and looked straight ahead, refusing to look anybody in the eye.

When they reached the final stop, Siddaiah tried to tell her that they had arrived and attempted to gently remove her hand. Ajji, without letting go of him, said, 'I am the only one who knows what happened. I am the cause of it all.' A steady stream of silent tears began to flow down her cheeks. They looked like streaks of water on the windows of the bus. Siddaiah looked at her in silence. Both the windows and her face had been so cleaned by countless monsoons that they looked perpetually streaked by lines of dirt.

'Kalpana is not dead. I want you to find her,' she finally said, when the driver came up to them and told them they had to leave.

SIDDAIAH GOT OFF THE BUS AND TOOK AJJI TO A TEA STALL inside the bus stand. He bought her 'buns' – the deep-fried variety – with tea. Ajji ate them with relish. She enjoyed being out of her village and having tea in the bus stand early in the morning. It almost felt like she was a working woman, she told Siddaiah with a pleased smile.

'The problem,' she suddenly said, 'began that morning before Kalpana went to school. My son was getting ready to go to his office and his wife was in the kitchen. I, as usual, was saying my prayers. Do you know any prayers to Devi? No? Siddaiah, you better learn before you get married. Girls these days don't know any prayers, and then what will you do?'

Siddaiah smiled. Most of the girls he saw in the bus seemed to be going from one temple to another. He had no doubt that his wife-to-be would know as many prayers as Ajji did.

'So I was sitting there,' Ajji continued. Murmuring her prayers, when Kalpana, out of sheer boredom, or mischief, decided to bother her. She was ready to go to school, had finished her morning tiffin and was wearing her school uniform. It had started to rain again and she knew that she would enter a classroom with numerous puddles around the feet of the children, like a map of many islands. If she and her friends got bored in class, they could wiggle their toes in those puddles and imagine that they were swimming. She was irritated that Monday had begun so early and had come upon her so fast. She watched Ajji saying her prayers, like she did day after day. Without really thinking, she asked, 'Ajji, what are you going on muttering?'

Ajji ignored her. She had practised this art for long. She was fully aware of what went on in her house and outside while she was in the midst of her prayers. She had the knack of stopping her prayer at a particular word and coming back after a chore to continue it right from that point. Normally, Kalpana would have got bored of trying to irritate Ajji and would have skipped away to school. But that day, she couldn't stop. She said, 'Ajji, tell me, you keep saying prayers the whole day. Why?'

Ajji started muttering louder. She looked at the ceiling, as if banishing Kalpana to the spaces between the wooden rafters and the tightly packed tiles. 'You sit there and watch, you little monkey,' she might have said. 'But destiny,' she might as well have added, 'works mysteriously.' Kalpana would not stop badgering Ajji, and Ajji would not answer.

Then, suddenly, Kalpana asked the questions that perhaps she should not have.

'Ajji, have you ever asked yourself if anybody is listening to your prayers? You keep saying these prayers, but where do they really go? Do you know? Do you?' Kalpana did a skip and a hop as she asked these questions. The rain looked like it was stopping and she was waiting to run away to school.

Ajji was furious. She caught hold of Kalpana, pulled her close and said into her face, 'You want to see where my prayers go? Do you?' Kalpana stared at her, seeing her gentle Ajji transformed. Ajji turned her around and said, 'Then go and follow these words and see where they take you.' She dragged Kalpana to the door and recited a line of her prayer clearly and loudly. She waved her hands dramatically, as if she were waving the words along. 'Now go. Go behind them and see where they go. Go and follow my prayer,' she said, even as the rain stopped and Kalpana stepped outside the house. 'Go and follow it if you can, you little devil,' she said more gently, watching Kalpana walk away in her fading top and bright red ribbons waving goodbye to her.

SIDDAIAH WAS AGHAST. 'WHAT? KALPANA RAN BEHIND A prayer? How can anybody follow a prayer? I am sure you are imagining this, Ajji. Something else must have happened.'

'I don't know what really happened,' Ajji replied. Her enthusiasm for the buns and tea had slowly dissipated. Too many people had filled the bus stand. She wanted to go back to her corner in her house. 'But I know within me that is what Kalpana did. She must have followed my prayer.'

Siddaiah was a young man for whom temples were more like places of entertainment, where one went to see dance and music performances or get some hot food. He said, 'But, Ajji, how can anybody follow a prayer? What is there to follow? I am sorry, Ajji, but this does not make sense. You are not the cause of Kalpana's disappearance.'

Ajji was not to be dissuaded so easily. 'Siddaiah, please listen to me. Please think. If we are going to find Kalpana, we have to ask ourselves what she would have done if she was following my words.'

'Which ones? Your prayer or your command asking her to follow your prayer?'

'See? That is exactly what I mean. If Kalpana could follow my command, why couldn't she follow my prayer?'

Siddaiah walked her out of the tea shop. He had work to do. He put her on a bus back to her village. 'I have called your son and told him you are here,' he said, 'in case he thought you too had gone missing. You should stay home, Ajji. We will do all we can.'

Ajji shrank further. She had confessed in the hope that her confession would lead to action. She clutched Siddaiah's hands and said, 'You are my last hope. You are my final prayer. I want you to find Kalpana. I know that she is running behind my prayer.'

Siddaiah was puzzled at first, then worried. *What an absurd idea! As if words travel somewhere! As if they go from one place to another! As if one can follow them and see where they go!* 'Senility strikes in different ways,' he told the driver later, as the bus wound its way along the many curves on the road. But he couldn't get over the image that Ajji's words had created. Words, like a bus—his bus—moved from one point to another, and following words was perhaps not very different from following the meandering trajectory of the bus over curvy roads.

SIDDAIAH DIDN'T REALLY HAVE TO EXERT HIMSELF. AFTER three days, Kalpana came back home. A bus labouring up the mountains stopped in the village at around seven in the morning. The village was up and running, smoke curling out from houses and dogs lazily spinning around in squares and circles. A young man jumped off the bus and helped a girl get down. He looked around and called out to a woman walking by, 'Is this the girl who went missing?' The woman came close to them and recognised Kalpana. She rushed to her, held her by her shoulders and asked her if she was fine. The young man told the woman to take her home, and with a shrill whistle, he jumped back on the bus. The bus sped off with a loud rattle and a whistle of its own.

Kalpana, in a muddied dress, her hair knotted into spirals of dirt, stared at the street as if it were an unfamiliar land. She heard a cycle bell at the end of the street, and suddenly galvanised, started walking towards her house. A woman washing the ground outside her gate saw her and ran towards her, shouting, 'Kalpana! Kalpana!' Hearing her, more women came running out of their houses. Dogs paused to look. The early morning cows stopped their unending search for truth in tufts of grass and turned their heads towards the little girl walking unsteadily towards her house, a few women following behind. Befittingly, Ajji was outside the house, offering her prayers to the mountains and the rising sun. Before she could grasp what was happening, Kalpana pushed her aside and ran into the house.

On the day of her return, Kalpana just slept. Her mother tried to feed her, but she too was pushed away. Not a word escaped her. Not a tear. People came in and out, whispering outside the windows and inside the rooms. They looked at Kalpana in fear. The local police constable huffed and puffed his way there on his bicycle, but Ajji did not even let him into the house. Father walked around the house saying that he always knew that Kalpana would be back, and Mother seemed to be doing all her chores in a daze.

The only person who was with Kalpana the entire time was her ten-year-old sister, Deeksha. She too was silent, not realising the enormity of what had happened. She first sat with Kalpana, holding her hands constantly. Then, when Kalpana pushed her away, she sat just behind her so that Kalpana would not have to look at her all the time. Deeksha was most delighted when her mother said nothing to her about going to school. She sat, watched and heard every little whisper around her.

All efforts to get Kalpana to tell them what had happened to her were in vain. Kalpana was completely silent, sometimes staring, without blinking, at the adults. She put up with her mother's hugs filled with unvoiced fears and ignored her father.

But it was to Ajji that she was the most rude. She pushed her away everytime Ajji came to hold her. She refused to look at her at all. Ajji realised this soon enough and went back to her space on the floor near the main door of the house, incessantly muttering her prayers.

The night of her return, Kalpana and Deeksha were asked to sleep together in the tiny room that was largely used for storage. Father had cleaned out the slightly rusting iron boxes and bundles of clothes that should have been thrown away long ago. He thought he was building a secure fort around his daughters. 'At least *now*,' his wife might have added.

The school principal came to their house the day after Kalpana's return. The doors were wide open, and suddenly, Ajji saw a bulky figure peeping into the hall. Ajji stared at her and called out to Kalpana's mother, 'Ey, come here.' The mother was flustered on seeing the principal in their house. It had always been so difficult to see her even in the school. And when, by chance, they met on the village streets or in a shop, the principal completely ignored her, just like she ignored the mothers of all her students. She saw herself not just as a teacher, not only as a principal, but more as a government administrator. 'If only I had done my civil service exams,' she often told her husband, using the incomplete thought not as a complaint but more as a way of scolding him.

She sat on the plastic chair under the fan. It was warm and sultry after the rains, but still too early to turn on the fan. She asked loudly, almost as if she were in a classroom, 'Where is she?' Kalpana was lying down inside, her black eyes wide open to every sound. Deeksha crept near the opening of the room but did not want to be seen by the principal. She turned to Kalpana and whispered, 'Principal has come.' Kalpana stared at her, not even blinking once to communicate that she heard her. Deeksha was suddenly overtaken by the fear that Kalpana had gone deaf.

'You can't hear?' she asked, and all she got back was a stare.

'Why don't you bring her out?' the principal asked loudly. Kalpana's father came out of the bathroom after a bath, bare-bodied, a towel wrapped around his waist. Seeing the principal, he bolted back inside and called out to his wife.

The principal turned to Ajji. 'You can't let the girl just sit like that. I can go and get her out!' As she got up, Ajji leaned over, caught her hand and pulled her back into the chair.

Mother came hurriedly back. 'What to do, madam, the girl just wants to sleep. She doesn't open her mouth. Not a single word ... no, not a single sound has come out of her. We don't know if she hears anything we tell her.'

'What she needs is to come back to school. Where is she? Let me go and tell her.' She got up more forcefully this time.

Ajji too pushed herself up to stand. 'No, she is not well, and she is sleeping. We should not disturb her.'

'Did you take her to the doctor?'

'A doctor came and saw her. He could find nothing wrong.' How could the mother bring herself to say what kind of questions the doctor had asked? And what he had asked the mother to check!

'Does she have a fever at least?' At least a fever. The principal needed a description of the illness. 'Dumb due to shock' was not in the Department of Education's approved list of reasons for sick leave.

Mother began to say no, but then Ajji jumped in.

'Fever, definitely. Comes and goes. Sometimes is there and sometimes not there. What to do? Who knows? Not even the doctor.'

'You should take her to the government hospital in Hebri.' *I go there*, she thought of adding, but she didn't think these people were important enough to share that information with. She got up and looked around the sparse hall—three pictures of gods and a short almirah in one corner, and Ajji's rolled-up bedding in another corner.

Mother said, 'Please, don't leave. Have coffee before you go.' The principal refused. But before leaving the house, she asked the questions she had actually come to ask. What did the police say? Did they find out where Kalpana had been for those three days? Had someone harmed her?

Mother trembled. Father came into the room, now neat and presentable, and said firmly, 'Nothing was done to her. Nobody touched a hair on her head. Please tell that to all your teachers and students. The police also agree with me that this is the right thing to do.' He was doing his job firmly, protecting his reputation and that of his family.

The principal smirked at him. She wanted to smile dismissively and walk out of the house with a flourish. *What stories this man was telling! As if nothing was done to Kalpana. Whatever it was, it was not good. Not good at all. You don't lose your voice or go missing or sleep continuously or have a fever for nothing.* She would call the police inspector herself.

At the door, she turned back, the sun filtering through the oily coating on her shiny black hair, and said, 'Send Kalpana to school. As you know, she cannot miss her classes beyond a point. Otherwise we will have to detain her this year.' She looked at the father, who had the temerity to enter into a conversation between three ladies. 'And you, you have to give a leave letter for her absence. We cannot give leave without that.' She paused and told Ajji, 'Government is very strict these days, what to do!'

Yes, what to do, what to do? With children, parents, teachers, and the stray dogs who sleep in the school's kitchen all the time? What to do about all this and so much more?

When she left the house, more light rushed in, as if it had been waiting for her to leave. Deeksha came out of the tiny room and looked out of the open door, into the grey skies and the mountain tops with toothpaste froth on them that morning.

IT WOULD SOON BECOME A HABIT, LIKE ALL HABITS. GET up, stare at the slowly revolving day and go back to sleep. Dinner was done by seven and mostly consisted of leftovers from the day. The lights would be off by 8.45 or 9 p.m. at the latest. In the rainy season, they did not even have to bother turning off the lights. The power would come and go, following the vagaries of lightning and thunder.

The night sounded like dripping dark light on the tiles of their house. The windows were kept open in the hall, but the small storeroom where Kalpana and Deeksha slept had only one small window. A creaky fan was placed on the floor, but the power was often not on.

When Kalpana went missing, Deeksha had not known how to respond. There was a sudden sense of fear that overtook her, and when she saw her mother crying, she too began to cry. It was the palpable fear around her that she felt more than any sense of what it meant to go missing. Those few days went by in a haze of people walking in and out, talking softly and patting her head as they passed her by. She felt like she was another piece of furniture in the house. Sometimes she felt some of them looked at her as if she too was a cause for worry—*will she too run away or go missing?*

She had been happy not to go to school. She enjoyed her classes, but the act of rebellion, of not doing what she was so routinely expected to do, made her joyous. One time, sitting outside her house at ten in the morning, she was mesmerised by the everyday life around her. Going to school meant missing out on all the sounds, on seeing people walking by, and smelling so many different smells, while she sat in a dark, musty classroom. That realisation had suddenly made her want to run towards the mountains.

After Kalpana came back, Deeksha got into another routine. Except now, she was around Kalpana most of the time. Deeksha was surprised that Kalpana did not speak at all—Kalpana, who had been so lively, so talkative all the time, telling her what to do and what not to do!

Deeksha was also very worried. How would Kalpana be able to tell them what had happened to her? How would she be able to go back to school? And most importantly, how could all of them live in this silence? Kalpana's silence had become their silence. Ajji just sat quietly, and her father was anyway out of the house most of the time. Deeksha wanted the laughter and the fights back in the house.

Deeksha had a doubt: what if Kalpana had lost her voice and her mind? One night, she resolved to make her sister talk. Kalpana was tossing on her mat, while Deeksha lay curled a few feet away on her own mat. She had felt sleepy and lain down, but sleep had escaped along with her roving, sideways glances at Kalpana. When Deeksha thought the others in the house had gone to sleep, she sat up on her mat. 'Akka, Akka,' she whispered dramatically, calling out to her sister. Kalpana was turned away from her and showed no sign of having heard her.

'Akka, turn around. I know you are not sleeping.'

Deeksha went closer to Kalpana, leaned over her body and looked at her face. She knew that Kalpana felt her weight. Kalpana's eyes were closed, but her mouth was set in a frown.

'Wake up. I am not going to sleep. Not till you speak to me.'

There was no response. Deeksha tried to tickle Kalpana on her tummy. Kalpana's arms shot out and roughly pushed her away. Deeksha fell on her back. After a few moments, she crept back to Kalpana, curled around her sister and held her.

'I am not going away. I want to be with you. Please talk to me. I can't talk to anybody else in the house.'

She could feel Kalpana tensing.

More hopeful now, she said, 'Talk only to me. Not about what happened. Tell me about anything—I don't care. I only want to hear your voice.' Kalpana tried again to push her away.

Frustrated, Deeksha said, 'Do you at least hear me? I am afraid that you have become deaf.'

Kalpana turned around. Her black, luminous eyes were two dark stars of the night. Her body shuddered as if she wanted to shout. She looked at Deeksha and lifted her finger to her mouth. And turned away from her.

Deeksha hugged her tighter. Kalpana pushed her away harder.

Deeksha rolled back on her mat. The sound of the crickets in the raining forest suddenly seemed to have become louder. The rain continued, a metronome of steadiness.

After many minutes of silence, Kalpana turned towards Deeksha. Deeksha was awake and waiting.

'You don't have to speak to me if you don't want to,' she said. 'But I will. I will tell you everything. I will tell you about the principal.'

Kalpana turned away abruptly.

'Okay, not the principal. What about your friends in school?'

Kalpana turned towards her.

'They all want you to come back. Even the teachers.' She smiled. She had never before talked to Kalpana's classmates, those who came to the house to see Kalpana. And visits by the principal and two teachers were in themselves events of importance.

Kalpana continued staring at her. Two lizards scampered across the ceiling, scuffling through the dust. Deeksha looked up. 'I hate lizards. You do too.' She had a sudden inspiration. 'If you don't speak, I will catch a lizard and drop it on you.' She giggled away her fear of catching a lizard.

Kalpana's eyes dared her to do it.

'Or I could just keep talking to you till you get tired of me.'

Kalpana waited.

Deeksha waited. 'I don't know what else to say now,' she said. Kalpana turned away.

Deeksha fell asleep, imagining the lizards flying away on the little cloud that had silently entered the storeroom.

ONE WEEK HAD PASSED SINCE KALPANA'S MIRACULOUS appearance. A routine had been set and nothing seemed to have changed. Except for the unbearable silence of Kalpana. Deeksha kept trying to make Kalpana speak but had not succeeded.

Siddaiah had come in between, sat with Ajji, peeped in to see Kalpana sitting in a corner, had a tiny cup of coffee, and left. Kalpana's friends hovered outside the house. Her teachers offered to talk to her. But nothing helped. Kalpana's father vanished every morning for his job in the neighbouring town, and the silence of the house was only broken by Ajji's muttered prayers, the sullen sounds of cooking from the kitchen, and the sound of the fans when they came on and as suddenly stopped when the power got cut. Deeksha was bored, tired of sitting around, lost in her repeated attempts to make her sister talk. She was waiting to go back to school.

The morning that happened, it was bright and already warm. Deeksha had her bath early, put on her uniform and picked up her bag. Her mother and Ajji held one hand each. Her mother said, 'I will drop you to school.'

Deeksha was aghast. She had wanted to skip and hop to school, stop to wave at the shopkeepers, shout out to her friends, and pat the cows that would be grazing all along the way. *She is becoming another Kalpana,* the old women would have said.

'No, Amma. No. I will walk by myself,' she protested. What a shame at her age to be seen being dropped to school by her mother!

Ajji tightened her hold on Deeksha till her arm hurt. 'Keep quiet, your mother will drop you.'

So, instead of a smiling morning jaunt to the school, it was a sulky Deeksha who walked behind her mother's shadow, hidden within the smell of woodsmoke that enveloped her mother. In a small act of kindness, her mother stopped a little distance before the school gate and told her to go on by herself.

Deeksha ran off happily without looking back. Her mother watched her go through the gate, picking up friends along the way like buzzing bees. The principal passed the mother as she was walking back. She wanted to ignore her and walk past, but suddenly said, 'Good.' It sounded like approval but was more like a rebuke.

That morning, Kalpana too left her house for the first time after her return. Her mother had given her dosas to eat and dragged her to the bathroom for a bath. 'We are going to the temple,' she said, 'and I am not going to enter with an unwashed girl.'

Kalpana would have said a great deal, if only she would talk. But for now, she just tried to make her face look angry. Words bubbled and boiled right up to the surface. She kept quiet, and when it grew unbearable to listen to her mother and Ajji, the dam burst and words fell as torrential tears down her cheeks. But not a moan escaped her.

Ajji called Siddaiah on the phone and asked him to send an auto. 'And also a good driver,' she added.

To Kalpana, who still refused to look her in the eye even after a week, she said, 'Fish curry when we come back. I made it, not your mother. Special only for you.'

Kalpana pushed her away and ran back to the storeroom. She did not want to leave the house. She did not want to see anything outside her house, not the shopkeepers or her dearly beloved cows on the streets.

The auto came at 11 a.m. Siddaiah's friend Babu was a burly, jovial man who walked into the house with a great deal of familiarity. Mother was looking hassled trying to get Kalpana to leave her room. Ajji was walking around mumbling her prayers. Babu peeped into the storeroom. 'Akka,' he said, addressing the mother, yet another universal sister. 'Come. It will get late if we delay. We have to reach before the main prayer in the temple.' The morning prayers in the temple culminated with the main rituals around noon.

Kalpana refused to move. She held on to a table on which were piled neglected years of accumulated household objects. Babu walked into the room and gently picked Kalpana up. He released her hold on the tabletop and carried her out. Looking at the shocked but thankful mother, he said, 'Ajji told me to do this.' Hearing this, Kalpana hit him on the chest, but by then he had carried her across the threshold, from the gloomy darkness of her room into the bright, hot sunlight. Kalpana immediately pushed him away—the shame of being carried by an auto driver! She who strutted to school, who could make fun of her teachers, and spoke to cows and butterflies. What a shame!

Kalpana ran into the auto and sat huddled in a corner. Ajji triumphantly told the mother, 'This is the only way.' Kalpana did not let Ajji sit next to her. When her mother sat in the middle, she uncharacteristically hugged her mother's arm tightly. It was so unexpected that the mother suddenly had tears in her eyes. The auto started with a roar, and her sadness was immediately lost in a burst of dust from the road.

They went to the larger Devi temple, which was on the way from their village to Hebri. Like in many temples in that region, once every week, after the morning prayers, the priest became an oracle. He would be possessed by the goddess and people would queue up to ask her advice. They would write their questions on a small sheet of paper and another person would read it out to the possessed priest, who would then transmit the answer from the goddess. Ajji's family, like almost all the families in the village, went to the oracle before any important event. They would go with questions on health, marriage, education, or anything else for which they wanted some advice. There was nothing that they hesitated to ask, although there were many people around them when they asked their questions.

The priest was preparing for the final rituals, decorating the Devi and the shrine. Already a group of people were standing silently, waiting for the main aarati. Another priest was lighting the wicks of the lamps that would be used for the aarati. The moment Ajji, Kalpana and her mother came in, all heads turned towards them. Some nodded at Ajji, and a couple of young mothers who were there involuntarily pulled their saris closer around their bodies. Kalpana stood with her eyes defiantly staring at the god, but then decided to keep them closed. She didn't want to see the Devi. And she definitely didn't want to see the people around her. With her eyes closed, holding on to her mother's hand, Kalpana experienced a new world of sounds and smells. The incense sticks, the burning of the wicks, the coconut oil being used in the temple kitchen, and the wafting fragrance of many different flowers. She could hear soft murmurs, the crinkle of plastic sheets, the breaking of a coconut, the meaningless whispers of people around, and the tinkling of a bell. This was her world, a new world of darkness. From silence to darkness seemed such a natural step for her.

The time for the puja arrived with a loud banging of a metal plate and the sound of little bells being shaken vigorously. The prayers of the priest mingled with murmured exclamations from the devotees around her. Kalpana opened her eyes a little at the prodding of her mother. She saw the shining Devi, small and petite, cloaked in bright red, encased in white and red flowers. Kalpana stared at the Devi's face, now reflected in the multilayered lamp, reflecting her million qualities in each flicker of the flames. Kalpana's mother was so deeply moved that her eyes filled up. Ajji was looking around at the people, and at Kalpana, her devotion always a bit grounded and pragmatic. Kalpana stared at the Devi and would have said this if she could have spoken: 'You cheated me. You cheat these people.' Thinking this, she felt the tears begin, and shaking off her mother's hand, she moved away.

Ajji followed her to the courtyard outside. 'Don't walk away like that,' she scolded. She made Kalpana sit on the porch outside while the sounds of the puja slowly subsided. The question-and-answer session would begin after some time. Already there were around ten people waiting in the queue.

Kalpana's mother stayed near the shrine, keeping an eye on Kalpana and Ajji at the same time. When the session with the oracle was announced, she called out to them. Kalpana refused to move. Ajji caught her hand and tried to drag her forward. Kalpana was obstinate and held on to the pillar. Ajji saw Babu loitering at the entrance with a couple of other auto drivers. She called out, 'Babu, come here.' She told Kalpana, 'He will carry you in again.' Kalpana hated her grandmother so intensely that her mouth moved and she might have shouted. But instead, two drops of spittle dribbled down her chin. Shaking Ajji's hand free, she walked towards her mother.

The session was already in progress. The priest, who was now possessed by the Devi, stood before the idol of the goddess. There was a queue in front of him. He was in a trance, shaking as if he had the shivers, and held a twig with leaves in his right hand. He would suddenly jerk his hand and lightly beat the twig against his body. In spite of herself, Kalpana was drawn to this man. He had been an 'ordinary' man, and now the goddess inhabited him! She felt afraid, but also curious. When he answered the question of someone ahead of them, his voice sounded different. 'Is the Devi really in him?' Kalpana so wanted to ask. But she ground her mouth shut.

Their turn came. When the man looked at her, Kalpana felt that he knew who she was. And what had happened to her. Her mother's question was read out by the person standing next to the priest: 'Will my daughter speak again?' Kalpana's mother pointed Kalpana out to the oracle. Her question drew the attention of everyone around them. It was as if all of them knew Kalpana and were waiting for the answer.

The oracle started shaking and convulsing. He mumbled a few words that nobody understood. He then stopped suddenly and said something to the assistant, who announced, 'Devi says that the girl will speak when she wants to.' The three of them bowed to the oracle, who suddenly grabbed some flowers and kumkum and spread the vermilion on Kalpana's forehead. He spoke to her directly and Kalpana thought it sounded like, 'If you don't want to speak, don't.'

Babu drove them back. Mother was thinking of the fish curry. She was content after her visit to the temple. She believed, simply and devoutly, that the Devi would take care of Kalpana. She neither rejoiced nor felt let down. She was equanimous, sitting patiently on the bouncing back seat of the auto. Kalpana, who was now leaning out and staring at the world around her and at the people who stared back, felt unreasonably happy. What transpired at the temple was an unexpected vindication, although it wasn't clear to her what the vindication was about.

It was Ajji who was most irritated with the Devi. On the drive back, she went on an uninterrupted monologue with the goddess, telling her that she felt let down, that she expected more from the goddess, that it was her duty to take care of young girls. Mother acted as if she didn't hear Ajji, and when Babu got a phrase in here and there, Ajji merely laughed loudly.

Just before they reached home, Ajji turned to Kalpana's mother and said, 'See, this Devi will make Kalpana just like her. Both two little devils.' Mother was aghast at this blasphemy. But Kalpana, not-so-little Kalpana, heard Ajji, and the first contour of a vanishing smile could be seen on her face for the first time since the day she went missing. Two little devils! Thinking of this made her think of Deeksha, and if life had been normal, Kalpana would have laughed loudly and skipped all the way home.

FISH CURRY WITH RICE WAS DEEKSHA'S FAVOURITE FOOD. She had it for dinner and was all smiles afterwards. She watched TV with her mother in the hall, accompanied by a running commentary from Ajji. Ajji had a comment about everything: the heroine didn't know how to act, the singer didn't know how to sing ... and even the photography was not good. Her final declaration was about the incompetence of the director. Through it all, Deeksha laughed. Once in a while, she remembered Kalpana and felt a bit guilty. But when she went to peep into the room, she found Kalpana close to the door of the storeroom, listening to the TV. Seeing this, Deeksha bounced back happier, till the morbid serial made her go and look out of the main door. She could hear the sputtering of her father's two-wheeler from a distance. As he walked in, she smiled at him and said, 'Super fish curry.' He smiled, lifted her and entered the house. Not seeing Kalpana with the others, he guiltily set Deeksha down and went to wash. Ajji rolled out her bedding and sat on it. The father peeped into the storeroom and saw Kalpana lying down.

Deeksha went into the storeroom. She spread out her mat and sat on it. Kalpana was turned away from her. She heard Father ask Mother, 'So, what did the Devi say?'

'He said she will speak.'

'When?'

'Soon, I think.'

'Not what you think. When, according to the Devi?'

There was silence, broken only by the sounds of plates and ladles.

'What is the matter? Did he say she will talk at all?'

'Yes, definitely. The Devi said ... said that Kalpana will speak when she wants to.'

'What?' Deeksha had rarely heard her father's raised voice.

'Yes, that will be soon. The other priest told me specially.'

'I hope so. I am getting tired of this circus. Every day in office everybody asks me the same question: has she begun speaking yet?'

'It's fine. Just a little more time. She is already doing much better. She sat in the auto and stared at everybody. When we came back, she enjoyed the fish curry.'

'I don't know. What to tell you? How can we even know she enjoys something when she does not even speak? I don't know.'

'*I* know,' the mother replied with a secret smile. 'I can hear her all the time even when she is silent. I heard her in the auto and in the temple.'

Hearing her mother's words, Kalpana turned in panic. She saw Deeksha sitting on the mat and staring at her. Deeksha whispered, 'You see? Mother can hear you even if you don't speak.' She paused to let the words sink in. 'So what is the point of you keeping silent?' she added triumphantly.

There was so much Kalpana would have said to this. In frustration, she banged her fists on her mat and turned her back to her sister.

Deeksha went to her, curled around her and said, 'I am so sleepy'.

She woke after a couple of hours, sweating. The power was off. The fan had gone silent. The sound of the crickets outside invaded every corner of the house. Kalpana was tossing and turning, and had pushed Deeksha away. Deeksha turned back to her and put her arms around her. She thought she heard a sound, a moan, from Kalpana. She held her tighter, and Kalpana stopped pushing. They both started breathing together.

'It's hot,' Deeksha whispered. 'But don't worry. The power will come soon.' But all that came was an extremely loud thunderclap that rolled in beats of metal sheets, shrill and loud enough to rattle the vessels in the room. Deeksha held Kalpana tighter. The sudden sound of a downpour fell upon them in thundering little droplets on their tiled roof.

'Water will cool better than any fan,' said Deeksha, trying to laugh. She tried to turn Kalpana over on to her back but didn't succeed. So she climbed over Kalpana's body to look at her face. Kalpana's eyes were closed. Even in the shy darkness of the room, Deeksha could see that tears had flowed down her cheeks. She softly touched Kalpana's face. Kalpana flinched and moved as if she were going to shove her away, but suddenly, uncontrollably, more tears flowed. Deeksha started crying too, and both of them, without knowing why they were crying, lay on their backs and wept softly. The rain increased in ferocity, and by the time it turned into a steady drumming, the girls too had stopped their tears.

'Please talk to me, Akka,' Deeksha whispered. Kalpana opened her eyes and stared at the ceiling.

'At least tell me if you can speak. You are not speaking on purpose? If you won't say anything, can you at least nod?'

Without looking at her, Kalpana nodded slightly. Deeksha was overjoyed.

'So you have not become totally deaf. I am so happy!'

Kalpana turned towards her and put her finger over Deeksha's mouth.

'Okay, okay, then you can also speak?'

Kalpana nodded.

'How do you know? Did you try speaking when we were not around you?'

Kalpana was amused and tapped Deeksha on the head. Deeksha held on to her hand.

'Why are you not speaking then?'

Kalpana remained silent.

'I don't understand it at all. First you go away without telling any of us. Then you suddenly come back, totally silent. Now everybody thinks you are dumb. Our principal said you have become deaf and dumb because you were caught in the rain for three days.'

Kalpana turned to her, angry and aghast. But she couldn't bring herself to open her mouth.

Hearing the insistent noises of a lizard on the wall, Deeksha said, 'Even the lizard is laughing. Tell me why you are not speaking.' When Kalpana did not reply, Deeksha hesitantly asked the questions she had been dreading to ask. 'What happened to you? Did somebody take you away?'

Another lizard replied to those questions. The rain stopped, the power came on, and the fan began its rackety sound in that silence.

'Okay, Akka. You don't speak. But I will keep talking to you. I will talk to you every night even if you beat me to make me stop.'

Kalpana smiled and held Deeksha's palms tightly. She turned on her side. The sisters now lay facing each other. Kalpana's smile was as good as speech for Deeksha. The more Kalpana was silent, the more Deeksha wanted to speak. As if her words could fill the silence of her sister.

'You are so famous, Akka,' she began. 'Because of you, I am also famous in school. Today, even the high school students were looking at me. So many of my friends smiled at me. My best friend, Kumari, held my hands the full time in class, and even when I was talking to her in class, the teacher did not stop me. Very good idea that you ran away, Akka.' Deeksha giggled and Kalpana shook her head.

'What? You want me to stop?' Kalpana shook her head again.

'Then why did you shake your head?' Kalpana stared at her as if she could will Deeksha into hearing the silent words bubbling inside her.

'Oh, how nice if I could listen to you. Like Amma can.' She thought for a moment. 'Can Amma really hear your mind?'

Kalpana shook her head again.

Deeksha could not be stopped. In urgent whispers, she told Kalpana about meeting the principal during the lunch break, about how some senior students insisted she join their team in a game of kho-kho, and how a whole bunch of her friends proudly walked with her along the main road of the village. It was exhilarating to be wanted so much, but she also added that she could not answer the one question everybody asked.

'All my friends want to know when you will come back to school, Akka.'

Kalpana shook her head again.

'You will not come to school? Ever?'

Kalpana nodded in the affirmative.

'Really?'

Yes, really, Kalpana would have said. *Really, really, really. Not to that school.* Deeksha started crying. 'If you don't go, I also won't go,' she declared, totally spent.

Kalpana moved closer and hugged her. She calmed her by rubbing her hand over Deeksha's thick hair. She wanted to say so much, so much to Deeksha, but she was also obstinate. She held Deeksha tightly, and the next morning, when their mother came to wake Deeksha for school, she saw the two of them sleeping, holding each other. Her heart lifted, and she found the first tune of a morning song settling on her lips.

THE DAYS WENT BY IN THIS ROUTINE: DEEKSHA WOULD RUN off to school in the morning, Mother would make Kalpana have a bath and eat her tiffin, and then Kalpana would sit in her room till lunch. One day, her father placed her school bag near her mat, telling her, 'You should read those books while you are at home. You don't have to speak to read.' It sounded halfway between a scolding and advice. Kalpana, when he was not looking, kicked the bag away from her. This was indeed blasphemous, since kicking a book was like abusing the goddess of learning, but she was in that kind of a mood.

After a few days of sitting in the room in silence, Kalpana became restless. She came out, but avoided Ajji. It seemed to her that Ajji was looking at her suspiciously all the time. As if she were going to try and trick her into speaking. Her mother was the ambivalent one. Every time she thought of forcing Kalpana to speak, her heart filled with the unknown fear of discovering what had happened to her in those three days. That was not a truth she was ready to hear. Her husband said she was being too soft, and Ajji had agreed. Kalpana had heard Ajji say, 'I can get Babu, that auto driver, to force Kalpana to speak.'

Mother had become worried. 'No, no, I think Kalpana has really lost her voice. Chennamma told me that people can lose their voice after some shock. There was even a film about it.' She looked at the TV as if, miraculously, that film would be showing on it then.

Ajji muttered her opinion about Chennamma. She had always thought that her daughter-in-law was too soft and gullible. 'Very surprising given the nature of the women in our community,' she might have said if her old childhood friend, who was no more, were sitting with her.

Kalpana started coming out of her room to watch the days go by. How much she enjoyed this voyeurism of the ordinary day!

The bustle of the early morning, the silence after the morning chores were done and her father and sister had left, the sounds of the puja performed by her mother and Ajji, and then the smell of cooking. Kalpana sat on the porch of her house, half in and half out, staring at the road, a passing two-wheeler or a woman walking by, and looking at the not-so-far-off mountains, and the cows and dogs that came sniffing near the main door. It was these animals that eventually got her to come out of the house. She went to feed the stray cows that came and stood outside, staring at her solemnly. It had rained earlier, and the smell and the mist rising from the earth were like a welcome embrace, inviting her back to the world.

The afternoons were the most difficult, at least till Deeksha came back from school. Initially, Deeksha tried to get her out of the house to play. But after days of resistance from Kalpana, their mother gave them a ludo set and told them to play with that. For Kalpana, the game was an escape valve for the pressure of the silence within her. It also disciplined her speech, for there were many moments in the game when she wanted to shout out in anger, frustration or delight. She converted all of these into physical actions, hitting the ground or suddenly jumping up and walking ferociously from one end of the tiny room to the other.

Deeksha, as if wise way beyond her years, told her mother, 'Akka is going to speak soon. I know.'

IN BETWEEN, SIDDAIAH HAD COME TO MEET AJJI AND ENQUIRE after Kalpana. Ajji took him out of the house, and Kalpana watched them speaking animatedly. Siddiah was busy trying to survive the cut-throat business of private buses. He told Ajji, 'Be happy, she is looking fine.'

Ajji told him that nothing was fine. 'The child has become dumb, has stopped going to school, and who knows what else!'

Siddaiah held his ground. 'Ajji, maybe it is just a cold. Standing in the rain for five minutes can give us all a bad cold. This girl was missing for three days in the rain. And that too in the forest! What if she was completely soaked? Maybe she got a bad cold that made her lose her speech. Once the cold deep inside her leaves, she will start speaking.' Siddu often spoke as if there was no distinction between hope and reality. He left hurriedly, adding, 'Better to go see a doctor now that the Devi has already seen her.'

Ajji told Kalpana's father that night about the need to go to a doctor. He said they had already done that when Kalpana returned. 'But now,' Ajji said, as if she had discovered a new secret, 'we have to go to a different doctor. I heard that too much time in the rain could have made her lose her speech.' She paused. Her son looked at her blankly. 'Due to cold, you know.'

The father was not amused. 'But she has no cold. She is totally fine.'

Ajji pounced on this statement and delivered her denouement with a flourish. 'But this cold I am talking about is the cold of the mind. You don't cough, sneeze or have phlegm. It lies inside your head and covers your ability to talk. She is not speaking because of this mind-cold.'

Kalpana's father stared at his mother. She never ceased to amaze him as much as she irritated him.

Ajji continued, 'And there is a doctor in the new private hospital in Hebri who is the best for this problem. Best in India, I am told.'

BUT BEFORE THEY COULD GO TO THE DOCTOR WHO WOULD cure the cold of the mind, Kalpana spoke. It was brief, very brief, and only meant for Deeksha's ears. Nevertheless, she uttered her first words in days.

It was another rainy night. Deeksha had not enjoyed school that day. The novelty of being Kalpana's sister had worn off. Her teachers were not as indulgent. The concern for Kalpana was transforming into jokes. They all revolved around being dumb, deaf, blind or otherwise 'crippled'. Two senior students had made fun of Deeksha's closest friend, Kumari, who had been afflicted with polio as an infant, and limped. These girls told Deeksha that maybe Kalpana, who had lost her voice and hearing and who knows what else, would soon become like Kumari.

So Deeksha was not feeling good that night. Kalpana was her usual oscillatory self, playing ludo and then turning away in silence. Deeksha, following their daily ritual, told Kalpana about her day in school. She told her about the incident with the senior girls with a lot of bitterness.

'Akka, you just sit here silently. But in school, when they talk to me, it is all about Kalpana, Kalpana. They are now making fun of you.'

She added, 'I am also getting tired. And angry. You are having a good time at home. I have to go to school. It is so boring now.'

She was silent for some time, as if deciding what to say before she said it. And then she did.

'It is like you are making fun of me. By not talking. I am telling you everything. But you are still silent. You don't tell me anything.'

Deeksha realised that she was going to start crying. She said, 'Why are you not speaking to me, Akka?' and gave in to her tears.

Kalpana held Deeksha's hand and lay on her back. She stared at the ceiling in silence. If only she could speak through her palms! After a long pause filled with Deeksha's sniffles, she turned on her side and placed her mouth close to Deeksha's ear. She whispered, but the sound that came out was deafening to her own ears after so many days of silence.

'Language is a lie. Every word we speak is a lie. Your books are lies. God is a lie.'

She spoke softly but clearly. As if she wanted to imprint her words on Deeksha's ears forever. Deeksha was shocked to hear her speak, but more confused about what she said.

'Is that why you are not speaking? But why?'

'Yes, because all language is a lie, and I do not want to speak lies.'

'But why now? What happened, Akka, when you were away? Did somebody tell you that language is a lie?'

Kalpana knew that if she continued, she would not be able to remain silent: that too was the devil's work of language. And she had resolved to live in a world of silence, come what may.

'The answer is known only to Ajji. Ask her. These are the last words I will speak—to you or to anybody else, Deeksha. And these words are only meant for you. You can never tell anybody else that I spoke to you.' She hugged Deeksha tightly, but Deeksha started crying uncontrollably. A miserable day had come to a more miserable end.

THE NEXT DAY WAS A DISASTER WAITING TO HAPPEN. Deeksha got up late, while Kalpana was still sleeping. A drizzle had persisted the whole night, and the morning seemed unusually grey. The water for her bath seemed colder than usual, and her tiffin was tasteless. Ajji ignored her even as Deeksha tried to catch her eye and find a way to ask her about Kalpana. If Deeksha had thought about it carefully, she would have known that her discomfort had begun the previous night. She had not understood what Kalpana had said. Could not even begin to fathom why Kalpana stopped speaking because of some crazy idea that she had about language!

The mood persisted in school. The first class was mathematics. Their teacher was an earnest middle-aged woman who had been an excellent student of mathematics in her school days but had not studied beyond a meaningless college degree. She was a good teacher, and patient, and had the capacity to let children make mistakes. Deeksha liked her class, but that day, she was least interested.

She sat next to Kumari as always. Deeksha was a friend and mentor to Kumari, who was prone to sickness and often felt sleepy in class. There were days when the two girls sat through class holding hands. There was a story behind this practice. The previous year, Deeksha had got to know Kumari better, and they would often sit and talk together. Two of their classmates came up to the girls one day, and one of them told Deeksha, 'Don't sit too close to her or touch her. You will also become a cripple.' Deeksha, in defiance, held Kumari's hands and hugged her closer. Kumari took a handful of mud from the ground and threw it at the girls. From then on, the two girls grew even closer to each other.

In the middle of the mathematics class, Deeksha suddenly whispered to Kumari, 'Do you think language is a lie?'

Kumari was puzzled. But she was used to Deeksha suddenly asking crazy questions.

'What language is a lie?' Kumari asked after a moment of silence.

'What do you mean by what language?'

'You asked me whether language is a lie.'

'Language—what we speak. Kannada language. English language. I was thinking whether it is all a lie. Is language lying to us?'

'You are saying language is lying? How can Kannada lie to us? Why should it lie?' Kumari started giggling. 'You are talking as if Kannada is a person.'

Deeksha was puzzled. She realised that there was a valid point behind her question, but felt that she did not know how to ask it properly.

The teacher saw the two girls whispering. She had been teaching multiplication and had written in big letters on the board: 25 X 36 = ?

'Deeksha,' she shouted. 'What are you sitting and talking? Are you listening to me?'

Deeksha stood up. 'Yes, Teacher,' she said, looking at the board and trying to solve the problem. She knew what would come next.

'So what is the answer to the problem?' the teacher asked, pointing to the board.

Kumari, hiding her mouth behind her palm, whispered, '900'. Kumari was like that. She could solve mathematics problems effortlessly, while Deeksha would splutter.

Deeksha never doubted Kumari. She said, '900, Teacher.'

The teacher was pleased, but not too surprised. Deeksha was a bright girl. 'Sit down,' she said, 'but don't talk.'

As she sat down, Kumari said, 'Was 900 a lie?'

'I don't know. You said 900. I believe you. Teacher believes the answer.'

'So 900 is right, correct? It is not a lie, isn't it so?'

Deeksha was silent. 'Okay, I am talking about language. Language we speak.'

'Why do you ask these questions, Deeksha?'

Deeksha kept quiet. She didn't want to tell anybody, not even her dear friend, that her sister had finally spoken. She thought further and said, 'From where did the teacher get that question? Why is she asking, what is 25 times 36?'

Kumari giggled. Deeksha was not to be put off.

'What if 25 is a lie? 36 also a lie? What is so true about either of them? Then won't 900 also be a lie?'

Kumari started laughing. The teacher caught her at it and was about to ask her to stand up as punishment, but remembered in time her polio-afflicted legs. Instead, she shouted at a boy in the back row who had blissfully gone to sleep.

THAT NIGHT, BOTH KALPANA AND DEEKSHA WENT TO SLEEP early. Kalpana had been taken to the private hospital that afternoon by her parents. Her father had felt awkward going alone with a mute daughter, so he took his wife along. 'Better to have a woman around' could have been his life's slogan. The doctor was an ENT specialist. He peered into Kalpana's mouth, into her ears and eyes. He tried to make her say 'aah' by opening her mouth wide, but Kalpana refused to let any sound come out of her wide-open mouth. He asked her to clear her throat, but she obstinately refused to produce the required noise. The doctor leaned over Kalpana and suddenly poked her with a tiny drawing pin. Kalpana couldn't hold back a faint shriek.

'Ah,' the doctor said, 'her voice is fine.'

'But she does not speak,' the mother said, her own voice sounding frail.

But the doctor found no problems. 'She is perfectly fine,' he confidently told her parents.

The father would not leave. 'But what about her speech?'

'It will come.' The answer seemed unsatisfactory even to his own ears. 'When it comes. You can't say anything about the body. Suddenly, it will start talking, and she will start talking non-stop.' He smiled indulgently at Kalpana, who stared back at him.

'Isn't there some medicine you can give?' her mother asked.

'Or do some tests?' The father was not to be left behind.

Nothing. Nothing at all. It seemed that there was nothing anybody could do to help Kalpana. Under pressure, the doctor finally said that maybe they should take Kalpana to a neurologist. But there was no neurologist in this hospital, and so they would have to go to the government hospital in the next town, or to the new private hospital that had opened recently.

Having nothing else to write, the doctor scribbled a prescription recommending that Kalpana see a neurologist. He told the parents as they left, 'She should gargle twice a day. Put some salt in the water.'

Kalpana had an absurd urge to laugh loudly, but she bottled the sounds that threatened to gurgle out. They came out nevertheless, as little teardrops, and seeing that, the mother too got tears in her eyes.

Kalpana was tired after the trip. She went to sleep early, firmly pushing away Deeksha's inquisitive questions.

She slept deeply. Until.

The lizards were at it again. Maybe it had something to do with the rains coming and going. Stopping and starting. Like the fan and the zero-watt bulb on the back wall of the house, a vain attempt to drive away the creepy creatures of the night.

Deeksha woke up feeling thirsty. How wonderfully quiet the house was! Even the sounds of the crickets had dwindled to a background frequency, not urgent in their insistence. She went into the kitchen and drank a glass of water. Kalpana was sleeping peacefully, curled up on her mat. Deeksha sat next to her, then lay down slowly, putting her arms around Kalpana.

Kalpana did not wake up. After a few restless minutes, Deeksha tried to gently turn her around.

Kalpana would not wake up, but neither could Deeksha go back to sleep. Frustrated, she began talking. She told Kalpana about the mathematics class.

'The teacher asked me in front of everybody. I had to answer. But the teacher doesn't know that I have the best mathematics student as my best friend! Kumari gave the answer in a second. I think even the teacher was surprised.' Deeksha giggled happily and tugged Kalpana even more forcefully towards her.

Kalpana groggily opened her eyes, and Deeksha said, 'I asked Kumari if 25 is a lie.'

Kalpana's eyes opened cautiously. She looked around the room. It seemed to be the middle of the night.

'I asked her if 36 is also a lie. The teacher wanted to know what is 25 times 36. When I said 900, the teacher said that it is correct. So 900 is not a lie, is it?'

Kalpana stared at her.

'So if 900 is not a lie, 25 and 36 are also not lies. 1 and 2 are also not lies.'

In the silence enveloping the two of them as one, Deeksha pronounced her judgement. 'So how you can say that language is a lie?'

Kalpana was unfazed. She had always been good at mathematics. She found the school mathematics exams too easy. She would have told Deeksha the answer to her query, but her obstinacy once again came in the way. She got up, turned on the light, and went to the stool in the corner. Underneath the stool was an old notebook. She picked it up, along with a pencil from Deeksha's school bag, which lay on the floor.

She wrote in Kannada: *1 + 1 = 2. Correct?*

Deeksha nodded.

Kalpana wrote: *2 is not a lie. 1 is not a lie. Correct?*

Deeksha nodded, though a bit cautiously. It seemed like a trick question.

1 + 1 = 3. Correct?

'No, that is wrong, Akka,' Deeksha whispered, looking furtively to see if her mother had got up to see why the light was on in their room.

3 is a lie then?

'No, 1 + 1 = 3 is not correct.'

Is it a lie then?

'It is wrong ... I don't know, Akka. You are confusing me.'

Kalpana patted her and gently rubbed Deeksha's face. She had wanted to say, 'Go to sleep,' and perhaps even hum a lullaby. A little tune to accompany Deeksha's dreams. Instead, she turned off the light and lay on her side, eyes closed, and wondered how much longer she would be able to keep silent.

Deeksha was disturbed. She had never thought 3 was a lie, but couldn't understand why 1 + 1 = 3 was not a lie. And if Kalpana was obstinate, so was she.

She turned to her sister and said with finality, 'Akka, you wait and see. I will show you that language does not lie.' After a pause, she said what she had really wanted to say all along. 'I will make you speak.'

Lying on her back, staring at the dark, splotched roof and listening to the lizards and the other sounds around her, Kalpana smiled. This changed the stakes of her action. Now, it was not just her obduracy, not her whim. It had become a challenge. Kalpana loved challenges and puzzles. She would sustain her silence, knowing that it was also a game between the two sisters. And she had never lost to her sister before.

THE NEXT DAY WAS A SUNDAY. NORMALLY, IT WOULD HAVE meant a trip to one of the temples nearby. But the sun had come out in the morning, and it looked like it would be a long, bright day. Such an opportunity could not be allowed to go to waste. The women hung washed clothes out to dry. Some brought out boxes of groceries to dry out, to get rid of the damp fungus that invaded every bit of their homes, and also the stored groceries. Ajji sat out in the sun the whole day long, watching every little movement around her. Deeksha dragged out two plastic stools and made Kalpana sit outside with her. Their mother was busy, and Father had gone out. Kalpana sat silently. Deeksha suddenly got up, took her stool and sat next to her grandmother. Ajji continued with her prayers, but looked at Kalpana suspiciously.

Unable to contain herself, she asked Deeksha, 'Did your sister say anything?'

'No.'

'Not even a word?'

'No.'

'Not even a sound?'

'Sometimes when she sleeps, she snores, just like you.' Deeksha laughed delightedly.

'So she has not said anything to you.'

'No, that is what I said.'

Ajji looked at her suspiciously. Deeksha seemed too cheerful. Her doubts increased when Deeksha asked, 'Why is Akka so silent? Why is she not speaking?'

'I don't know,' Ajji replied.

'She was fine till the day she went missing. What happened to her, Ajji?'

'You should ask her.'

'I did. She doesn't reply. But you are old. You know things we don't know.'

'I am not that old,' said Ajji, and Deeksha started laughing. Kalpana, sitting some distance away by herself, stared at her, irritated by her camaraderie with Ajji.

'Please tell me, Ajji. Everybody in school asks me, and I don't know what to say.'

'I don't know, Deeksha, believe me.' Uncharacteristically, Ajji pulled Deeksha closer to her.

They sat in silence. Kalpana was annoyed by what she saw. She got up and started pacing around. She picked up a stone and threw it at a tree. And then heard Deeksha ask, 'Okay then, Ajji, tell me what you think of language.'

Ajji was puzzled. 'Language?'

'Yes. We speak Kannada, right? So, what do you think of Kannada?'

'I think it is a beautiful language. It is very musical and soft.' She added slyly, 'Like its people.'

'So that is all you think Kannada is?'

'Yes. I don't know much. I only studied till the fifth standard.' She peered at Deeksha and something struck her. 'You are in the fifth now, aren't you?'

Deeksha nodded. Ajji thought of herself as a young girl in the fifth standard who enjoyed going to school, crossing the river in a small boat every day to get there. What a pleasure all that had been, but after the fifth standard, she had to stay home.

Wistfully, she told Deeksha, 'You are so lucky, Deeksha, to be able to go to school.'

'But that is all you know about Kannada then?' Deeksha would not be sidetracked.

'Yes,' Ajji replied. 'Why are you asking me all this?'

'Homework.' Deeksha knew that 'homework' was the safest excuse for her to do anything she wanted. The power of homework was even greater than the power her father had over her. Whenever he began shouting at her, she would say 'homework' and he would instantly stop.

Kalpana, who had heard Deeksha's questions, came to stand close by, but with her face turned towards a brown mushroom that was growing out of the ground.

Deeksha felt more energised by Kalpana's proximity. 'What about English then?' she asked.

Ajji had a quick answer, something she had said many times before. 'I don't know any English. I am not educated like you and your sister.'

'I have a doubt about Kannada. I don't know if it is better than English.'

'I am sure it is much better.'

'Actually, my doubt was whether Kannada is a language that can ever lie.' There, she had said what she wanted to.

'Lie?'

'Yes, does a language lie?'

Ajji became angry. 'What has a language got to do with lies? Who is teaching you all this nonsense?' She looked at Kalpana, who pretended to search for birds in the sky.

'Why are you asking me all this?' Ajji asked impatiently.

Deeksha was quick to respond. 'My friend in class told a lie and it was in Kannada. So Kumari and I were talking—'

'Kumari is no good. Why is she talking to you about—'

'No, Ajji. I was the one who asked her. Don't say anything about Kumari.'

'Even if the student told a lie in class, why are you blaming it on Kannada?'

'Yes, Ajji, that is exactly what Kumari told me.'

'Oh, she did. Good girl.'

'Should our language be blamed or the girl who lied, that is what I asked Kumari.'

'The girl, of course. Why blame the language? Specially our own Kannada.'

'True, Ajji. But another classmate asked us, if the girl did not know Kannada, could she have told a lie?'

Ajji was furious. She got up from the chair, kicking it over. What were they teaching in schools these days? She walked angrily into the house.

Deeksha looked at Kalpana with a new thought.

'Yes, if she did not know Kannada, could she have lied?'

Kalpana looked back at her proudly. Her face shone as if she had herself spoken those lines. She nodded encouragingly.

'So, is the girl lying ...'

Kalpana nodded vigorously.

'... or is it the language that is lying?'

Kalpana clapped and moved to hug her sister, but Deeksha pushed her away and walked inside. 'Now my head is going to burst. I am so confused.'

That night, when Deeksha lay down on her mat, Kalpana gave her a sheet of paper, on which was written: *Very good, but Ajji has not told you what happened to me. She knows.* After Deeksha read the message, Kalpana took it and tore it into little bits. Deeksha was irritated. She said, 'Next time, use the slate.'

THE BEGINNING OF A NEW WEEK DID NOT PORTEND THE beginning of a new life for Kalpana. Having seen her step out of the house and seeing her camaraderie with her sister, her parents had thought that she would soon be ready to go to school. Ajji said that she knew it was just a matter of time, the mother was grateful to the gods, and the father said, 'Enough of this drama.'

On Monday morning, Kalpana was up early, but refused to go to school. When her father came to scold her, she ran into the storeroom and sat in a corner. Deeksha dressed silently, picked up her school bag and left without even looking at her sister.

Deeksha was bursting to tell Kumari what she had thought of the day before. When she saw Kumari outside her house, on the way to school, Deeksha called out to her. The first words she spoke on seeing her were, 'Do you know how to lie?'

Innocently, Kumari replied, 'Of course. I do it all the time.'

'Give me one example of your lying.'

Kumari thought about this. 'I told my mother I was having a headache last night. But I was fine. I didn't want to read, and she keeps saying I should read.'

'So you told a lie.'

Kumari felt a bit guilty. 'It was not fully a lie. I think I had *some* headache.'

'No, that is still a lie. Good.'

She said 'good' in English and felt like a teacher herself.

Puzzled, Kumari asked, 'Why good?'

'No, what I mean is, you told a lie. And you told the lie in Kannada.'

'Yes, Deeksha. My mother only speaks Kannada.'

Deeksha stopped and held Kumari firmly by the hand. They were just outside the school. Deeksha whispered dramatically, 'Do you see? If you did not know Kannada, you could not have lied.'

Kumari thought for a moment. 'Yes, true.' She thought some more. 'But so what?'

'This is what I told my Ajji. Did you lie or did Kannada lie?'

Kumari felt a sudden burst of exhilaration. 'True, true,' she cried. 'If you don't know the language, you cannot lie.'

She pulled Deeksha closer to her.

'See, there are so many street dogs. They do not lie. They do not know Kannada!' Joyously, both the girls started jumping up and down, giggling in tune with their jumps. An attendant working at the school came over and asked them to keep quiet.

Kumari, in a singsong voice, told her, 'We can't keep quiet. We are too happy.' The woman stared back at them, wondering what could make little girls so happy.

THEIR HAPPINESS DID NOT LAST. FIRST OF ALL, THEY WERE drained by their moment of insight. And three tedious classes did not help. They ate their lunch quickly and decided to meet the Kannada teacher.

Bravely, and for the first time in their school life, the two of them walked to the staff room, a room filled with tables and chairs, where the teachers sat. It was primarily a place for the teachers to have their lunch and doze under the fans between classes.

One of the junior teachers, a girl who had just completed her degree, saw Deeksha and Kumari standing outside the door and peeping in. She went to them and asked what they wanted. They told her that they wanted to ask the Kannada teacher something. The junior teacher did what she would never again do. She went to the Kannada teacher and stood respectfully before him. He was the oldest teacher in the school and had been there ever since the school opened in the village. He had two more years before retirement. His was the most comfortable chair and also the most favoured space in the room—right under a working fan. The junior teacher stood there, unsure of what to do, since he seemed to be in the midst of a deep nap. The other teachers around her looked away. Before the young teacher could turn back and tell the girls to come back later, Deeksha walked up to the Kannada teacher and called out, 'Sir.' One tiny voice was enough. He opened his eyes and saw the young teacher and the two students staring at him.

Deeksha quickly said, 'Sir, we have a doubt. Can we ask you now?' The teacher, who barely remembered the girls, was extremely irritated. In earlier times he would have shouted at them, but now he calmly (thanks to his blood pressure medicine, his wife would have said) replied, 'Not now. Ask in class.' He looked at the young teacher who was standing next to them. Addressing the students but looking at her, he added, 'And never enter the staff room.' The other teachers stared at the two girls in surprise. It was the first time students had barged into the staff room with a doubt. A doubt! What a surprise! The mathematics teacher pointed to Deeksha and told her colleague sitting next to her, 'Very bright girl.' Deeksha felt ashamed, and whispered to Kumari guiltily as they walked away, 'That is also a lie.'

The Kannada teacher, Mr Upadhya, would regret his action in the staff room. His was the last period of that day for Deeksha's class. He disliked the last period, since the heat by then would have enervated even the most obedient student. He too would be waiting to go home by that time. That day, as he entered the class, he recognised Deeksha and Kumari. The two girl were sitting on the front bench. Both of them had their hands up in the air even before he sat on his chair. By the time the class could settle, Deeksha was up and saying, 'Sir, doubt, Sir. You told us to ask in the class.'

If not for the heat and his general mood that day, Upadhya would never have agreed immediately. He would have first established his authority, and when he was ready, he would have asked the class in general (and not these two students) whether anybody had any questions. But that day, he was feeling too lazy and tired to assert his dominance. The first question took him by surprise.

'Sir, what is Kannada, Sir?' Deeksha said.

Puzzled, he replied, 'A language.'

'Sir, why do we have this language, Sir?'

Some of the students snickered.

'To speak to each other. To write poetry. To tell stories.' He paused. 'What exactly is your doubt?'

'Sir, Kumari'—Deeksha pulled Kumari up to stand alongside her—'Sir, Kumari was saying dogs do not speak Kannada.'

The whole class started laughing. The teacher was hesitant to smile, unsure whether the students were making fun of him.

'Of course a dog cannot speak Kannada.' He couldn't resist adding dismissively, 'If it did, it would have been sitting along with you in class.'

The children roared with laughter and Upadhya was pleased. It lulled him into a false sense of security.

Deeksha said, 'Sir, why Kumari said that was only to point out that dogs do not tell lies.'

Upadhya stared at her, unable to understand what she was trying to imply.

Kumari spoke up bravely. 'What I was saying, Sir, was that a dog cannot lie because it cannot speak Kannada.'

Unfortunately for the two girls, the other children started laughing again. Upadhya felt that there was something aimed at him in that comment.

'What do you mean?' he shouted. 'What does lying have to do with the language?'

Deeksha put up her hand again, but without waiting for his approval, jumped in. 'This is the doubt we have, Sir. Somebody said that language itself is a lie. Is that correct?'

Upadhya was furious. He had always felt that his students were least interested in the Kannada class. The government also did not care, and even the people in his village wanted the children to only learn English at school. He felt that parents believed that having a Kannada teacher was a waste, since they all knew the language and the children spoke it at home. Even other teachers openly said that the Kannada class was 'timepass.' Everybody, even the principal, seemed to agree that his classes were less important than the science and mathematics classes. So he saw Deeksha's comment about the language as a dig at him.

'Language is a lie, is it? Is it?' He got up threateningly and moved towards the two girls. He caught Deeksha's hand and pulled her to the front of the class. 'Why don't we ask the principal? She can answer your question! And also decide what to do with the two of you.'

Kumari, who was holding on to Deeksha's hand, started crying. Seeing her, Deeksha too started wailing. Seeing the two of them cry, some of the other girls in the class started shouting, 'Sir, Sir, leave them.' The boys in the class sat up straighter and grinned.

The crying was too much for Upadhya to handle. He made the two girls stand in front of the class and asked them to do sit-ups. Deeksha turned to him and said, 'Sir, you cannot ask Kumari to do this. Her parents will complain to the principal.' Upadhya panicked and rushed them back to their seats.

He wanted to shout at all of them. He wanted to tell them that he was not going to waste his life on such worthless students. At the same time, he remembered that he had already spent his one—and only—lifetime with impossible brats like these. This realisation, at the end of a tiring day, drained the last bit of his energy. He sat down on the chair and closed his eyes. The students fell silent, and the only sounds were of hundreds of little shuffling feet all over the school waiting for the final bell to ring.

Upadhya opened his eyes. He saw the children staring at him, some with fear and some with glee. Whatever he did would be another source of entertainment, another joke about the Kannada class.

Deeksha bravely got up and said, 'Sorry, Sir.' The whole class, in unison, for reasons unknown to them, repeated, 'Sorry, Sir.' Upadhya's mood fell further. He had spent his whole life in this school, teaching students what they didn't want to learn. He could quote the texts of the earliest Kannada writers, like Pampa and Ranna. He could talk for hours on modern Kannada poetry and novels. But what a waste, what a colossal waste. None of his students became scholars or writers. Or, if any of them had indeed become one, he was not aware of it. The most famous student from their school was somewhere in California, and he had donated ten used computers a couple of years ago. Obviously a science student! What a waste, what a waste of life, walking every day to the school, shouting at the kids and fighting with various principals about government rules.

But in the midst of all these thoughts was another one, which made his life seem even more worthless. He had understood Kumari's question. He was furious because he didn't know how to answer it in a way the children would understand. He looked at the class of ten-year-olds staring expectantly at him. All of them, without exception, were scrawny, dark, with eyes wide open, desiring to see a new world. But he, the great teacher, had failed them. He did not know the answer to the most basic question.

Kumari got up awkwardly, seeing that Deeksha was still standing, and voiced the question, as if clapping a lid over his thoughts. 'Sir, we are sorry. We only wanted to know what a language is.'

Deeksha jumped in. 'Yes Sir, we only wanted to know what Kannada is. Why is it different from English?'

The two girls sat down on their bench. The children sat still, looking at Upadhya. The teacher stared back at all of them. He picked up the duster filled with chalk powder, which hid erased meanings of years past. His hand shook. He looked down at them and smiled. His spirit lifted the evening light streaming into the class. He got up from his chair. The children smiled, seeing him smile. Unaccountably, Upadhya felt lighter. His students had finally asked him something. They had actually asked him a question about language. They had asked him this question not to make fun of him but because they wanted to know. He would never have guessed that such a simple question would make him feel so good. He had been brought back from his cynicism by two tiny, shrivelled girls, one of whom couldn't even walk properly. He did not know how to immediately answer the question, but he would know, he would learn. That moment felt like liberation. He told Deeksha and Kumari, 'I will tell you tomorrow.' He had wanted to declare that he did not know the answer, a declaration that would have cleansed his soul. But he couldn't disappoint those eager little faces. He turned to the board and cleaned it once again of all the traces and dust of earlier marks till the final bell rang.

That night was long. Deeksha was so excited to tell Kalpana about all that had happened that she even forgot to whisper. She talked and talked, and Kalpana listened and listened. Words bubbled inside Kalpana's head, wanting to rush out, wanting to embrace and envelop Deeksha. What a crazy girl Deeksha had turned out to be! Kalpana was afraid to laugh or smile with her mouth open, for she knew that the words inside her were just waiting for an escape. Finally, it became too much for her to control. She got up hurriedly, ran into the bathroom and vomited out sound after sound, all of which were nothing more than disguised words. Her mother, hearing her vomiting, got up and came to the bathroom door. Kalpana stepped out, smiled at her and nodded her head. She didn't know what else to do, so she flashed a sign, the way she had seen Indian cricketers do on TV: thumbs up. Mother wet a towel and gently massaged Kalpana's face. Deeksha nuzzled up to her and held her hand, declaring, 'I will go to sleep now.'

WHEN DEEKSHA CAME BACK FROM SCHOOL THE NEXT day, she brought Kumari with her. After they had finished a glass of milk each, Deeksha announced grandly, 'I want all of you to come to the hall.' She dragged her reluctant mother from the kitchen and a placid Kalpana from the storeroom. Ajji was sitting on the ground near the front door, peering into the vastness.

Deeksha made her mother and Kalpana sit on the ground. Walked across the room and pulled out her slate. She asked Kumari to stand next to her. She balanced the slate on the plastic stool and said, 'I am now going to take a class.'

Mother was pleased. She asked, 'So, what are you going to teach us?'

'Today I am going to teach you what language is.'

'We already know that,' replied her mother, happy to be part of a game with her daughter. Ajji, who had stubbornly looked away, turned towards the slate. Kalpana moved away from her mother, went to the far side of the room and leaned against the wall.

'No, Amma. Do you know what language is?'

'Language is Kannada.'

'What is Kannada?'

'It is something ... that all Kannadigas speak.'

'Why is it different from English?'

Ajji asked impatiently, 'Do you go to school to ask questions or learn answers?' Mother frowned at her. This was, after all, the first class taken by her daughter!

'My teacher—'

'Who?'

'Kannada teacher, Upadhya Sir.'

'Yes, that old man,' Ajji mumbled.

'He said to ask questions is good. And because Kumari asked this question, he told us all about Kannada today.'

She beamed and looked at them. They all turned to look at Kumari, who smiled happily at them.

Mother asked, 'So, what is Kannada?'

'First, he said, Kannada is made up of Kannada sounds. When we speak in Kannada, we are making sounds that are special to Kannada.'

Ajji was sceptical and made a growling noise.

Kumari quickly added, 'See, that is also language because it is sound.' She looked around for the effect of her statement.

Deeksha added, 'But is it Kannada?' She came close to Ajji and laughed. 'No, that is only Ajji's language.'

Even Ajji smiled at her wit.

Kumari asked her audience, 'How do we know if Ajji's sound is Kannada or not-Kannada sound?'

Deeksha looked at the three of them and said, 'Don't worry if you don't know. Only our teacher knows the answer. Kannada teachers know what is a Kannada sound and what is not a Kannada sound.'

Kumari added, 'And English teachers know what an English sound is.'

Deeksha said, 'Ajji knows what *her* sound is.'

Mother shushed her. They fell silent.

Mother asked, 'That is all? Class is over?'

'No, this is a rest. And now Kumari will give all of you one biscuit each. While you eat the biscuit, think of a question to ask.'

Kalpana took two biscuits from Kumari and motioned to her to bring the slate over. On it, she wrote: *Dogs make sounds. So is there a dog language?*

Deeksha made a big show of reading the question loudly and then dramatically wrote the answer in Kannada: *YES*.

Kumari limped over to the slate, rubbed the word out and wrote: *NO*. She told Deeksha, 'You forgot, Deeksha, what the teacher said. First sound and then word.' Upadhya had written the word 'mara' for tree. He had made all the children chant, 'Mara, mara.' Then he made them say, 'Ra, ra.' The children had never had so much fun shouting in class. The teacher in the neighbouring class came over, saw the children shouting and Upadhya watching them silently, and went back shaking his head.

Deeksha added, 'Sir told us that mara is different from ra. Mara is a Kannada sound and ra is not.'

Kumari looked at all of them as if ready to pronounce something important. 'So we say mara and not ra. Mara is a word in Kannada.'

Kalpana waved at her impatiently. Deeksha understood. 'So we can tell you that there is no dog language because there are no dog words.'

Kumari nodded. 'They just go bow-bow.'

Mother was excited in spite of herself. She hadn't ever felt that these two girls knew so much. She got up and hugged both of them, and said, 'You are both so clever!'

Deeksha pushed her back to her place on the ground. 'You can't hug your teacher. We will punish you if you do that again.'

Ajji laughed aloud. 'Yes, yes, good idea,' she said.

Kalpana gestured for the slate again. She wrote, *Language produces lies. It is the cause of lies,* and sent it back. Deeksha read the words and wiped the slate clean. She sent it back to her through Kumari. 'You have to ask a proper question. Otherwise Teacher will get angry.'

Kalpana wrote: *Isn't language the cause of all lies?*

Deeksha read that out loud like an announcement. 'Kalpana wants to ask this question.' On an impulse, she turned to Ajji. 'Ajji, should we answer it?'

Mother muttered something.

Deeksha was not amused. 'In my class, you have to stand up to answer.' But smiled as she added, 'Since you are a very old student and you are also my mother, you can sit.'

Deeksha looked at Kalpana and continued, 'What my akka wants to say is that language is used to make lies. Correct, Akka?' Kalpana nodded in amazement. Was Deeksha listening to her mind like her mother had claimed she could? Was her refusal to speak a waste if both of them could hear her thoughts?

Ajji was getting angry. She said, 'This is all nonsense. Words describe this world. If the world is true, so is language.'

She pointed to Kalpana. 'Kalpana,' she said. 'That is a word. It means this girl in front of us here. If you say words are lies, then Kalpana is a lie. Is that so?'

Kalpana knew it would only be a matter of time before the floodgates opened. It was becoming impossible to remain silent. She grabbed the slate and wrote one word. Deeksha read it, frowning.

'Ganesha,' she read. 'Ganesha, the god.'

Kumari jumped in. 'That is very good, Akka. Ganesha is our god. If I say the word Ganesha, that means he is here, just like the tree.'

Deeksha immediately realised that this was the question they were all waiting for.

She hesitantly asked, 'Ganesha is a lie? Or is not a lie?'

Mother got up quickly. 'Deeksha, don't say such things. Enough of this lesson. Go read what is meant for your age.'

Kalpana dragged her mother down. She looked at Ajji angrily.

Deeksha said, 'Ganesha is a word, right?'

Kumari chirped, 'Ganesha is a Kannada word. A Kannada sound. You remember the song "Ganesha bandha ..."'

Mother was irritated. 'Ganesha is real, not a lie. Like Kalpana is real, Ganesha is also real in the same way.'

Kalpana shook her head. She walked hurriedly to the slate and wrote a big *NO* in Kannada. As if to emphasise her point, she also wrote it in English.

Ajji was furious. She grabbed the slate and threw it across the room. It broke into pieces. She raised her hand to smack Kalpana, but Kalpana ran behind her mother and into the storeroom. Mother was very upset, but beyond a point she couldn't say anything to Ajji. Deeksha and Kumari ran out through the main door, Ajji's gaze on their backs. They stood outside the house and stared at the mountains.

'I have to get another slate,' Deeksha said.

Kumari was puzzled. 'Why did Akka say Ganesha is a lie?'

'I don't know. I think she had a fight with Ajji. She has been like this from that day.'

Kumari was thoughtful. 'I think Akka was saying that we cannot show Ganesha like we can show a tree.'

'Maybe she is asking, "Where is Ganesha? Where are all the gods? We know that the word "mara" points to a tree, but what can we point to when we say "Ganesha?"' The moment Deeksha uttered the last question, she realised that was exactly what Kalpana wanted to ask.

Deeksha and Kumari sat down outside the main door and watched the mountains. The sun was setting behind them, and it looked as if the shadows of these mountains would soon come lapping at their feet. Ganesha was forgotten when Kumari's mother called out to her from the road. Kumari limped away, telling Deeksha, 'I think our class went off well. We should both become teachers.'

She went home and announced to her parents that she would become a teacher. Her father said, 'So you can waste your time on other people's children!' Her mother glared at him, but Kumari's dream of being a teacher made her blind to the moment.

Kalpana lay on her mat that night, feeling restless. She did not sneak out to the hall to watch TV. She ate her food and went back to the room. She opened her school bag for the first time since coming back home and pulled out her notebook. She found her pencil and sharpened it. She wanted to write all that she could not say, but her fingers overtook her mind. She began by writing *mara* and then drawing a picture of a tree. She wrote *Ganesha* and began drawing a picture of him. She drew the elephant trunk, but her anger overtook her. Unable to write or even draw, she started to scribble ferociously on the page. She calmed down a bit, turned the page over and started doodling—aimlessly but intently—on every little space that dared to exist on the page. Kalpana scribbled and doodled till all the pages of the small notebook had been filled. It was a release, it was as if she had spoken and said all that she had to say.

Deeksha came over and slept on Kalpana's mat. Kalpana had dozed off, but Deeksha's hands on her shoulder woke her. She opened her eyes and lay still. Deeksha whispered, 'Tell me what really happened. If you don't want to speak, write what happened. What happened with Ajji? What happened to you in those three days?'

Kalpana sat up. She looked at Deeksha, who was staring at her intently. She felt moved, and more like a mother to her sister. She took her school bag and pulled out another notebook. She opened it to an empty page and wrote: *Ajji sent me to follow Ganesha.*

'What?' Deeksha jumped up and stood on the mat. 'Ganesha the god?'

Kalpana thought for a moment. *No, I went in search of Ganesha the word.*

All she had done was play with Ajji. Invigorated by the mountains, the skies, and Ajji's seriously comic face when she prayed. How could she have known? She was playing a game, singing a song, but Ajji had said what she shouldn't have.

Deeksha didn't understand. 'You followed a word?'

Kalpana nodded.

'But how can you follow a word? Akka, you are making fun of me.'

Kalpana thought some more. She realised that she had expressed herself wrongly. *I followed the sound of the word,* she wrote.

Deeksha was puzzled, but what could Kalpana tell her when she could not utter a single word? Would she tell her that she had skipped behind the word, searching for Ganesha the god by following Ganesha the word? And what possessed her to follow the sounds along the road, off the path that led to the forest, running behind the echoing sounds of Ganesha that had been picked up by the rustle in the leaves, buffeted by the winds and the rain, to become one with the song of the birds, lost in the growl of the mountains? How she ran behind the elusive sound, hearing it resonate so close to her that it seemed possible to touch. How she ran skipping with a joyful heart, seeing the word like another butterfly waiting to be caught! She had almost caught hold of it, and she could clearly see it hovering nearby. Catching it would have shown her the real Ganesha, would have shown the god hiding behind a human sound. She saw the sound glimmering, heard Ajji's voice run behind it, reached out for it, and fell down a deep gorge, sliding through mud turned to slush by the incessant rain.

Her fall was stopped by the trunk of a tree that had collapsed on the ground. Suddenly, the word had stopped fluttering, and there were no butterflies around her. The morning seemed so dark in the jungle. She became aware that she had run far from the village. Suddenly, there was no longer the call of a reverberating 'Ganesha' that had so craftily drawn her into the jungle, only the sudden, shrill sounds of insects. It needed only another moment for Kalpana to imagine snakes slithering towards her and tigers roaming around for food. She screamed and panicked. How was she going to tell all this to her little sister?

Deeksha felt disturbed by the fear in her sister's eyes. She asked, 'How can anybody follow a word or even a sound?'

Kalpana was silent. Then resolutely, she wrote *mara* on a new page and drew a picture of a tree and an arrow from the word to the tree.

Deeksha understood instantly. 'Very nice, Akka. The word "mara" is like an arrow.' She stood up excitedly and walked to and fro. 'I get it. I understand now. You are asking whether the word "Ganesha" is also like an arrow.'

Kalpana nodded vigorously.

'And you are asking, where is the god Ganesha standing? Like the tree is standing?'

Kalpana clapped softly. She pulled Deeksha close to her. Deeksha flushed with pride. Her elder sister, who used to tease her all the time, now seemed so different!

Deeksha thought for a moment. 'But why do you say that? Ganesha is there, and we have seen him. We see him in the temple every time we go.'

Kalpana shook her head angrily. She wanted to shout out that it was all a lie. She beat her fists on her thighs and the pillow. Pushing Deeksha away, she curled up on her mat. It took her a long time to fall asleep.

How could she sleep remembering the betrayal of the word? If she were older, she might have said that she ran behind the sound of Ganesha like a lover, like the many gopis who ran behind Krishna. She would swear that it was the reverberating words that enticed her to follow them, the chants of 'Ganesha, Ganesha, Ganesha' like a never-ending string that pulled her along. She knew she only had to reach out to the sounds to see and touch Ganesha. And yet, when the time came, all she found was the dark pit of a brooding, wet forest. Soon, she understood that it was not the big animals that scared her, but her imagination of a thousand little worms of all sizes and shapes. When she had got over the first shock, she stood and looked at the forest around her. It was surprisingly benign. She shouted and shouted till her voice dribbled into a hoarse silence. Kalpana knew that she could not climb up the steep slope, but thought she saw a path. With her school bag held close, she ran down the path. But it was not really a path, and she ran in vain till she collapsed under a tree, tired and scared. Later, after drinking the water that dripped off the leaves, she continued walking in what she thought was the direction of her village. Late in the evening, the rain came again, and darkness crept in suddenly and noiselessly, petrifying the little girl. She cried, whimpered, and finally collapsed under a huge tree with thick foliage. When the rain stopped and a million crickets began their calls, Kalpana thought that her life was over.

She remembered how she had so cheerfully set off for school just that morning. But she was now lost in the forest, all because of a word, all because of Ajji's foolish beliefs. In a moment of bravery, she had stood under the tree and shouted, 'Ganesha, Ganesha, Ganesha,' hoping that the god would hear her and would come to show her the way out of the forest. If not as an elephant man, at least as a dancing butterfly. But there was not even an echo, and the words dried out. There was no Ganesha coming for her. She would soon lose not just the god but also his word, his sound within her.

Thinking about that night, lying under the creaking fan, Kalpana started crying, sobbing uncontrollably. Deeksha rushed to her, enveloped her with her body and, without knowing what she was doing, began to rock her sister back and forth.

WHEN DEEKSHA WOKE UP THE NEXT MORNING, IT WAS still dark inside the room. She could see the light of dawn in the hall and hear the first birds that were already up. She was lying on Kalpana's mat, and Kalpana was sitting, leaning against the wall. She had a notebook in one hand and a pencil in the other, and she was intently drawing and scribbling in the book, page after page.

Deeksha tried to see what Kalpana was doing, but Kalpana pushed her away. Deeksha went out and lay down under the fan in the hall. Ajji was lying on her mattress in a corner of the room, and Deeksha could see that she was not really asleep.

There was an appointment with the neurologist at 4 p.m. that day, at the new private hospital near Hebri. Father had taken half-day leave. Babu came in his auto to take Kalpana and her parents. Deeksha had just come back from school. Her mother said as she was leaving, 'Stay inside. Don't step out.'

Deeksha was pleased. Unexpectedly, she had Ajji to herself. The night before had been painful, seeing her ever-cheerful sister sob so bitterly. She had held her, cried with her, but she did not know what else to say or do.

Deeksha dumped her school bag in the hall and sat looking out of the open door at the mountains. The first few evening clouds had gathered near the mountains, and they would soon come down to their village. Ajji walked around the hall but was slyly watching what Deeksha was doing. She stopped in front of Deeksha, standing between her and the open door like a giant shadow come to life.

'Kalpana was making so much sound last night. Was she talking to you?'

Deeksha cheerfully replied, 'No, I think you must have heard me speaking to her. She has become fully dumb, I think. I even pinched her, and not a sound from her. What to do, Ajji?'

Ajji became angry. 'Don't call her dumb. She is not. She is adamant like my husband was. She is just like her ajja. If he decided to stop talking, nothing could make him. If he was angry with me, he would not talk to me for days.'

'Kalpana is like my ajja!' Deeksha giggled. She had no memory of her grandfather, but thinking of Kalpana as an old man, someone who must have looked like Ajji, was enough to make her laugh.

She thought for a moment and said, 'He did not speak at all? Or only to you?'

Ajji glared at her, but did not answer. She continued her pacing.

'Ajji, Kalpana is so angry with you. What did you do to her that day?'

Ajji's fury was quick in erupting. She rushed towards Deeksha, took her hands in her own and shook them. 'Do?

What did I do? I did nothing. Kalpana was going to school and something happened to her on the way.'

'But she told me that you said something to her.'

'Ha! So she spoke to you.'

'No, she wrote that. Now she keeps writing and drawing. You told her something about Ganesha.'

Ajji began to cry softly. Seeing her, Deeksha forgot all the questions she had for her. She came closer to her and put her head on her lap. Ajji said, 'I am not responsible. Why would I harm my dear child?'

'But what happened, Ajji?'

'You wouldn't understand.'

'No, tell me. I won't tell anyone.'

'If your father comes to know, who knows what he will do? And your mother will anyway blame me.'

'I promise I won't tell anybody.'

'There is nothing to tell, Deeksha,' Ajji said, relieved that the words bottled inside her, her constant anguish, could now find a voice. 'You know that every morning I say all my prayers. When I was offering a prayer to Ganesha, Kalpana, who was waiting for the rain to stop to go to school, kept pestering me. She was not letting me say my prayers. I got irritated when she asked, "Who is listening to your prayer? Where does your prayer go? Where do your words go?" I ignored her, but she became more irritating. The moment the rain stopped, I shouted out my prayer into the wind and the clouds. I told her, "Now go. Go and follow these words." I said it as a joke. I did not imagine that this little girl would indeed go searching for the gods who listen to my prayers. Kalpana laughed when she heard my words and ran away to school. That is all I know. That is all I did. How am I to be blamed?'

Deeksha said, 'She ran behind the words? She followed them to see your gods?'

'No, no. I was not serious. I don't know where words go. And even if she ran behind them, why was she missing for three days?'

Deeksha sounded morose. 'Maybe she really found where they went.'

Ajji frowned. 'If she had, she would be a saint and not a dumb girl. She would have found Ganesha himself.'

'But, Ajji, Ganesha is in the temple. Maybe she went there.'

'No, she was not in any temple. We searched everywhere.'

Deeksha thought for a bit. 'I don't think she found Ganesha. She wrote that Ganesha is a lie.'

'Oh, that is what your class to us was about!' Ajji pinched Deeksha's ears lightly.

'No, that was about whether a dog can speak Kannada.'

'You be careful, Deeksha. Stop thinking about all this. Why are you asking what is Kannada, what is language? We know what they are. You grow up and you will know. Don't unnecessarily ask these questions.'

'But, Ajji, you are old and you still don't know the answer.'

Ajji replied calmly, 'I am not educated. I have not gone to school. What do I have? Only my prayers.'

'But you know language is not a lie. You know Ganesha is not a lie.'

'Yes, that I know. I am not educated, but I have lived for seventy years. So I know.'

They both sat silently as the darkness came in waves of croaking frogs, spluttering buses and faintly ringing bells from the temple. Deeksha waited in the hope that Kalpana would come back healthy. That the doctor would cure her of her foolishness.

Ajji pulled herself up. She put on the light in the hall and went to light the lamp. As soon as she had, Deeksha asked, 'So, Ajji, is Ganesha really in the temple? Do my prayers go to this Ganesha? Or to some other Ganesha?'

What she had wanted to ask was whether Ganesha was just a word. Whether God was just another word, like every other. Whether prayers were just more words with no gods to hear them. Ajji kept quiet, as she recognised that these were questions that did not demand a reply.

THE TRIP TO THE DOCTOR HAD NOT BEEN VERY HELPFUL. The specialist was brusque and treated Kalpana and her parents like village idiots. After listening to what had happened, the neurologist did his usual round of basic tests to see if Kalpana would respond. He could find nothing wrong with her.

He told the father that Kalpana was physically healthy. 'But mentally,' he continued, 'I can't say. If she has had a shock, then she might have lost her voice. We will have to do some brain tests for that, but you can't do them here. If something has happened to her brain, then we will have to see what to do. Since she is not speaking now, we can try a speech therapist.' He paused and let the words slowly simmer. He was exclusively addressing the father and didn't see Kalpana's growing irritation towards him. 'But the problem is that we don't have any of these facilities here. The best place for you to go is Bengaluru. And you will have to stay there for some time, since she will need that time to get better.'

Mother finally spoke. 'Will she get her voice back if we do that?'

'That I cannot say. Even God cannot say.' The doctor looked irritated.

Kalpana glared at him and made as if to get up. Her mother pulled her back down into the chair.

Father was disappointed. How could he leave his job and go to Bengaluru? Where would they stay? And where would he get the money for all these tests? He said, 'Doctor, is there no medicine that you can give her? Something that can make her speak.'

The doctor was already scribbling something. 'I will give her something to calm her, to help the shock wear off.' The three of them stood up, and Father took the prescription. 'Be patient,' the doctor murmured to their tired, stooping backs.

They went to the pharmacist right outside the hospital. The man behind the counter looked at the father with concern. 'You are taking any other medicine? For BP?'

Father was puzzled. 'No.'

The pharmacist said, 'I am making sure. This medicine has side effects if you take it with BP tablets.'

Mother immediately jumped in. 'What is this medicine for?'

'Nothing much. But it can make you feel very sleepy. Your husband will sleep far better with it, but don't make a habit of it.' He grinned at them till he saw the expression on the mother's face.

Father, now worried, said, 'It is for my daughter.' As he said that, all three of them turned to look at Kalpana. So did two other onlookers loitering in the store.

'Your daughter? What happened? She is not sleeping well?'

One of the onlookers told the mother, 'Just give her milk with turmeric before she goes to bed. She will sleep very well.'

The pharmacist was not done. 'I don't think this medicine is right for your daughter. What is her problem?' Again, all eyes turned towards Kalpana. She walked away from the store, her mother hurrying behind her.

Father was caught in no-man's land. He said, 'Okay, give me just two tablets. I will use them if there is an emergency.'

He paid for the tablets. An older man, who was leaning against the counter and reading *Prajavani*, the daily Kannada paper, added, 'Take her to the Devi temple. They can cure whatever problem that girl has.'

Babu drove three silent people back to their house. Kalpana was becoming disinterested in what the doctors had to say. She knew what the problem was, and medicines were no answer. Father was still thinking about Bengaluru and Mother was wondering when Kalpana would go back to school.

'Did the doctor say everything is fine?' Babu asked.

Father grunted a reply. It sounded like yet another burst of the auto exhaust.

The medicine was put in a little box with other bits of forgotten tablets. When Kalpana had stretched herself on her mat, Deeksha came and sat next to her. She told her excitedly that she had spoken to Ajji and what Ajji had said. 'I know what you did,' she whispered. 'You followed Ajji's prayers to see if they would take you to Ganesha.'

Kalpana was too tired to respond.

'Don't worry. I will find the answer for you, and then you can begin to speak,' said Deeksha with great confidence. Kalpana smiled at her sister's enthusiasm. 'I will follow the prayers and show you where Ganesha is,' Deeksha declared proudly. Kalpana was aghast and hit her, not so gently, on her shoulder. She shook her head vigorously: *No, no, no.*

Deeksha looked at her and said, 'You hit me so hard,' and they both fell on their mats, laughing. As Deeksha drifted into sleep, she knew that she had a new question for her Kannada teacher.

WHEN UPADHYA ENTERED THE CLASSROOM, HE SAW DEEKSHA jump up with her hand stretched to the ageing, tiled roof. With a little more energy, it seemed as if she could have flown to the roof. Her eyes were shining, and she had a wide smile. Upadhya was happy to see this. That one cathartic class earlier had changed his mood. It did not matter to him much if the students were interested in listening to him or not. All he wanted to do now was perform, show the students the pleasure he got in reading poems and stories. So he was inclined to be indulgent to his newly-found undeclared patron, Deeksha.

Kumari also jumped up and stood beside Deeksha. She had no question to ask, but wanted to show her solidarity.

Deeksha said, speaking quickly, 'Sir, Sir, I have another question.'

The other students laughed. Even Upadhya smiled. 'What is it this time?'

'Sir, I ... we,' she added, looking at Kumari, 'we want to know where a word goes.'

The class burst into laughter again.

Upadhya asked them to keep quiet and listen. 'What are you really asking, Deeksha?'

'Sir, when I throw a stone, you can see it fall somewhere. Correct, Sir? Then, when I speak, where do my words go?'

Kumari was not to be left behind. 'Sir, suppose I say a word. Does it fall from my mouth?'

Upadhya was puzzled. But he said, 'Let us ask some other student to answer this question. Does a word fall from your mouth?' He looked around as if expecting somebody to answer.

The class was quiet. Upadhya picked out a boy who had always done well in his class.

'Manjunatha, you tell me. When you say a word, does it fall?'

Manjunatha stood up. 'No, Sir, there is nothing to fall. If I say table, a table does not come out of my mouth.'

Everybody laughed loudly. A couple of the boys drummed an approving beat on their desks. Deeksha and Kumari smiled. Imagine a table coming out of Manjunatha's thin, elongated mouth!

Kumari was undaunted. 'Sir, forget about a table coming out of his mouth. You please ask him if a word comes out of his mouth or not.'

Deeksha added, 'Yes, Sir, you ask him that.'

A set of girls sitting next to Deeksha and Kumari clapped.

Upadhyay was not pleased. 'No clapping in class. This is a serious discussion. Do all of you know what a discussion is?' There were some hesitant nods.

'So, Manjunatha, tell these two girls whether words come out of your mouth.' Seeing that Manjunatha was silent, he added, 'Try saying a word, any word.'

Two of Manjuantha's friends said, 'Table, table.'

Manjuantha slowly pronounced the word 'table' and acted as if something fell out of his mouth. He mimed catching it as it fell and bent over as if the word was very heavy. The whole class clapped.

Kumari, looking at Manjunatha, said, 'The word came out of your mouth.'

Deeksha added, 'It is like spitting. Your mouth was open, and you were spitting out the word.'

A silence fell over the class. They did not understand fully, but it sounded like a serious 'discussion'.

Upadhya was pleased. 'Yes, like spit. And spit falls.'

Deeksha interrupted, 'His word came to me, Sir. It came to her and to you. So words do move.'

Manjunatha sat down. He had not thought of such questions. He had only wanted to crack a joke and make his friends laugh.

Kumari then asked, 'So, Sir, what we want to know is how this word moves from him to you.'

Suddenly, for the first time in their memory, Krishna, a tiny dark boy, stood up and said, 'Sir, I think words are carried by spit. When I heard what Manjunatha said, it was his spit that fell on me.'

Upadhya was amazed at what was happening around him. In all his struggles to get his students to enjoy the language, he had never met with such responses.

Another boy got up. 'Sir, that is not correct. Words are not carried by spit. If that were the case, we would have to take a bath each time we heard a word.' He looked like he was seriously concerned.

Upadhya went to the board and drew a mouth, and at some distance from it, an ear. He explained how the word produced from a mouth was heard by an ear. A word travels like a stone, he said, although we cannot see it like we see a stone.

Krishna stood up again. 'Sir, so if there is nobody to hear, will the word move?'

Deeksha turned to look at Krishna. Who was he?! He had asked her question. 'Sir, Sir,' she jumped in, 'if nobody is there to listen, where does the word go?'

Upadhya knew where words went. They went round and round in his head. They spoke, laughed and cried within him. They came out of his mouth, ears and nose. Sometimes whispering, shouting and screaming. They surrounded his face, tickled his greying beard and irritated his throat. Words, words, words. That fell over one another and sang songs within him. They made his eyes twitch, irritated the soles of his feet and sometimes made him scratch. But how could he say all of this to these little children? How could he remove the romance of words, make them just another falling stone or a stream of spittle aimed at the ground? He kept quiet.

Till Kumari in a tiny voice said, hesitatingly, 'But if I say a word, I can hear it. Even if nobody else does.'

The bell rang, and the students got up, much slower and quieter than they usually did. It was as if the sound of the bell had become a heavy rope that slowly drew them out of the room. In a true sense, sounds and words had entered into the lives and imaginations of these little children.

Deeksha insisted that Kumari come with her and tell Kalpana all that had happened in class. The three girls sat outside Deeksha and Kalpana's house as dusk gave way to a night filled with lights sporadically popping up along the main road. Kumari said, 'I know where words go. They go out of your mouth and come back into your ear.' Both Kumari and Deeksha felt unaccountably sad, as if in solving this problem they realised that life would not be as much fun as before.

But Kalpana was having none of it. She brought the notebook from the storeroom. She drew an open mouth and a word tumbling out of it and going back into the ear. She showed it to the two girls, and they nodded. Then she drew a face with a closed mouth and a word going from the tongue inwards and up to the ear. And she pointed to herself.

The girls understood immediately. Kalpana drew another picture of a word coming out of a mouth. One path took it back to the ear, while other paths took it away in many other directions. Kalpana stood up and opened her mouth wide, as though she were screaming. Deeksha and Kumari looked at her, captivated by their own little angry goddess, eyes closed and arms spread out, screaming at the mountain with not a tiny sound escaping her. Kalpana's silent scream bounced off the mountains and echoed back in rolling sheets of thunder and rain. The three girls ran past Ajji, who stood at the door, muttering words meant for invisible ears.

THE THREE OF THEM SAT IN THE STOREROOM. DEEKSHA SAID they should all play ludo. Her mother generously deep-fried goli bajji for the girls, as well as a few for Ajji, whose favourite snack it was. Life, it seemed, was not totally lost, and the past was regained in little measures of repeated comforts.

In the midst of playing, Deeksha suddenly stopped. She went to a corner of the room and picked up a plastic water bottle from a bag filled with vessels, bottles, and all those things that her mother could not bring herself to throw away. She opened the cap and peered into the bottle. She showed it to the other two and declared, 'You see that this bottle is empty.' The two of them nodded. Deeksha huddled closer to them, the three of them looking like three pegs of a tent, and said, 'I was thinking of a way to catch the words as they go from my mouth to you. I will speak into the bottle, and then we close the cap.'

In response, Kumari smiled so widely that it was as if her soul came shining out of her mouth. She didn't have words to tell Deeksha what she thought of her idea. Kalpana nodded like an adult.

So, into the open bottle Deeksha spoke. She kept her mouth at a little distance from the opening. Kalpana pushed her face towards the opening. She gestured that the words would fall outside the bottle. Deeksha put her mouth to the lip of the bottle but found that she couldn't utter the words clearly.

'What word are you going to say?' Kumari asked. Kalpana and Deeksha looked at each other.

'Ganesha,' said Deeksha. 'Ganesha, Ganesha, Ganesha,' she muttered into the plain little plastic bottle with a half-torn sticker and a blue cap. She uttered the words with her lips just touching the opening of the bottle, and quickly screwed the blue cap back on. Suddenly, there was a power cut, and in the darkness, Deeksha put the bottle in the middle of the triangle they had made. All three girls stared at it, waiting to see sudden flashes of light emanating from the word of god bouncing inside the bottle.

Nothing happened. They kept the bottle near their ears, hoping to hear some rattling whispers. Kalpana shook the bottle and imagined marbles rolling inside. She shook her head, dejected, and put the bottle back on the ground. Kumari's mother called out to her from outside the door. The rain had stopped and the crickets began their march into the night. As Kumari left, Deeksha told both of them, 'We will keep it like this. Maybe the sound will become louder.'

All three nodded wisely. Kalpana felt so proud of her sister that she almost opened her mouth to say, 'You are so much cleverer than me.'

AS THE DAYS WENT BY, KALPANA WAS ALMOST FORGOTTEN at school and in the village. Her family went about their daily lives as usual. Kalpana had become another human oddity, an example of the magic of unexpected happenings.

Siddaiah dropped by one day to inform Ajji of a new doctor. 'Doctor of the mind,' he whispered loudly. He said he would send Babu to take them to the doctor. Ajji had slowly lost faith in him and nodded her head irritatedly. As if in reply to his suggestion, she asked, 'What happened to your plans of getting married?'

The plastic bottle with the sound of Ganesha lay mutely on the ground. One dark morning, when Kalpana got up, she accidentally stepped on the bottle and heard the plastic getting crushed. Even with all her anger at Ganesha, she felt bad that she had somehow stamped on the god himself.

A couple of days later, Kumari came to their house with a glass bottle. It had been a bottle of jam, but every bit of the jam had been wiped clean by her. The bottle had been washed and dried, but still had a fading, partly torn label: *Kissan*.

Kumari gave Deeksha the bottle and said, 'You should now speak a new word into this bottle. A glass jam bottle may be better than a plastic water bottle. Maybe your words will also like jam, like you do.' Kumari and Deeksha giggled, remembering how much they liked to lick off the last unseen bits of the bright red jam.

Kalpana nodded. She wanted to say, 'Don't say Ganesha. That word is of no use.' Instead, she stared mutely and intensely at Deeksha, willing her to listen to her inner words.

Immediately, Deeksha responded. 'We can say "mara". If we speak that word inside this bottle, maybe a tree will grow. Let us see what happens with this word.'

That dusky evening, Deeksha muttered 'Mara, mara, mara, mara, mara' into the empty jam bottle and quickly screwed on the cap. Like a seed planted in the mud, they carefully kept the bottle on a shelf, away from 'Kalpana's kicking legs', in the words of Deeksha. Words that were accompanied by yet another ever-springing giggle.

'Should we pour water in it?' Kumari wondered.

Instead, what they decided was that Deeksha would monitor the bottle every day to see if the word had started growing like a tree. They looked at the empty bottle wistfully. Had the words settled down? Would they take root? Would they, one bright morning, see the word transformed into its meaning and then see a little tree growing inside that bottle?

Kalpana showed the girls what she had written in her book: *Words are like seeds*. They nodded wisely, as if they understood the full significance of her words.

Kalpana had used up three of her notebooks, filling them with furious scribbles. The pages were filled with diagrams, badly drawn pictures, scribbles and alphabets that seemed to burrow into one another. But her agitation had not decreased. She was finding it more difficult to control the words that threatened to burst forth. She thought that if she uttered one word, it would be the end. Her decision to not speak would become a joke. But her body was paying a price for bottling the words inside her. When she could no longer convert her agitation into the squiggles in her notebook, she started poking herself. It began as an accident. While walking outside one day, she stepped on some sharp gravel. Her soles felt as if they had been pierced by many thorns. Later, in her agitated state, she began poking the soles of her feet with her pencil. And then she started writing on the soles of her feet. She discovered a great release in this act, as if she had finally found the right punishment for language, as if she had found the right slate to write words on. She could write what she wanted on her soles and then rub them out viciously, scraping her soles on the floor or on the grassy mud outside the house. She felt a great sense of power and liberation. She had language under her control. She could write her thoughts and feelings but, at the same time, not allow anybody else to read them. She would sit with her left leg folded and write furiously on the sole of that foot. She would soon feel that the right foot was not being used at all. Her body could sense the imbalance of the sensations in the two soles. So she started using her left hand to scribble on her right sole. Whenever she felt she had to respond to something—particularly when she heard her mother and Ajji talking to each other—she would start writing on her foot. It was becoming less painful, and the skin was hardening. But in all that pain, not a single sound was squeezed out of her.

After three days of staring at the bottle and seeing nothing inside it, Deeksha thought it better to keep the bottle in the kitchen. She told Kalpana, 'I think it needs more light. Have you ever seen any tree growing inside a house?' Kalpana had become indifferent to the bottle by then. Deeksha put the bottle on a shelf, away from the many little glass bottles of mustard, dal, chilli powder, turmeric and other spices. She told her mother that it was homework and that she shouldn't touch it. 'Don't even go near it,' she added. Her mother only remarked that the bottle was 'fully' empty and wondered what her children were learning at school.

SIDDAIAH CAME BACK AGAIN ONE NIGHT. HE HAD TAKEN A friend to the 'doctor for the mind', and during that visit he had mentioned Kalpana's case to him. The doctor, he informed Kalpana's father, told him that it was a common problem and could be cured. He also said that he would make all the arrangements to fix a time with the doctor. When Kalpana's father thanked him, he said, 'What thanks? She is our girl.'

Ajji felt proud and told the father, 'He is a good boy. Find a good girl for him.'

They went to the doctor the next evening. Siddaiah had sent a friend of his to meet Kalpana and her parents at the hospital. There was really nothing for the friend to do, but he hung around awkwardly for a while, then began speaking on his phone.

The doctor was a young man. He was originally from this region too. That much was clear from his name: Dr Nayak. He looked at Kalpana with interest. She seemed very bright, although unnecessarily angry. Kalpana's father told him what had happened.

Dr Nayak was gentle and seemed genuinely concerned. 'Was she speaking properly before she went missing?' he asked.

Kalpana's mother smiled with a tinge of sadness. 'She spoke too much.'

'And from the time she came back, she has not spoken?'

'Yes, not a single word.'

Dr Nayak asked Kalpana to open her mouth. Asked her to say 'aah'. Kalpana opened her mouth passively.

'You have to try. Try saying aah.'

Kalpana said 'aah' within herself. She could feel the throat muscles contract and felt the air flowing along her throat. But no sound emerged.

'Can you shout?' The doctor smiled at her. 'Scream as loud as you want. None of us will object.' The parents too smiled. Kalpana opened her mouth wider and screamed very loudly. Her face showed the effort: her eyes grew wide and her cheeks vibrated. But not a sound came out of her mouth.

'Looks like this could be a problem with her vocal cords, or it could be neurological. Some damage due to the shock.'

He picked up Kalpana's arms and, while measuring her pulse, pricked her slightly with a needle. Kalpana reacted but made no sound. She thought, *What a doctor. He thinks he can trick me!* She looked down to hide the glee in her eyes.

'So, do you know what happened to her?'

Father had answered this question a thousand times. 'No. She left for school as usual. But it looks like she did not reach the school.'

'And this was in the morning, right?

'Yes. Nobody saw anything.'

'Then what happened?'

'We knew that she was missing when she didn't come home in the evening. We searched all over. The whole village searched for her everywhere.'

Kalpana's mother remembered that day and her eyes misted. 'It was raining heavily that day,' she added.

'How many days was she missing?'

'Three days.'

'And no news on those three days?'

'No, doctor.'

'Then what happened?'

'That morning, after three days, Kalpana was found lying on the ghat road about twenty kilometres from our village. Thankfully, the bus driver saw her and stopped the bus. She was shivering, wet and covered in mud. They brought her on the bus to our house.'

'Was she hurt in any way?'

Both the parents quickly and simultaneously said, 'No.'

'Please think. This is most important. Whatever happened to her, you have to tell me. Otherwise I cannot cure her.'

'No, nothing happened.' The father looked at the mother, willing her to speak as a woman about a girl.

Mother said, 'Nothing. Her clothes were not torn, but they were muddy and dirty. She smelled of rain and leaves.' She smiled at Kalpana, who smiled back.

'And she did not tell you anything.'

'Not a word.'

'She did not make a sound.'

'No. When she saw me, she hugged me very tightly and cried. But after that, no sound and no tears.'

'Did the police find out anything?'

'No. They had no idea. We were the ones who went searching for her.'

'Did a doctor examine her after she came back?'

Father looked at Mother again. Kalpana had allowed nobody near her except her mother. That evening, a government doctor had been brought to the house by the police.

Mother said, 'Yes, a lady doctor examined her.'

Kalpana bent her head, feeling shameful. How that doctor had prodded and looked. And asked her questions.

'And what did she say after the examination?'

'That nothing was wrong.' Mother couldn't say what she wanted to say. Not to a male doctor with her husband and daughter there: that her little girl wasn't touched or harmed in any way.

'So we do not know what happened in those three days.' He turned to Kalpana. 'Can you tell us what happened?'

Kalpana stared back at him.

'Something happened to you. It was a shock for you. That is why you have lost your voice.'

Unaccountably, she thought of Deeksha and felt the beginnings of a giggle inside her.

'So when we discover what the shock was, we will discover how to cure you.'

Father was very impressed with the doctor. He would definitely recommend him to his friends. But then he remembered that, unfortunately, this doctor was a doctor only for the mind.

Kalpana nodded as if she understood. If she had decided to speak, she could have taught him a lot about speech and silence.

'I will ask you questions to find out what caused the shock. And you nod if I am correct.' Kalpana nodded.

'Did somebody take you away that morning?'

Kalpana showed no response. 'Did a man or men take you? Have you heard the word "kidnap"?' He turned to the father.

'What do they say for kidnap in Kannada?' Father looked at Mother. Her Kannada was so much better. But Mother couldn't immediately think of the word for kidnap. Or maybe she didn't want to acknowledge that possibility.

'If that is what happened, tell us without being afraid. We are here to protect you.'

Kalpana smiled at him.

'Is that yes or no?'

She smiled more broadly.

'Why are you smiling?'

She looked at him blandly.

A sudden thought struck the doctor. 'Did you not want to go to school?' He looked triumphantly at the parents.

Mother immediately said, 'No, she always enjoys going to school. She likes it far more than sitting at home.' She too shared her daughter's excitement for school. She had often wished that she could have gone on studying.

'Ah, yes. Maybe you can also study to be a doctor!' He thought he had cracked a joke, but Kalpana merely stared back at him.

The doctor had spent enough time with her. He told Kalpana's father that they should come back for more tests. When Father asked what those tests would be, Dr Nayak said that he and his assistant would do some tests to discover any hidden trauma.

Mother looked worried. Seeing her expression, the doctor laughed. 'No, we won't give her any shock.' She looked blankly back at him. 'Based on the tests, I will decide on medicines for her.'

'Would that be medicines for the throat, doctor?' asked the mother.

Dr Nayak laughed. 'The throat is the least of her problems. It is her brain that speaks, not the throat or the mouth.'

They left, the parents disappointed with the end result. But Kalpana seemed very happy. She was overjoyed not because she had managed to keep silent but because of what the doctor had said at the end. It was the brain that spoke! She had been wrong all along. Words don't fall out from the mouth. They fall out from the brain! How wonderful! Suddenly, a great sense of sadness and anxiety fell upon her. If only she had continued speaking, she could have asked the doctor about the brain. How much she had given up just because she had stopped speaking! Sometimes it wasn't even clear to her why she was refusing to speak.

But by the time she bounced back home in Babu's auto, her spirits had raced back. She told herself that if she had not stopped speaking, she wouldn't have met the doctor and wouldn't have learnt that it was the brain that spoke. Now all she had to do was to find a way of communicating this to Deeksha.

HER VISIT TO DR NAYAK WAS A KEY THAT UNLOCKED DOORS that the doctor could not have imagined. This one visit had many consequences for Kalpana. First, she decided to get more notebooks to write her thoughts in. The days of scribbling her anger and fear were over. The second consequence was that she decided to find a way to go back to school, but without speaking.

The third consequence was catalysed by Ajji in an indirect manner. A couple of days after the visit to the mind doctor, the wife of the local priest stopped outside their house and called out to Ajji. When Ajji went up to her, she said, 'The priest was saying that he hasn't seen you at the temple for many days.' She always referred to her husband as 'the priest'. Peeping into the darkened insides of the house, she added, 'Everything is okay at home?'

Ajji went to the temple that evening. It was on a small, elevated hillock. There was nobody there except for the priest.

Seeing Ajji, he said, 'So you came. How is everybody?'

He gave her a packet of god's blessings: a combination of sugar and coconut pieces, packed neatly in small paper covers. Ajji pulled out a crumpled ten-rupee note that had been tucked into the innumerable folds of her saree and put it on the offering plate.

A young couple came into the temple. They took one of the packets and walked away to circumambulate the shrine.

'I sent for you, Ajji, because I heard that your son took your granddaughter to a mental doctor.'

Ajji nodded. 'I hear he is very good.'

'He may be. I don't know. But why are you taking the girl to a mental doctor? I have never heard of anybody being cured by going to such doctors.'

Ajji had no answer. A dog entered and lay down across the entrance to the temple.

'I don't remember the girl coming here. We can take care of her problem. Sometimes they get possessed, as you know.'

Ajji nodded vigorously. 'My son—'

'Yes, your son. He works in the town, so he thinks he knows more than us.'

'No, it isn't like that.'

'I am not saying come to the temple. Or go see the tantri, who will tell you exactly what the problem is and what to do about it. I want to only tell you one thing. We had a person like this in our family—older than your granddaughter. She too lost her voice, and then her mother sent her to a music teacher. That girl got back her speech by learning to sing!'

The couple had gone once around the shrine and were now standing next to them.

'Wonderful, isn't it?' the priest remarked, not just to his human audience but also to the deity of the temple and the many smaller deities distributed all around him.

Thus it was that Dr Nayak unintentionally became the cause for Kalpana to go to a music teacher.

The fourth unintended consequence was catalysed by Deeksha. When she heard the half-digested sounds of 'mental doctor', Deeksha was petrified. She had heard it from a teacher who, on seeing Deeksha walk by, told her colleague, 'They took her sister to the mental doctor, it seems.' Deeksha's only awareness of 'the mental' was associated with a 'mad' woman who used to sit outside the temple many years ago. She was an old woman in tattered clothes who slept there and ate what people gave her. She never spoke, but used to grunt, particularly at little children. So this woman was used as a convenient threat by young mothers who could not control their kids.

When Deeksha heard her teacher, she immediately remembered the old woman. Nobody knew who she was or where she went. One day she was there and another day she was gone. Deeksha had a horrible image of Kalpana sitting outside the temple, grunting at little kids. Had Kalpana become a 'mental case', a phrase that she and her friends used as a form of light-hearted abuse for students they didn't like?

Deeksha walked back home filled with fear about Kalpana. But she also resolved to help her sister, whatever happened. She would make her speak. She would make her smile and dance. By the time she reached home, she knew how she was going to do it. She would force Kalpana to teach her.

THE NOTEBOOKS AND PENCILS WERE THE EASIEST TO organise. Kalpana took two of Deeksha's notebooks, and when Deeksha protested, she gestured to her to ask her mother. Deeksha was secretly pleased and hoped Kalpana would write instead of making those horrible scratches in the book. Kalpana opened the newly khaki-sheet-bound book and wrote the first line: *It is the brain that speaks.* Thankfully, she had learnt the Kannada word for brain at school.

She showed the line to Deeksha, who smiled seeing the sentence. Would this be her sister's first steps towards a normal life? She laughed and said, 'Is this the first line of a joke?' Kalpana drew a face with a flat, squiggly brain on top and a closed mouth. She then drew an arrow from the brain to the mouth. The arrow looked more like a pipe. She mimed words flowing from her brain to her mouth.

'I thought we spoke from here,' Deeksha said, pointing to her vocal cords.

Kalpana nodded. She drew a tube from the brain going through the throat to the mouth.

Deeksha didn't understand the point of it. She stood up and adjusted her dress as if she were onstage. She closed her mouth tightly and traced her fingers from the brain to the mouth. Kalpana nodded encouragingly.

Deeksha opened her mouth. 'You are saying words come from my brain. So I can close my mouth and talk.'

She closed her mouth again and made animated expressions. She started nodding vigorously, as if agreeing that words were tumbling down from her brain into her mouth. She puffed up her cheeks as if struggling to keep the overflowing words inside. Then she opened her mouth and produced squeals like sharp raindrops falling all around her. Her mother came running in, thinking that something had happened. Deeksha was laughing and Kalpana was smiling.

Deeksha told her, 'Amma, you should try filling your mouth with your words.'

Mother shook her head and went back to her TV show. Her daughter was only in the fifth standard and she was already not able to understand her! She converted this thought into words for Ajji. 'What they teach girls today!'

Deeksha was struck by Kalpana's idea. She was acting, no doubt, but for a moment it had seemed like words had indeed filled her puffed-up mouth. Suddenly, more saliva had been generated and those words flowed into her stomach along with the saliva. She remembered her class discussion. Were words really carried by spit?

Kalpana wrote on the sheet: *Brain speaks. Brain also hears.*

She connected the tube from the brain to the tongue and extended it to the ear. All of them as little independent objects inside the head.

Deeksha said, 'You speak with your mouth closed, only you can hear.'

Kalpana nodded. They both sat in silence, each one thinking.

Deeksha hesitantly said, 'But I speak to myself.'

Kalpana got up excitedly, clapping. *Yes, yes, yes.* Her head bobbed up and down.

Deeksha too jumped up. 'Yes, we keep talking to ourselves all the time.'

She did a little jig and skipped around the room. She hugged Kalpana tightly and ran out.

She saw Ajji, Mother and Father sitting tiredly in front of the TV. She went and stood in front of the TV and spoke like a news announcer.

'I want to tell you that Akka has been speaking all this time.'

Father was most surprised. But he saw so little of his daughters that he didn't know if she was joking or not.

'Yes, she speaks the whole day.' Deeksha looked at Ajji and Mother.

Both their faces fell. They knew Kalpana had not been doing that. Father asked Mother, 'What is this girl saying? You knew? Why did we go to the doctor then?'

Seeing her mother's face, Deeksha hastily said, 'I have just discovered that Kalpana keeps talking to herself all the time. She is constantly talking, but only she can hear herself.'

Her father was furious. He got up from his chair and raised his hand as if to smack Deeksha. She slipped under his raised arm and would have run away, but his palm caught her on the back. Father had only wanted to frighten her, but Deeksha felt the blow and started crying.

Mother shouted at Father, while Ajji muttered curses at all of them.

Father picked Deeksha up and said he hadn't meant to hit her. Deeksha clung to him and told him, 'I am only telling the truth. She can speak. She speaks. But she doesn't want to speak to us. To anybody.' She would have liked to say, *Her words are for herself alone, and all we can do is wait till she gets tired of speaking only to herself.* But Deeksha could not say that—not then.

Kalpana had come out into the hall and was watching them silently. Her mother could not control herself. 'All because of you. Why can't you just speak like a normal girl?' Kalpana looked at the three adults and felt that they were all staring accusingly at her. She felt a sudden sense of betrayal and ran into her room, ready to burst into tears.

Why couldn't she just speak? Yes, why couldn't she? Why should a little girl decide to extinguish the fire in her life—her speech? Maybe Mother would have understood if she had been in the forest that night, sitting under the tree, imagining unimaginable creatures entering her body. Or the day after she went missing, when she went along each clearing, thinking that it was a path, looking vainly at the sky through canopies whose leaves no longer looked green but black. Shouting for people who had all gone into hiding, whose houses had all dissolved in the rain till there was no one left but little Kalpana—short, thin, scrawny, only a little girl in the middle of a gigantic, wet forest.

The next day had been better. The sun was out and the birds were making sounds she had never heard before, vying for Kalpana's attention. She had survived the night, dozing on and off, stumbling through the forest, her voice fading after hours of shouting to unseen people and, most frequently, to her unseen god, Ganesha. She was lost and ready to lie down and wait for the terror to envelop her. But suddenly, the sun came through, came down the leaves, crept along the bark of the tree under which Kalpana lay, and tickled her eyes. When Kalpana opened her eyes, she could have sworn she saw the sun standing in front of her, smiling so brightly that it hurt her eyes. She looked around and found she was surrounded by mango-laden trees, the forest mango so famous for pickles. She ate her fill and stuffed her bag with more. Walking now with a purpose, as if she could discern houses in the distance, she saw the forest for what it was. She found a half-cracked jackfruit lying on the ground and tore at it. No fruit had tasted more divine.

By the time evening came, the clouds rolled in, the darkness began to rapidly fall and her tired voice could not shout any more. But Kalpana was not a coward. She had survived one night and she would survive another. She found a huge banyan tree and remembered her teachers telling her that banyan trees could be hundreds of years old. This fact about its old age comforted her. If that tree could survive untold nights in the forest, day after day, rain after rain, so could she. She half lay, half sat, hugging the trunk of the tree. The night was not easy. The rain stopped, and just as suddenly, the clouds vanished to reveal the moon, which lit up the forest. Kalpana felt a great sense of joy in the midst of her fear. Her foremost thought was that if she had been at home, she would never have seen this sight. She stared at the stars for so long that she felt she had become one of them. If only she could fly above those trees and shine like the stars above. As she fell asleep, she had an idea, but before she could fully grasp it, she had vanished into the world of black sleep.

So why can't you just speak? Kalpana felt a great sense of injustice and would have given in to a fresh bout of crying if Deeksha had not come and lain down beside her.

'I am sorry, Akka. I should not have said that. That was your secret.'

Kalpana remained silent. After a long pause filled only with the background noise of adult murmurs from the hall, Deeksha said, 'But I was so happy that you have not lost your voice. Or forgotten your language. I was only scared of that.'

So saying, Deeksha started crying. 'I was afraid you would never speak and would become like that mad old woman outside the temple.'

Kalpana started laughing, her throat moving silently. She pulled Deeksha close to her. Oh, how much she wanted to whisper into her ear.

Deeksha sat up. 'Akka, I have a great idea. I know what to do. You don't have to open your mouth at all. After all, you are always speaking to yourself. Your brain is speaking to your ear. So, what I think is, we can put a mic in your brain and connect it to the TV. Then you can sit quietly and we can listen to you clearly! We can even hear you speaking from inside the TV!' She jumped up and down, clapping her little hands. 'This is a good idea, Akka. What do you say?'

The three adults sitting gloomily in the hall heard loud laughter from Deeksha. And then more sounds came, in rolling peals, sounds bouncing off each other with great delight. They listened to the sounds more closely, but there was no way they could tell which was Deeksha's laughter and which could have been her sister's.

Kalpana came closest to breaking her vow then. When the laughter had died down, she leaned over to whisper in Deeksha's ear. She would have said, 'For your idea, here are my words as a gift to you,' but at the last moment, she turned away, curling her body to hold back the words that so desperately wanted to escape her. She was fast losing control over her words, which now seemed to have an independent will of their own.

Deeksha too thought that Kalpana was going to say something as she moved closer to her. When Kalpana turned away at the last moment, she felt a terrible sense of disappointment. Managing to control herself, she weakly asked, 'But why are you so angry about speaking? I don't understand at all, Akka. I don't understand why you are doing this.'

Kalpana got up from the mat and picked up her notebook. In the reflected light from the room outside, she started writing. She clearly remembered the exact moment when she had lost the will to speak. And she did not want to forget it. She wrote:

Prayers are lies.
Where is god to listen to all our prayers?
How can we think that god will help us pass our exams?
Or take care of our stomach aches?
Who are we speaking to when we pray?

On the third day in the forest, feeling hungry and sick, Kalpana had felt a deep sense of loss. She experienced a sense of nothingness, a feeling of being nothing at all. She saw herself as a leaf on the soggy earth, slowly rotting. She felt cast out and betrayed. Betrayed most of all by the words that she believed in, that she so unthinkingly followed. Words that resonated in every nook and corner of a human being. She felt betrayed by Ajji saying false prayers all the time. By her parents for taking her to so many temples and making her chant prayers that they themselves didn't understand. She felt most betrayed that her prayers had let her down in the forest. That not a single god had heard her screams, cries and pleas. Her terror had been her own, with not a hand to hold. She was convinced that all those prayers and songs for unseen gods were a lie. The belief that her prayers were heard by them was a lie.

On that day, lying under another shady tree, feeling sick after eating too many mangoes and drinking from a stream of brownish water, after listening once more to her feeble shouts that found no other listener, she lost her belief but discovered a new sense of anger. She promised herself that she would find her way out and show the world the lies of language, and of the prayers they so believed in. She stopped shouting, stopped calling for Ganesha, and instead listened to the massive silence of a million creatures around her. She realised that none of those creatures spoke like humans did, and that thought gave her a great sense of peace. If they couldn't speak, then they couldn't lie. *They cannot lie. They cannot lie.* That became her new refrain.

Later in the afternoon she saw a tall tree with sturdy branches close to the ground. She began climbing the tree with some difficulty, but as she went up higher, she began to feel that she could hop from one branch to the next with ease, like yet another insect on the huge, canopied tree. Once she had climbed above the dense foliage, she discovered that she could see the vast expanse of the forest. The view calmed her and she felt one with the forest. Her fear vanished, almost turning into joy. Many minutes later, as the clouds rolled in yet again, this time almost as a duty, she thought she saw a light. She stared at it, and in the encroaching darkness of the evening, she thought she could see a bobbing yellow light in the distance. She was sure she could see a road some distance off. Energised, she scampered down, tearing her dress here and there, scratching her arms and elbows, and with a new spirit, she walked in the direction of the road. But the rain started, the darkness fell with a force that seemed to suffocate her, and she spent another night shivering in the cold. Her ordeal would not be over till the next morning, when she woke up to the sound of a bus labouring over the mountain.

KALPANA TOOK OUT HER NOTEBOOK AND WROTE DOWN THE thoughts that had filled her mind on that last day. Those thoughts that had made her promise herself that she would never again speak in the land of liars. That she would be like the animals and insects around her that did not speak, that did not have a language, did not have gods to mutter prayers to, and thus could not lie.

When she was discovered on the road, recognised and brought back to her home, everything she had felt in the forest was shown to be true. None of the people hovering around her understood her silence. Nor her pact with the millions of other living creatures around her to be one like them. To live in silence and in truth. Instead, their language only betrayed their fears and the lies of those fears. They wanted to examine her body. They wanted to know if any man or men had carried her away. 'Did they do something to you?' they asked, as if that was the most important question for all of them. Kalpana, in her silence, pitied them. After the first few days, she would have said this if she could have spoken: 'It is not their fault. It is only the fault of their language. Just because they have words within them, they speak them without knowing what they say.'

Watching the parade of people who came to look at her after her return, in a daze of lost sleep and a cold that had entered the depths of her bones, she had a thought that she now remembered as she wrote in her notebook.

Do we decide to speak or do words decide when to come out of our mouth?

It was this question, even though not fully understood by her, that made her decision not to speak easier to bear. In her forced silence, she found her will, her true voice. She would not be a slave to words that, without her bidding, would rush out and say what they wanted.

Deeksha read the words aloud.

'Is this a riddle?' she asked. Kalpana shook her head.

'I am the one who speaks, Akka. Isn't that so? When I speak, it is not Kalpana speaking.' She paused. 'Or Ajji speaking.' She laughed.

Kalpana wrote: *When you don't want to speak, do you still speak?*

'No. If I don't want to speak, I do not.'

Kalpana realised that Deeksha would not understand. As yet. She wrote: *Try being silent. Don't speak for a day.*

'I won't do that. Mother will become totally scared!'

Kalpana showed Deeksha what else she had written.

Prayers are lies.
Where is god to listen to all our prayers?
How can we think that god will help us pass our exams?
Or take care of our stomach aches?
Who are we speaking to when we pray?

Deeksha read all the lines.

'I agree, Akka. As Upadhya Sir would say, good questions!' She paused. 'But they are all wrong. Don't ask me why. I don't know.'

Deeksha felt that she was being asked to say something about a topic she did not want to speak about. So far in her schooling, it was the answers that had been either right or wrong. Now all these questions themselves seemed to be wrong. She loved going to the temples, putting flowers in her hair, eating the sweets she got there. She even liked to see the little Ganesha with his nice tummy. Somehow she felt Ganesha looked a bit like her, except for the elephant trunk. She smiled when she thought of his trunk. So adorable and so friendly. These questions from Kalpana did not make sense to her.

'I talk to Ganesha,' she confessed. 'I told him about you. Asked why he did not take care of you.'

Kalpana was surprised. She wrote: *So what did he say?*

Deeksha was hurt. She thought Kalpana was making fun of her.

'He said that you will be fine.'

He told you this in Kannada or in some other language?

Deeksha looked at Kalpana defiantly. 'Yes, I heard him in Kannada.'

What was his voice like?

Deeksha thought. She screwed her eyes shut. How had Ganesha sounded to her? She opened her eyes and said, 'Sounded just like you.'

Kalpana was stumped. She wanted to crack a joke. She was tempted to call her sister stupid. Or worse, a liar. When she had this thought, she suddenly stopped. She became aware of what she was doing. She was using language to hurt her sister. She stopped writing and smiled at Deeksha.

Deeksha persisted. 'Write something.'

Kalpana shook her head. To Deeksha, Kalpana suddenly looked like Mother. Not in the way she looked, but in the tiredness of her age.

Deeksha tried again. 'Please, write something.'

Kalpana refused.

Deeksha said, 'Okay, in that case, I will go talk to Ganesha instead.' She lay on the mat next to Kalpana, turned away from her and started muttering some gibberish with the sound of 'Ganesha' thrown in between.

DEEKSHA AND KUMARI WALKED BACK FROM SCHOOL TO Kumari's house. Kumari wanted Deeksha to taste a sweet that her mother had made the previous day. They put the sweet into their mouths and sat outside Kumari's house on a small cement platform.

Deeksha began by saying, 'Kumari, we have another question for Upadhya Sir.'

'What is it?'

'Do we speak or do words speak?'

'Hmm, that sounds like a riddle.'

'No, it is not a riddle.'

'Then it is nonsense. Words cannot speak.' Kumari started laughing at her own words.

Deeksha was irritated. 'What I mean is, do you decide what to say? What not to say? Don't you sometimes feel that you shouldn't have said something, yet you did?'

Of course, yes! Both of them remembered many times when words had escaped them and they felt that they should have kept quiet.

'Kalpana is right, I think. Words come out by themselves.'

Kumari was aghast. 'No, Deeksha, I do not agree. I am the one who speaks.'

They sat silently, furiously thinking.

Then Kumari said, 'How can words decide which word should come out of us?' They thought about this for some more time.

'I have a question,' Kumari said. 'Does the mouth decide to open and then speak?'

Deeksha had a quick answer. 'The doctor told Kalpana that it is the brain that speaks. Maybe the brain tells the mouth when to open and when to close.'

'So it is the brain that speaks,' Kumari declared. This sounded so absurd to them that they burst into a fit of giggles.

Kumari's mother came out and asked, 'What do you girls keep talking about so much?'

Kumari had the safest answer. 'We are talking about our homework.'

Later that night, Kumari's mother told her husband, 'Schools nowadays must be doing something different. I have never seen girls enjoy doing homework as much as Kumari and Deeksha.'

The two girls decided to play a game of dice. They drew a picture on the ground with their fingers and used cowrie shells as dice. Deeksha was distracted while playing, and soon Kumari felt her disinterest.

'You don't like this game?' she asked.

'No, no. I was just thinking. What if words make the brain speak? Maybe language has more power than our brain.'

Kumari thought for a moment. 'Yes, Deeksha, without language, what can the brain do?'

The two girls sat in silence, looking at the mountains and listening to a herd of cows going home, their tinkling bells a lullaby for the setting sun.

Deeksha said, 'Seems like the brain is more powerful than Ganesha.' Both felt a sense of sadness settle on them.

As Deeksha left for home, Kumari abruptly turned to her and said, 'Then let us build a temple for the brain. If Ganesha can have a temple and if the brain is more powerful than Ganesha, then we should also have a temple for the brain.'

That was enough for both of them to start squealing and for Kumari's mother to wonder again about what was so funny about their homework.

As they parted, they decided that on the coming Sunday they would build a temple for the brain, who it seemed was more powerful than their favourite god.

That night, Kalpana listened silently as Deeksha recounted her conversation with Kumari. Kalpana had changed over the last two days. She had realised that the moment she started writing, she had fallen back into the grip of language. She was silent, no doubt, but was no longer free from language. She looked older and wiser to Deeksha's constantly probing eyes. The whole day, she just sat on the mat, leaning against the wall, her notebook on a small, sloping table in front of her.

After Deeksha told her about the temple for the brain that they would build on Sunday, she smiled spontaneously.

'You will be the priest,' Deeksha added, and Kalpana laughed. Tiny little sounds struggled to escape her, escape from her.

But then, later, as the sisters were about to fall asleep, she remembered Deeksha's question and wondered if language had control over the brain. If that was the case, then they would have to build a temple for language. A temple for Kannada—imagine! She smiled as she curled up on her mat.

UPADHYA FINALLY CAME THROUGH. THAT DAY IN CLASS, HE wanted to teach some new words to the students. He had originally begun with an ambitious idea, to teach them one new word a day, inspired by the Government of India's initiative to introduce one Hindi word a day in Central government offices.

But, unlike the government, Upadhya soon gave up. He decided that it was more important to keep using one word in different sentences and contexts over many days instead of needlessly accumulating words, one each day.

But on that particular day, inspired by the previous class, he decided to go back to introducing a new word. He chose 'election'. He wrote the word in Kannada on the board. A group of boys at the back were talking to each other and laughing. Upadhya shouted, 'Chandru, get up!' Chandru was shocked into action. He was not aware that his teacher was even conscious of his existence in the class or that he knew his name.

Deeksha, who was watching this, reacted first. Before Upadhya could say anything to Chandru, she jumped up with her hand extended in the air, shouting, 'Sir, Sir.'

Upadhya ignored her and told Chandru to read the word aloud. Chandru's reading skills were not as sharp as they could have been. Put in the spotlight, he started stammering. He looked around the class and saw unknown backs and unknown faces. He saw all these children every day, but he had never seen them as he saw them at that moment, standing up and looking down at all of them.

Upadhya would have scolded him, but Deeksha intervened. 'Sir, Sir,' she said again, and Upadhya turned impatiently towards her.

'What do you want?'

'Sir, I don't have a question.'

That was a surprise. Upadhya looked at her, knowing well that Chandru was still standing.

'Sir, you said stand up to Chandru and he stood up. It was like ... like ...'

Kumari jumped up beside her. 'It is like this. If you tie a rope around a cow and pull at it, then it also stands up.'

Deeksha patted Kumari. 'Correct. It is like a rope.'

'What is?' asked Upadhya.

'The word, Sir. It's like a rope. You said stand up and he stood up. Just like the cow.'

Upadhya told Chandru to sit down.

Deeksha clapped her hands in delight. 'See, Sir, you told him to sit, and he sat. Why did he do that?'

'Because I told him to.'

'So who made him sit down?'

'I did. I am the teacher. I told him, and so he sat down.'

Kumari was undaunted. 'Sir, what she is saying is that the words you said made him sit down. It was your words and not you, Sir.'

Upadhya was stunned for a moment. These two girls were in truth two little devils. It was impossible that they had thought of this by themselves. But he was also secretly pleased, a pleasure that renewed his commitment to this dialogue.

'We will ask Chandru,' he said. Chandru was petrified. He had thought he had escaped the teacher, and now his name was resounding through the classroom again. He jumped up quickly, knocking his bony thigh on the table in front of him.

'Chandru,' Upadhya asked, 'why did you stand up?'

'Because ... because you told me, Sir.'

'So you got up because I told you?' He paused. 'Or because you heard the sound "Get up"?'

Chandru was confused. What was the difference between Sir and his words?

'Because of you, Sir. Because you told me, I stood up.'

'If Deeksha had told you the same words, would you have got up?'

Chandru looked at Deeksha. Like the others, he had not registered her presence consciously. They were both short, dark and skinny. Would he have stood up if she had told him to? He kept quiet.

Upadhya turned to Deeksha. 'See? Chandru will only listen to me, not to you. We both say the same words, but he will only obey me. So it is not language that makes him stand or sit.' He remembered that Chandru was still standing and gestured for him to sit down.

Deeksha was deflated. She had thought her idea was an inspired one, a great insight. What Kumari had said also seemed right to her. Language was a rope and you could make people do things by pulling on that rope.

She thought of Kalpana and knew what she wanted to say. She stood up again and said, 'Sir, if you were silent, he would not stand up.'

Upadhya ignored her. Or acted as if he didn't hear her. Or perhaps wanted to show that her words were not the rope that would make him act.

Kumari was convinced. As the two of them walked back home after school, her limping gait making her body swing like a metronome, she said, 'You are right, Deeksha. If I tell you to stop, you will stop. If I say run, you will run. Words make you do these things.' She stopped and looked around. 'I wonder how animals do anything.'

They reached Kumari's house and went straight to the backyard, where a few hens and chickens with long strings attached to their feet were busily hopping around. They sat in silence and watched and wondered why these chickens did what they did. The birds in the tree nearby also looked on silently, and then flew away, as if responding to inaudible calls.

That night, Deeksha told Kalpana about the class. 'You are right, Akka. It is only words that control us.'

She thought awhile and added, 'Not even our parents control us. They need words to shout at us.'

Deeksha remembered the glass jar. She ran to the kitchen and brought the bottle back carefully. The two girls looked at the empty bottle. In the fading yellow light in the room, Deeksha thought she could see something growing.

She was excited. 'Mara the word is becoming a real mara!'

Kalpana was sceptical. She silently handed the bottle back to Deeksha, motioning to her to keep it back in the kitchen.

Hearing what Deeksha had to say about control, Kalpana remembered the time in the forest when she had wanted to lie down and never get up. Her fear of snakes and tigers overtook her mind. She could not fight any longer, and the silence and approaching sleep seemed so welcome. She knew that it was just a matter of time before she gave in and lost the will to move, whatever the consequences. Words were her only companions then. It was repeated words of exhortation that made her get up. Words were what pulled her out. She kept murmuring to herself, 'Get up. Walk. Home is close.' When everything else had deserted her, only her words brought her out. She knew this well. She didn't know how, but she knew that without words, humans were not even animals.

But Deeksha was not done for the night. 'See, Akka, I went to the kitchen to keep the bottle. You didn't tell me to go, but I still went. Why? Because you told me to go using your hands and face. So I went, even though no words told me to go.'

Kalpana was stumped. She did not know what to make of this observation. Deeksha had acted without anybody telling her to do so. Kalpana had been so angry at words that she had forgotten how faces showed anger. She knew well how to make the street dogs jump just by lifting her hand. So what was her anger with language really about?

She had nothing to say. Or do. Or even feel. She went and lay on her mat silently.

Deeksha was delighted. She had tested her sister. She was surprised that she was thinking like her sister now. She had never even considered asking questions in this manner earlier. Between the three of them, they were coming up with so many new thoughts! Where did these ideas come from? As she fell asleep, she recognised that she knew the answer to this question. It was the brain! Everything was the brain. And they were going to build a temple for it on Sunday. She fell asleep peacefully.

Kalpana woke up abruptly, at around 3 a.m. She had found the answer to Deeksha's question. It had been spoken to her in the silence of the night and within the cavernous space of her skull. She could hear the answer so clearly. The voice must have been hers, but she was still so sleepy. She thought about what she had heard in her head, smiled and lay back, tossing and turning till she fell asleep.

The next morning, when Deeksha awoke, Kalpana was already up and writing in her notebook. Deeksha sat up on the mat and Kalpana pointed to what she had written.

When you followed my action, you first spoke to yourself. In your mind, you said, 'She is asking me to go to the kitchen.' So words still made you act. Your words and not my actions.

She had drawn a sketchy picture of a cat below the sentence. She didn't know why, but somehow she felt that the words she had written were incomplete.

IT WAS ONLY A FEW DAYS LATER, AS SHE SAT, TIRED AND muddy after building the temple of the brain, that Kalpana actually understood why she had felt her answer was incomplete. She realised that words needed a body to act, needed something that would obey the command to stand up. She finally understood her problem. In the forest, there was nobody who could act on her plea. Words were a rope that emanated from her mouth, but there was nobody at the other end of it. There was no Ganesha at the end of her words who would do her bidding. Those three nights, her voice had been a lonely signal sent into space. Only the darkness, and the trees, plants, rocks, and who knows how many mute creatures heard her.

FATHER DECIDED THAT IT MADE NO SENSE FOR KALPANA to stay home. She had reached an awkward age, was entering her teens. Life would soon become different for her. Already whispers of what had happened to her floated everywhere, always below the surface.

He never knew who or when somebody would ask, 'Did you find out what really happened?' What could have happened? He was happy, though guiltily so, that Kalpana couldn't speak and tell them about those three days. Who knew, finally? Perhaps it was better not to know.

So he decided to take Kalpana to Bengaluru. He had spoken to a cousin who lived there. The cousin had said that he would get him a place to stay for a month and then they could decide what to do about Kalpana's treatment. Deeksha's school was a problem, but he was confident that the principal would let her go, given the circumstances. As he told his wife: 'Anyway, what does she learn that is so important in the fifth standard?'

But before these decisions could be made, Ajji succeeded in her mission. From the time the priest had told her to teach Kalpana singing or at least take her to a music class, she had been pestering Kalpana's mother to find a teacher. Mother did not believe that Kalpana would go to any class, but she didn't oppose Ajji. Recognising this, Ajji finally took it upon herself to find a teacher for Kalpana, and she thought that she had found the right person in the village. She told Mother, who then suggested it to Kalpana as if it was a passing thought. But Kalpana refused to even listen to her. Her husband, too, was uninterested in talking about it.

So Ajji responded to her son's declaration that he was thinking of moving them all to Bengaluru by telling him it could wait. 'We have found a music teacher for her,' she said.

Her son laughed. 'You expect her to sing when she cannot even talk.'

Ajji told him that was precisely the reason. 'Children are not born speaking. They first make noises. They first sing.' He laughed again and said that he had never heard children sing. Ajji was furious. In front of his wife, she told him, 'You did not speak till you were three years old. We thought you were born dumb. Your father had given up on you speaking at all. But I took you with me to bhajans and yakshagana. You always used to enjoy the music. That is how you learnt to speak. Don't forget that.'

Father merely said, 'You women do what you want.'

So the two women went to meet Gangamma, a person who could well have been a synonym for music itself.

GANGAMMA LIVED IN A HOUSE THAT WAS SURROUNDED BY wilderness. It was within the village, but set apart from the other clusters of houses. It was not a large house, but it had plenty of open space in the front as well as the back. There was a fence in the back that was a vain attempt to stop the wild growth behind the house. A small pond had formed in that wild patch, and in the rainy season, it sounded as if she was living in the midst of a colony of noisy frogs and countless insects. As Gangamma would have said, there was a sense of inevitability in this, that she stayed in a place that naturally produced a million shades of sound. After all, that was what her music was about.

Gangamma was well known in circles that knew about her kind of music. She did not sing in temples or at weddings or family functions. She was from a family of nomadic singers who mostly sang medieval Kannada poetry, more about people than gods. They would insult the gods, or praise them, and these were not the songs of Brahmins and priests. They were singers who lived on the margins of any society they belonged to. As Gangamma enjoyed saying, 'We are outside religion, outside jati. We are outside your society. We are outside everything you can think of.' That was the way she spoke and that was what she sang.

There were many singers like Gangamma in various parts of Karnataka. They came from very poor families and would supplement their income through farming labour. But singing was their passion, and what set them apart from countless other performers was the content of their music. They would be called to sing at all-night fairs and festivals. Entire villages would come to these fairs, and many of them would stay back to listen to these singers. For they sang about the world, the cosmos, the labouring women, the working body, and the dying body. They sang about the self, the sameness between humans, and the ways by which society had destroyed humanity. They did not sing praises to gods, they only sang songs that challenged the gods to make them better humans. They sang sitting on a crude stage, but their minds and voices danced in ways unimagined. People would walk up to the stage and add their offerings to the money strewn around the singers. What they earned varied from generous contributions by landlords or their pious wives to those of poor labourers who would give what they could.

Gangamma did not take on students. She did not see herself as a teacher. In their community, the singers taught only their family members, who would then continue the tradition. She was also constantly travelling with two of her nephews, who played percussion for her. There were no girls in her family for her to take on as apprentices. She earned enough in the non-rainy season since there were quite a few fairs during that time. In the rainy season, she would spend more time in her village and, other than sporadic singing, she sat silently, listening carefully to all the sounds around her.

People in the village respected her but also kept their distance. She was not a 'normal' family woman. After all, she was neither married nor a mother.

That fine morning, when Ajji and Kalpana's mother went to meet her, Gangamma was out in the back of the house, removing weeds that had crept from the edge of the forest right into her land. She was surprised to see the two women.

Ajji began. 'We live on the other side. Near the temple.'

Gangamma nodded. She knew who they were. She had also heard about Kalpana's disappearance and her reappearance.

'You may have heard about my granddaughter.'

Gangamma nodded again. Her dark face was dotted with tiny droplets of sweat from her exertion, and Ajji had a suspicion that she was chewing tobacco.

'Kalpana is her name. Nobody knows what happened to her during the three days she was missing. She came back, but has not spoken a word since.' She quickly added, 'She was not harmed by anybody or anything.' She paused, making sure that Gangamma understood the significance of what she had said. 'We have gone to doctors, but none of them are of any use.' She paused again, and said what she thought the fearsome woman in front of her might appreciate: 'I thought she may have been possessed by a bhootha.'

Mother looked at her in alarm. This was new. She had not heard Ajji say anything about Kalpana being possessed by spirits. 'So I went to the temple priest,' Ajji continued, ignoring Mother. 'The priest told me that Kalpana should learn to sing.'

Gangamma grimaced. She spat a stream of saliva behind her. Ajji was delighted; she had been proven right that Gangamma was chewing tobacco.

'Sing? You said the girl cannot even speak.' Gangamma's voice sounded deep and majestic. Hearing her, Mother felt like a little girl.

'Yes. But he said that only you can make her sing.'

Gangamma looked at her sceptically. 'He didn't say that I can make her speak?'

The two visitors kept silent.

Gangamma was firm. 'I don't teach anybody. I don't have students. I don't like children.'

Ajji persisted. 'But only you can teach a dumb girl how to sing.'

'How is that possible? Did the girl speak properly before?'

Mother jumped in. 'Akka, you could never stop Kalpana or her younger sister from speaking. All the time speaking and laughing.'

'So why is she not speaking now? Is she going to school?'

'No,' replied Mother. 'She is not going to school and just lies on her mat. Her sister, Deeksha, keeps talking to her all the time. I have heard them laugh. I once saw Kalpana laughing, but no sound came from her mouth.'

'What can I do, sister?' said Gangamma, suddenly feeling a kinship with this gentle woman. 'I am only a singer, and you say that even doctors haven't been able to help her.'

Ajji said, 'I think Kalpana can speak, but she has decided not to.'

Mother nodded. 'I too think that she is purposely stopping herself from making any sound.'

Gangamma was curious. 'You mean the girl can speak but she is choosing not to?'

Both the women nodded. 'That is what we think,' said Mother. 'We asked the younger one, but she will only tell us what her elder sister wants her to say.'

Gangamma was definitely interested now. 'I have not seen a child who can control her speech. What strength one needs to not utter a word! Nobody has that much control. Definitely not a little girl.' She sat in silence. She thought that anyone with that much control over words could become a great musician, but she did not say that out loud.

Gangamma got up to spit the tobacco out on the weeds. She came back and, standing over the two women, said, 'Nobody has that much control. I only know of one case of a rich zamindar who stopped speaking to his daughter in order to punish her. He never uttered a word to her till he died.'

Ajji nodded as if she knew well the power of using silence to punish.

'But that is different,' continued Gangamma. 'Because he spoke to everybody else. In fact, he started speaking more to others to further punish his daughter.'

Mother was disturbed. She could not understand why anybody, particularly the father of a girl, would do that.

'Kalpana is not like that,' she murmured, without knowing exactly what she was responding to.

Gangamma ignored her. 'I am interested. This girl must be very strong. I wonder what really happened to her.' She stared intently at Mother. 'Are you sure you don't know?'

In a small voice, Mother said, 'Yes, Akka, I really don't know. Maybe she will tell you.' She sounded hopeful.

Gangamma turned to Ajji and asked her the same by raising her eyebrows.

Ajji shook her head. 'Of course not,' she added unnecessarily.

'So you are not really interested in teaching the girl to sing. You only want her to begin speaking. Like I am another doctor.'

Mother looked at Ajji for help. She didn't know what the right response was.

Ajji said, 'Frankly, yes. We want her to speak, first of all. She has to go back to school. But we also think it will be good if she can learn singing. After all'—she looked slyly at Gangamma—'singing is more important than speaking. Am I not right?'

Mother added, 'Yes, it is important that she speaks. She has to go back to school.'

Gangamma said, 'And you have to know what happened to her in those three days.'

Ajji was dismissive. 'That is in the past. We are not interested in knowing what exactly happened. We are only worried about the future of this girl.' She paused and placed her right palm on Gangamma's right palm. 'Only you can help. Only you can understand what this girl is going through.'

Gangamma was embarrassed. She felt the cold, shrivelled touch of Ajji and pulled her palm away, saying, 'Bring her and then I will tell you whether I can teach her or not.'

KALPANA REFUSED TO GO FOR THE SINGING LESSONS. HER mother pleaded and Ajji shouted, but she was her obstinate self. She guessed what the project was about, and she decided that she would not be tricked into speaking. Mother took Deeksha outside the house and whispered to her, 'Try to make Kalpana go for the music class. Gangamma never takes students, but she has agreed to meet Kalpana. This is our best hope.' Deeksha felt important, like she was doing an adult's job, although she was unsure whether Kalpana should learn singing.

That night, Deeksha lay curled up on her mat, remembering the chattering of the lizards and wondering where they were hiding. Kalpana was back to doodling in her notebook. Deeksha said, 'I heard you are going to take singing lessons.' Kalpana vigorously shook her head. She wrote a big *No* in her book and showed it to her sister.

Deeksha nodded and said, 'Akka, I think you are right. Singing is also like speaking. If you sing, you may as well speak.'

Kalpana thought for a moment, puzzled.

Deeksha said, 'Do you think I could be a singer?'

Kalpana shook her head vehemently.

Deeksha was silent. Then she added, 'I wish I could learn singing. If you go, can I also come with you and join your class?'

Kalpana shook her head more vigorously. She was getting tired of so many movements of the body when a simple word would have solved her problem. How wonderful language was, she thought wistfully.

She looked at Deeksha suspiciously. She had never thought Deeksha had any interest in music.

Seeing her hesitate, Deeksha added, 'And the teacher is a crazy old lady. She lives next to the forest and sings all night. Ajji said that she can understand animals and insects, and she sings to them. Oh, how nice it would be to sing to these forest animals!'

Kalpana turned away from Deeksha and went to sleep.

ON THE FOLLOWING SUNDAY, THE THREE GIRLS BUILT THE temple of the brain. They went to an open area near their house. It was close to the main road going through the village—an open patch of land with a tree, and grass around it. Sometimes, the cows in the village would graze there. Kalpana and Deeksha left their house late that morning when they heard Kumari calling out to them from outside. They walked up to the tree under which they had decided to build the shrine for their brain god. Deeksha had said, 'We don't have money to construct a building for the temple. Let us use the tree as the building.'

They picked up a few flat stones. They built a small shrine by placing some of the stones on the ground and some on top, for the roof. Larger bits of stone functioned as the walls of the shrine. It now looked like a tiny doll's room, with one side open.

Kumari and Deeksha had discussed the kind of idol they wanted. They had seen drawings of the brain in some science posters pasted on the school walls. These posters had been sent by an NGO from Bengaluru, and they consisted of colourful images of the solar system and the organs of the body, maps of India, and a set of pictures of famous Indian freedom fighters. Deeksha and Kumari had passed by the poster on the organs of the body innumerable times but had not once stopped to look at it carefully. After they decided to build their temple, they stood in front of the poster and stared at it every time they passed by.

The brain looked funny. It had an odd shape—almost like a head. Or like a piece of clay on which there were many crooked roads. They had thought the brain was hard, like their head, but the poster described it as greyish in colour and soft to the touch.

The softness of the brain was a problem for their temple. Gods were made of stone, and the idol in their temple would also be a stone. They were worried about the softness until Deeksha said, 'Ganesha's tummy must also be soft, no? But, on the idol, it is hard because it is stone.'

Kalpana had little to contribute. Like a true high priest, she had decided to watch over the two as they built the shrine.

Deeksha and Kumari found the solution for the shape of their idol. They traced the drawing of the brain from the poster. Then they decided to stick the drawing on a rock that looked somewhat like a brain. That would be their idol. Kalpana went searching around the tree for a stone of the right shape. She found one, half sunk into the mud. When she pulled it out, hundreds of ants ran out from beneath the stone. She was happy with the stone. If she could have spoken, she would have said, 'This is a living stone. It is the right model for the brain.'

Despite her attempt to act aloof, Kalpana was very glad to be part of the project. Having the brain as a god was her answer to the problem of prayers. Ganesha might be a god, but he could not be seen by any of them, unlike the brain, which could be seen by all. They knew where the brain was, how big it was, and its colour and weight. Could they say that about their gods? Deeksha and Kumari cleaned the stone, but they also liked the ants scurrying on the stone as if they were all in a great hurry to go from one point to another. They tried to stick the picture of the brain on the rock with a small tube of gum they had brought with them. It was all imperfectly done, but looking at it, the three girls felt they were almost in the presence of a god. Instead of letting the brain hide inside every head, they would keep it in the open and other children would come to see their brain instead of the gods in the temples.

Kumari, increasingly excited, said, 'It is good that our idol is black. If the brain was removed from our head and kept under the sun for one day, it too would become dark like us.'

Deeksha and Kumari gave the idol to Kalpana. She solemnly placed it inside the shrine. Deeksha ran to a shrub nearby and picked out a few fragile flowers. She placed them on the idol. She imagined hundreds of ants and bees following her to the shrine. There was no coconut to break in front of the idol, as they had seen being done in the temples. But Kumari found a large, dry seed nearby. They threw it on a stone, but it did not crack open. Impatient, Kalpana took another stone and used it to crack the seed open.

Deeksha and Kumari clapped. Their temple was now officially open. They decided to bring kumkum from their homes and smear it on the idol. Red streaks on a black idol were always so striking!

'That way, people will know this is a temple,' Deeksha explained to Kumari. In response, Kumari limped over to some creepers that were vainly trying to climb the trunk of the tree, and came back with a few red berries. She crushed them on the idol and spread the crushed remains all over. The picture of the brain was now covered in splotches of red and fleshy little bits of fruit.

All three of them stood in silence before the idol. Each of them had their special thoughts.

Kalpana thought that if it was the brain that spoke, this would be a talking temple. She imagined cows and goats standing in front of the temple while the brain spoke to them. She opened her eyes and thought the idol was laughing at her vision.

Deeksha prayed to the brain, asking it to give Kalpana her speech back.

Kumari closed her eyes and murmured, 'Please let me and Deeksha be friends forever.'

The three girls sat around their shrine. Kumari said, 'I wish we had some biscuits. It would have been good to offer them to our god and then eat them.'

Deeksha ran to her house, past Ajji, who was standing at the door watching the girls, and asked her mother for some biscuits for the three of them. Mother counted out three flat pieces of

Parle-G and gave them to her. Deeksha squealed, 'Three more! Three more!'

She ran back to the girls. All of them stood, and Kalpana offered the biscuits to their idol. She then solemnly distributed the biscuits among them. They sat near the shrine and ate their biscuits while listening to a sudden influx of excited birds that swooped down on the tree. Two dogs sauntered over and looked at them in the hope of getting something to eat. The girls looked at the mountains, the beginnings of clouds behind the peaks that would reach their village by the evening. All of them—humans and dogs and birds and, not to be forgotten, ants—silently sat and waited.

Their mother come out of the house and called out to them. As she walked back to the house, Kalpana decided she would meet Gangamma. She would not sing; she was determined about that. But if this was the way to get Deeksha to learn music, she would go with her. It was the least she could do for her little sister, for having made her the priest of their temple.

GANGAMMA WAS ALL THAT DEEKSHA HAD IMAGINED. Mother took both the girls to meet her a day after the inauguration of their temple. She was extremely surprised that Kalpana had agreed, although the agreement was communicated in silence and with a sullen face. Deeksha was going to Gangamma because she wanted to help Kalpana, and Kalpana agreed to go because she wanted to help Deeksha have a chance to learn music. Such was the impact of Gangamma on their lives even before she began their classes.

Mother had taken some bananas with her. As the three of them walked through the village, people turned to look. Some shouted out a greeting and some just stared. When they saw the three of them take the path leading to Gangamma's house, they were extremely surprised. Gangamma's house was the only one on that path, and those living in that part of the village had never seen the mother or the girls in their area before.

Gangamma came out of her house on seeing them. She was sitting on the porch by the time they reached her. Mother asked the girls to prostrate themselves before Gangamma and give her the fruit. Gangamma asked the two girls to sit. Mother hesitated and said, 'I can come later and pick them up. Or I can just sit here.'

Gangamma said, 'No, no, you go back. The girls know their way back.' She looked at them. 'Correct?' The two girls nodded dumbly, already in awe of Gangamma in her bright red saree, a big round red mark on her forehead, draped in necklaces and bracelets. Deeksha thought that she looked almost like one of the goddesses, or at least, like the pictures she had seen of goddesses.

Mother hesitated. Gangamma said, 'Don't worry. I will make sure they get back safely.'

Mother said, 'About their fees ...'

Gangamma waved her away. 'We will talk later,' she said. She waited till Mother had said farewell to her daughters and walked away. It was early evening, and it was sunny and sultry. Gangamma turned her gaze to Deeksha first.

'You are ...'

Deeksha didn't understand.

'Your name?'

'Deeksha.'

'Have you learnt music before?'

Deeksha shook her head.

'Do you want to learn singing?'

Deeksha vigorously nodded in the affirmative. To emphasise her interest, she also smiled widely. Gangamma frowned at her. She then turned to Kalpana, who was staring broodingly at her.

'Your name?'

Kalpana remained silent.

'Your name?' she asked louder.

Deeksha intervened. 'She can't speak.' Paused and added, 'But she can hear.'

Gangamma laughed. 'You can't speak but you want to sing? How is that possible?'

Kalpana was silent.

Gangamma was not done. 'How can I teach you? What can I teach you?' Suddenly, she shouted, striking her right palm on the ground, 'You are wasting my time. Do you know who I am?'

Deeksha instinctively clutched Kalpana's hand. Kalpana stared back without flinching. But her dark eyes had changed. Gangamma stared intently into those eyes, and felt drawn to them. It seemed to her that Kalpana was pleading with her, as if telling her that she was in a situation where it was impossible for her to speak. And seeing Gangamma, she was all the more convinced that she would not let a single sound escape her.

Deeksha saw Gangamma staring at Kalpana and Kalpana staring back at her. Gangamma's face softened. Suddenly, she smiled. She put her hand on Kalpana's head like she was blessing her. Kalpana's eyes filled with tears. Deeksha was right—people could read her mind and listen to the voice within her. Deeksha had teased her that Mother could hear her speaking, but now Kalpana felt that she could read Gangamma's unsaid thoughts. When Gangamma placed her palm on top of her head, she could feel the enormous empathy flowing through it.

Gangamma then placed her hand on Deeksha's head. 'Now I take both of you as my students,' she declared. She laughed and added, 'I must be the first teacher to teach music to a dumb girl.'

She looked at Kalpana. 'Or, at least, to a girl who does not want to speak.' She turned to Deeksha and said, 'We will see how to teach singing in silence! Won't that be easy!'

Gangamma did not teach singing in the first class. She asked Deeksha about school, who her friends were, and what she spoke to Kalpana about. Deeksha told her that Kalpana would write if she wanted to communicate something, but Gangamma said she would not use writing as a medium to communicate with Kalpana.

Gangamma also asked Kalpana about her classes and her friends. Kalpana just stared at her. Gangamma then sat close to her, held her tiny wrist in her hand, and asked her about her disappearance.

'Do you remember what happened to you on the day you went missing?'

Kalpana pulled her hand away. Gangamma gently held both her wrists.

'Fine, we won't talk about that. I want you to say "aaa" within yourself so that we don't hear it at all.'

Kalpana opened her mouth and uttered a long 'aaa' that only she heard.

Gangamma said, 'Good. Now we will see how this dumb girl will sing.'

As they left, Gangamma gave one banana each to the two girls. The girls refused, since they had brought the fruit as an offering for their teacher. Gangamma insisted. Holding a banana each, they left, their heads buzzing with the new experience. They went to the end of the road and turned. Their mother was sitting on a stone around the corner. She was talking to another middle-aged woman.

Deeksha said, 'See, Amma was waiting for us here secretly.'

Kalpana nodded. She knew that her mother would not have abandoned her, not after what had happened. She felt a sense of happiness. She was outside and, for the first time, with somebody other than her family or Kumari. She was delighted that she did not feel awkward about keeping quiet. Her absolute silence was teaching her something about speech—that there was too much redundancy in people's speech. Why speak so much, and all the time, she would have asked if she could have spoken.

THE NEXT DAY, DEEKSHA EXCITEDLY TOLD KUMARI ABOUT her music class. Kumari looked at her in admiration. After a few minutes of silence, she added, 'I like music too.'

Deeksha spontaneously decided that Kumari should join them. 'You should come for the next class. You will like the teacher a lot. She is quite scary to look at.' She laughed as she said this.

Kumari said, 'My father will not allow me to go. I only come to your house.'

Deeksha was not scared of her own father, let alone Kumari's. 'Don't worry, Kumari. I will tell your mother.'

In the Kannada class that day, she remained standing after the other students had sat down when their teacher entered.

'What now, Deeksha?' asked Upadhyay with a smile.

'Sir, before you start, I just wanted to ask you one question.'

'If you think you must ask, then ask.'

Deeksha pulled Kumari up. 'Sir, you said that language is sound. Kannada is Kannada sounds.'

Upadhya nodded, but without committing to anything. He did not want to guess what new question these two devils had dreamt up.

'Sir, we want to know whether singing is also a Kannada sound. When we sing, Sir, we also make sounds.'

One of the boys in the back row made a sound like a groan. Everybody laughed.

Deeksha turned to the boy. 'See, Sir, that sound he made. Is that a Kannada sound or ... or an English sound?'

'When you sing, that is called music, Deeksha. It is not language.'

Kumari piped up, 'But why do you say that, Sir?'

Upadhya had a ready answer. 'Because it does not have any meaning, like words do.' He was pleased with himself that he could answer a complex question in such a simple manner. He asked the boy who had made the sound to stand and sing.

'Sing what, Sir?' the boy asked, trying desperately to remember any song.

'None of your film songs, Chandru. Just sing a tune.'

Chandru made some sounds. Deeksha shouted out, 'Sir, that is not music.'

Sir said, 'You see the difference? He just made some sounds. There were no words. There was no meaning to what he sang.'

Krishna stood up and announced, 'Sir, the meaning was that he was in pain, so he made that noise.'

Kumari started laughing, and the other students followed. Even Upadhya smiled. He would never have imagined Krishna uttering a word in his class a month ago.

Deeksha, perhaps as expected, had the final word. 'Sir, if music is not language, then music is not a lie.' She sat down, looking triumphantly at Kumari. Upadhya did not get the point, nor was he interested in continuing that point further. He wrote a new sentence using the word 'election' on the board and asked the students to try and understand the sentence.

That night, Deeksha came to lie with Kalpana on her mat.

'I want to tell you, Akka, that singing is not like language, because Sir said that music, unlike words, has no meaning.' She raised herself on her elbows and looked at Kalpana intently. 'So music is not a lie. You can sing, Akka, even if you do not want to speak.'

Kalpana shook her head.

Deeksha was irritated. 'Oh, you are so ... so ...' She thought furiously, and knowing there was nothing else she could say, she hissed, 'If you don't speak, your voice will die.' She thought for a few moments and then continued, 'Even if you decide to speak later, nothing will come out of your mouth. You will be like a big radio box without any radio station.'

So saying, she turned away. Kalpana grinned, imagining herself as a radio box and Deeksha and Kumari as little radio stations. She went over to Deeksha, lay on her mat, and held her as they both fell into the arms of musical dreams.

KALPANA HAD SO MUCH TO SAY, AND SHE DID NOT KNOW how much longer she could bottle up her words. But that night, thinking about an empty radio box, she decided to do something to let those words gush out. She leaned over Deeksha as she lay on her side, and just as Deeksha was entering the world of absolute silence in her sleep, she told her everything she wanted to say. Her mouth moved, her throat constricted and expanded, her fingers twitched, and her whole body participated in the dance of speaking. Everything was there except for the sounds of the words. Kalpana poured all her silent words into Deeksha's ear. Deeksha fell asleep to the rhythm and cadence of those unheard sounds. Kalpana knew that one night, sometime in the future, Deeksha would hear all these silent words as she slept.

Kalpana felt cleansed. Felt a great weight off her head, mind, stomach and hands, as if unsaid words had occupied all those spaces in her body. She was also at peace after telling Deeksha about all that had happened to her. As she dozed off contentedly, she realised that her jaw was feeling sore.

ON SUNDAY MORNING, BRIGHT AND BLUE, THE THREE GIRLS walked to Gangamma's house. Kumari had failed to convince her mother to let her learn singing. Her mother had blamed it on her father, saying he would not agree. Deeksha had bravely told Kumari that she would convince her mother. She had gone to their house on the way back from school, but seeing her stern, irritated face, she had kept quiet. So, the two of them decided on the easier path. They told her mother they were going to play with Deeksha's sister.

Deeksha told Kumari's mother: 'Akka is very happy when Kumari is with us.'

BUT GANGAMMA WAS NOT HAPPY TO SEE KUMARI.

'Why is she here?' she asked, seeing another wayward child in front of her. Her house would soon look like a school!

Deeksha told her that she and Kumari did everything together. She told Gangamma about the temple they had built and about Upadhya Sir. And how Kumari had asked all those questions about language.

'She likes music and wants to really learn it. But her father does not want her to.'

Kumari sat petrified, staring at the woman before her, who that day was dressed in a bright yellow saree and a purple blouse. She had a big, round mark of kumkum on her forehead and a large necklace made of wooden beads that would have weighed down a weaker neck. Her voice was powerful, and Kumari thought that maybe Gangamma spoke with a mic hidden in her mouth.

Gangamma turned to Kumari and asked her why she liked music.

Kumari did not know what to say. 'I-I like it,' she stammered.

'But why?' thundered Gangamma.

Kumari had no response. She had never actively listened to music in her house. Music always came unbeckoned into her world. Many nights she would listen to songs that floated near her ears, songs from faraway temples and yakshagana performances that went on through the night. She would lie awake, trying her best to listen to the music that had dodged mountains, trees and houses to reach her. When there was a sudden silence, till the next wave of sound reached her, she would imagine the music in her head. She didn't know how to say all of this to Gangamma.

'Do you listen to music in your house?' Gangamma asked.

'No, Ajji. But I have heard songs from the temple. From yakshagana. I have heard it at night, when I am trying to fall asleep.' Encouraged by Gangamma's gaze, she added, 'I listen to songs even when I am asleep. I hear others singing inside my head.'

She started giggling and Deeksha joined her.

Gangamma smiled and placed her palm on Kumari's head. She was happy to see these three girls. Kalpana looked at Gangamma with eyes unclouded by any unspoken thoughts; her face seemed as if it had been washed by fresh clouds.

Gangamma made all of them sit straight. She told them to breathe in and out. 'Breathing is most important,' she said, and to Kalpana, as a special aside, she added, 'Breathing is like speaking.' Kalpana nodded, not understanding what Gangamma had said. She was just so happy to be back in a class with other students, even if they were only Deeksha and Kumari.

'Music is about sounds,' Gangamma said, 'and I will teach you to make the proper sounds.'

Deeksha interjected. 'Ajji, our teacher Upadhya Sir said language is also about sounds.'

'Yes, but music is different.'

Gangamma looked at the three eager faces staring at her, waiting for her to tell them how music was different. She wanted to explain it to them, but couldn't find the words. So, suddenly, she sang a note. It was a clear sound, sharp in pitch, and slowly became louder. The three girls were smitten and watched her as if they were watching the progress of the sound emanating from her, as if they could see the sound beginning from her stomach and rising upwards. They looked at her with open mouths, listening to that sound. Gangamma stopped and smiled at them. 'See, that is music. And when I am speaking to you now, this is language.'

Kumari immediately responded, 'I want to learn the way you sing.'

Deeksha added, 'It felt like you were poking me with a pencil.'

Kalpana nodded. She again felt a desire to say something. Words were beginning to bubble inside her. That sound had been a call that created flutters in her stomach.

Gangamma was pleased with the girls' response. 'It is not difficult to create that sound. Each of you try to make a sound you like.' To Kalpana she said, 'Make a sound that only you can hear.' Kumari looked at Kalpana with surprise. She tapped Deeksha on the arm and pointed to Kalpana, who was miming singing. Deeksha whispered, 'She talks like this all the time! You watch her enough and you can hear her.' The ripples of her laughter sounded as clear as Gangamma's notes.

IT WAS INDEED A BIG CHANGE FOR GANGAMMA TO TEACH three kids who had no exposure to music. Gangamma had not learnt music from any teacher in a formal manner. Her father had been a singer, part of a family of nomadic singers. When they travelled, they would stay out in the fields or sometimes, after they had become somewhat popular, in houses that were empty, which their patrons would arrange. Their performances would start at night, sometimes after nine, and go on till dawn. There were no microphones in the beginning, and her father, with his team of two percussion players, would sing through the night. Her father saw their music primarily as a prayer, a prayer not to the many gods and goddesses but to the souls of humans, to the soul within each person.

Gangamma was his only child. Her father had not wanted to teach her singing or have her follow in his footsteps. But that was not really in his hands. Her mother used to say that her child was born singing. Her first sound in the world was not a cry but a song. Gangamma liked this narrative, although she knew how much her mother liked to tell stories. She accompanied her father from a young age. And when her father collapsed and died in the midst of a performance, she and her family knew she would carry on his legacy. She did not marry and did not even think of having children. In a roundabout cycle of cosmic events, these three girls had come home to roost in her singing den. Gangamma understood the worth of each girl very quickly. She realised soon that if there was one among these three who could really sing, it was Kumari.

Within a few days, the girls had become very comfortable with Gangamma. One of their first classes was about letting the girls make any kind of sound they wanted. Kalpana intensely watched the other two produce all kinds of sounds.

Gangamma said, 'We are all prisoners of language.' Deeksha looked at Kalpana and Gangamma smiled. 'Except for this brave girl,' she said, pointing to Kalpana. 'So the first thing to do is to get out of the prison of your language.'

Kumari put her hand up. Gangamma laughed. 'This is not a class, Kumari. If you want to say something, then just say it.'

'Why are you saying language has imprisoned me? I am not in jail.'

Deeksha giggled, but stopped when she saw Gangamma looking at her.

Gangamma said, 'Unless you get rid of language from your head, you will not sing. Singing is pure sound. How can I explain this to you?'

All three girls leaned forward and looked at her expectantly.

Gangamma found the words. 'Every living thing makes sounds. Even animals, birds and insects make sounds.'

'Except our sister,' said Deeksha, drawing Kumari into a familial embrace.

Gangamma was not to be distracted. She caught hold of Deeksha's hand, willing her to be silent for a moment. 'Everything on this land makes a sound. But humans are the only ones who do something with these sounds. They speak. They create language. Languages may be different, but sound is made by every object in this world.'

Kumari looked solemnly at her. 'What about dumb people? My father sometimes shouts at me saying that I am dumb.'

'Dumb people also speak within themselves. They may not be the sounds we make. But we should also realise that it is only great people who can stay silent when they can speak. You know, there are many who take a vow of silence and will not speak.'

The girls didn't understand her completely. They half-heartedly shook their heads.

Seeing their faces, Gangamma thought of saying something else. Turning to Deeksha, she said, 'Music is like friendship. You give your sound, your music, without wanting anything for it. When you speak, you are using your language to tell Kumari something. But when you sing, you are not doing it to tell her anything.'

Gangamma paused. She had lost the kids. They stared at her blankly.

The last thing she attempted to say was this: 'Singing is not talking. It is not telling anybody anything.' She stopped, feeling confused herself.

She remembered what her father had once told her. This was after a performance where the audience seemed uninterested. Gangamma was fuming at them, but her father had only said, 'We sing not for them. We first sing for our soul, and if others like it, they can listen.'

So she told the kids, 'We don't sing to or for others. We sing for ourselves first. But when we speak, we speak to and for others. Think about this, even if you don't understand it right now.'

As the children got up to leave, Gangamma gave them three hard guavas from her tree. Kalpana bent and touched Gangamma's feet, and Gangamma saw tears in her eyes. 'You have to practise singing this one sound I taught you,' she told Deeksha and Kumari. Kalpana smiled, imagining her parents' response to Deeksha's practice. As they trooped away, Gangamma called out, 'Kalpana, you can come for lessons when your sister goes to school. Instead of sitting at home, you can come here and sing.' She paused and added, 'Even if you only want to sing silently.'

WHENEVER POSSIBLE, DEEKSHA AND KUMARI WOULD VISIT their temple. Despite the alternating rain and sunshine, and curious grazing creatures, the shrine survived. One Sunday evening, the three of them went and sat in front of it. Deeksha had surreptitiously taken one dried golden-yellow raisin from the kitchen. She placed it on the idol. The picture of the brain that they had stuck on the rock had become pulpy and was half-eaten. Now the stone looked much more like the brain in the poster—a bit mushy and soggy.

Kumari had brought a packet of turmeric that her mother had got from the temple. She smeared it on the idol. Kalpana drew some figures around the shrine, like a compound wall drawn in the mud. When Deeksha looked closer, she found that it looked like 1 + 1 = 2.

'Akka,' she said in surprise, 'you are teaching our brain mathematics!'

Kumari skipped happily on one foot. 'The brain needs mathematics more than it needs your raisin.'

Sitting on the slightly damp ground, with a stick as a pencil in her hand, Kalpana felt as if the land itself was her notebook. She had not been aware that she was scratching out numbers in the mud until Deeksha pointed it out. Kalpana had always enjoyed her mathematics classes and was very good at it. She had forgotten this in her bitter battle against language, but in that instant, she realised how much she missed her mathematics class. Gazing at the idol of the brain, she became aware of an evolving thought: Mathematics was not like Kannada. Mathematics was not used for writing prayers to the gods. Her teacher had always said mathematics was only about the truth. Kalpana had never understood her. She decided to bring her mathematics book and do the problems in it, using her stick on the open land all around her.

That night, she wrote in her notebook: *I want to go to school but only for the mathematics class. I will not attend other classes. Tell Amma to talk to the principal.*

She showed this to Deeksha.

Deeksha said, 'Akka, you can't come to school if you don't speak. They will make fun of you.'

Kalpana wrote: *I don't mind.*

'I don't think it's a good idea. Go to all the classes,' Deeksha added.

Kalpana shook her head—a vehement no.

Deeksha went out and called her mother. She showed her Kalpana's note. Mother was surprised to see so many pages filled with writing and tried to read them. Kalpana grabbed the book from her.

'Amma, I told Akka that it is not a good idea to go to only one class. The principal will not agree. Everybody is scared of her.'

Mother too agreed that it was not a good idea.

Then Kalpana wrote: *Tell the principal that the doctor told me to sit in the mathematics class.*

Mother and Deeksha were stumped. They stared at Kalpana, trying to see how her mind worked in such ways.

Kalpana wrote: *Mathematics is good for the brain and, therefore, for my speech.* She drew a smiling cat next to the sentence.

THE WEEK AFTER PORTENDED MUCH OF WHAT WAS TO follow. As Gangamma would have said, there comes a time when nothing can be done. When things 'just' happen, and those who are part of it watch the events like they are bystanders and onlookers. Gangamma would have also said, 'Sometimes, when that happens, and when you know you should stop something happening but are powerless to do anything, you can only sing. Singing must have been born out of frustration.' Gangamma was right, and it was Deeksha who pointed this out to her when Gangamma finally voiced her thoughts to the three girls. Deeksha nodded sagely and said, 'Yes, yes, when you are frustrated with language.' As if she really knew what she was talking about. But Kalpana knew that those words were meant specially for her.

All this came later. First, it was the principal's turn. She sent word to Kalpana's father that Kalpana should restart her classes. On a Monday, on the way to his office, Kalpana's father went to meet the principal. School had started after yet another festival break, and the voices of a few teachers wafted by. Father had never been to the school when the children were all so quiet, and he felt like he had come to an ashram instead of a school. The principal made him wait outside her office for quite some time. Finally, he courageously told the peon outside her room that he was getting late for work and would be leaving. Hearing him through the creaky, swinging doors, the principal called out to him to enter.

She was sitting behind a large desk, with an open window behind her. There was an old ceiling fan above the table that once in a while created little swirls of dust like baby tornadoes. In front of her desk was a row of benches, one behind the other. Father stood looking at them, unsure of what to do. The principal's office looked like a modified classroom.

The principal said, 'Sit down,' pointing to the bench closest to the table. Father sat in the middle of the bench, seeing the imposing face of the principal looming in front of him. He looked around him, as though puzzled.

She looked at him as if he could not understand the obvious. 'The benches are here because this is also the meeting room with the teachers.'

Father imagined the teachers sitting like students in the principal's class and smiled involuntarily.

She thought he was laughing at her office—or worse, her school. 'Our teachers are very good. We have even got a certificate from the department in Bengaluru.'

Father nodded and added, 'Yes, I have heard the department in Bengaluru mention you and this school. They know you are doing a good job here.'

The principal stared at him suspiciously, unsure if he was making fun of her.

Father explained, 'I work in a government office, and we deal with the department in charge of school education.'

She called out to the peon and asked him to get two cups of tea.

Father said, 'I am sorry. I have to leave for my office.'

But they sat till the tea came in tiny little cups. It was milky and sweet, and smelt of the smoke of countless wood fires. The principal put her cup down and said, 'Your daughter has to come back to school. She has been away for too long. We can consider all these days as sick leave. But no longer.'

Father replied, 'I cannot force her to do anything. We are still going to the doctors. She is not able to speak, and I don't think it is a good idea for her to sit for classes until she is ready to do so.'

The principal was stern in her reply. 'Students don't speak in class. If she can listen, that is enough. She can listen and understand, right?'

Father nodded. 'But still ...'

'No "but still". It is for her own good. Otherwise we will have to fail her, and she will have to redo this year. That is not good, is it?'

Father became worried. He had not even thought of the possibility of his daughter repeating a year. He spoke hurriedly. 'I am sure there will be no need for that. She has always been a very good student. If you let her take the exam, she will pass it easily even if she doesn't go to classes.'

The principal leaned forward. 'You are saying that classes are not necessary? And what our teachers teach is useless?'

'No, I didn't say that, madam.' Father added the 'madam' in desperation. 'I am only thinking of the government rules.' He nodded sagely. 'Yes, the government rules. For sick students. Especially girl students.'

The principal looked at him doubtfully. Maybe he knew rules that she didn't. She was worried, since there were so many different schemes for girl students.

'I don't know about these rules. You can send me a copy of the rules and I will see. But how can she write exams if she has not been in class? It would be an insult to my teachers.'

Father was a quick thinker. 'If I get permission from the teachers, would that be okay?'

That was the wrong thing to say. 'No, no. You please do not go and talk to my teachers. It is not for them to decide. I am the principal, you know.' She then thought of a conciliatory half-measure. 'I am saying this only for the good of Kalpana. And also because I am a mother of girls. I know how these girls feel.'

If she thought that this subtle way of telling him that he was not a woman and so could not understand his daughter would make him back down, she was right on target. Father squirmed on the bench. The suggestion that he as a father did not know what his daughters *really* wanted made him uncomfortable.

The principal continued, 'I know how girls feel. They will feel like all their friends have left them. What is the point of keeping her at home all the time. Like being locked up!' Father looked at her guiltily. 'Yes, like being imprisoned. Kalpana is a clever girl, although she used to talk too much. And now, not talking at all! Have you thought about what the poor child is feeling? That she has lost her voice and now also her friends.' And then, with a flourish, she added, 'And now even her education is lost.'

She got up from her chair and walked towards him. 'I think it is for her mental good that she should come back to school.

It is not good for a little girl to stay at home—especially when they are this age. Don't worry. We will take care of her. Maybe if she attends classes and is with other children, she will even get her voice back.'

She stood towering over him, and he felt like he was back in school, crouching on the bench, trying to avoid the teacher's eyes. He got up awkwardly and said, 'I will try to convince her to come to school.'

The principal leaned away from him, creating an invisible path for him to walk past her. 'No convincing. She is just a child, she cannot decide these things. Just tell her.' As he walked away, she added, 'Or tell her that Madam Principal will come to the house and drag her to school.'

He turned back with a smile, but saw from her grim face that she meant every word. He hurriedly left the school.

SO IT WAS THAT ON A WEDNESDAY, A DAY CHOSEN BY AJJI as an auspicious one for rejoining school, Kalpana was taken to school by Deeksha, her mother and Ajji. Kalpana had refused to go, and her father's threats had had no effect. Nothing would make her go back to her classes. On Monday evening, after he had come back from the office, he spoke to Kalpana about what the principal had said. For no reason, she would lose a year, and he would not let that happen. Her mother joined in when Kalpana started shaking her head vigorously. Then Ajji shouted out from the hall, unnecessarily loudly, 'If she refuses, I will call Babu, who will pick her up and take her to school.'

Hearing this, Kalpana started crying and ran into the storeroom. Father was embarrassed and didn't know what to say. Mother tried to console her, but Kalpana refused to budge.

That night, after all the lights had been turned off, Deeksha crept close to Kalpana and held her. Kalpana tried to push her away, but Deeksha whispered, 'I won't speak. I just want to sleep here with you.'

They both lay on their backs and soon started breathing in unison. In and out their breaths went, and soon the breaths began to sound like words, like thoughts they wanted to hear.

Deeksha said, 'If you come to school, you will be a hero. Everybody wants to meet you.'

Kalpana shook her head.

'The girls will bring you sweets and you can give them all to me.' Deeksha giggled as she said this. Kalpana tried to push her away.

Deeksha was persistent. 'How long will you stay at home? You are missing out on so many lessons in school. All the teachers keep asking about you and when you will come back. Do you want to be like Amma and Ajji? At least Amma has work to do the full day. If you also sit at home, you will become like Ajji, all the time mumbling prayers. And we will all call you Kalpana Ajji.'

Kalpana started giggling along with Deeksha. She would do everything she could to not become like her grandmother. The source of all her troubles! And she was getting restless sitting at home. She sat with her eyes closed for a few moments. When she opened her eyes, Deeksha could see that she had decided on something.

Kalpana picked up her notebook and wrote: *I will go to school only if we can continue to go to singing classes.*

Deeksha was delighted. She would have Kalpana back with her to go to school, and she could also keep a protective eye on her. On the one day Kalpana went to school by herself, see what had happened!

On Wednesday morning, even the clouds were welcoming, as they left the sky in peace and went to hide behind the mountains.

A night drizzle had washed the road, so it looked like it had been specially laid out for Kalpana. Her mother had washed and ironed her uniform. Ajji plucked a red hibiscus flower and put it in Kalpana's hair. Her father awkwardly patted her oiled head, saying, 'Good, good.'

As they walked to the school, two dogs ran towards them and trotted along. Old Gundappa, riding his cycle, saw Kalpana walking, so he got off and walked along with them. Kalpana felt that the people in every house on the way were peering out, silently watching this little procession. She knew worse was to come at school.

Mother took Kalpana directly to the principal's office. Ajji stood outside the school, staring sternly at every entering student. Deeksha ran off to her classroom. The principal was happy to see Kalpana. She was also pleased that Kalpana's mother had come. She made her sit on the bench and spoke to her about running the school.

'So difficult, finishing cooking and cleaning at home and then taking care of the school. Children are not easy, as you and I know. But I have to deal with teachers also. Not easy, not easy,' she boomed, wiping her sweating face with a hand towel that she kept tucked into the waistband of her saree. Kalpana sat silently next to her mother. The principal came close to her and made a move as if she was going to pinch her. Kalpana leaned away.

The principal asked the mother, 'Does she make any noise at all?'

'Yes, she does,' Mother replied.

The principal raised her voice and addressed Kalpana. 'So you have forgotten how to speak?' Kalpana just stared back at her.

Mother murmured, 'She can hear well. She just won't speak.'

'Ah, hearing is enough. As I was telling your husband, children are not supposed to speak in class. Only listen. And write down what the teacher says. Can she write?'

Mother nodded. 'She has been writing. She has filled many notebooks with her writing.'

Kalpana kicked at her mother, her legs hidden below the bench. But the principal was already distracted. She told Kalpana to go to her classroom and told the mother, 'Don't worry. She will start speaking very soon.' Seeing Kalpana's defiant face, she added, 'I will make sure of it. Don't worry.'

Mother walked with Kalpana to her classroom and stood outside as she went in, as if in a rehearsal for giving a daughter away in marriage. She didn't want to leave, and if they had allowed her, she too would have sat in the class. Kalpana turned and waved her away. As she turned to leave, the mathematics teacher came in. She had been teaching mathematics for years. When she saw Kalpana's mother, she held her hands and said, 'Don't worry. We will take good care of her.' Looking at Kalpana, now surrounded by other children, she added, 'She is such a good student.'

Kalpana was happy to be back with her classmates. A group of them stood around her, some plucking at her hair, others trying to say something without knowing what they should. When adults spoke about Kalpana, there was always a dark space, a place where children's ears were not welcome. So her classmates didn't know what to ask, but they stood around her. Some boys grouped together at the back of the room. Kalpana, now trained to remain quiet, found herself a bystander, watching everything around her in silence.

The teacher came in and the students dispersed to their benches. The teacher said, 'We must welcome Kalpana back to class.' Everyone clapped and Kalpana incongruously thought of the flag-hoisting ceremony on Independence Day, when the children would all clap after the flag had been successfully hoisted. The teacher walked up to Kalpana and gently escorted her to the front of the class.

'Kalpana is a brave girl. Because of an accident, she has lost her voice. So all of you must be nice to her.' She looked down at Kalpana and asked, 'Kalpana, you can hear everything I say?' Kalpana nodded.

Suddenly, two boys at the back chanted, 'Speech, speech.' The class fell silent, as if collectively embarrassed. Kalpana looked at the boys, picked up a piece of chalk and wrote on the board: 'Shut up', which in Kannada was written as 'Mouth shut'.

All the girls clapped this time. Before Kalpana had even started lessons, she had caused a gender divide!

Lunchtime was when girls from other classes came to gaze at Kalpana. Afterwards, Deeksha took Kalpana with her and Kumari to a corner of the school compound. They sat under the shade of a large peepul tree. Seeing that Kalpana was an object of interest, Deeksha asked her to sit on a large stone that looked a little like a throne. Kalpana sat there regally, not looking at anybody directly but casting her gaze benevolently on all who came. Some girls stood a little distance away and tittered, while others came to talk to Deeksha but had eyes only for Kalpana. Kumari sat next to Kalpana as if she were her guard.

The climactic moment came when Upadhya walked out of the staff room and up to the girls. He patted Kalpana on her back and took Deeksha aside to ask, 'Any improvement in her speech?' Deeksha replied in the negative, and for a moment, felt like she had become an adult.

When the school bell rang at the end of the day, Kalpana, Deeksha and Kumari came to the school gate to find Mother waiting for them. She walked them to Gangamma's house, although she managed to say that it was unnecessary to go to music class on that day itself. She gave each of the girls a banana to eat on the way.

Gangamma was happy to see them. She was very glad that Kalpana was going back to school. She knew it would only be a matter of time before the words rushed back into her, and however obstinate the little girl was, the words would flow. There was nothing greater than the power and autonomy of language. This had become clear to her when she decided not to sing after her father died and after a fruitless search for a husband for her. Her mother had said that if she stopped singing, maybe somebody would come to marry her. Gangamma had stopped then, but had always regretted it. She didn't sing for two years, but she suffered so much during that time with the imprisoned sound inside her that when her body revolted one early morning, the sounds of her vomiting had the rhythms of a song. After that, she had felt like she had been reborn. So she knew that poor Kalpana had no choice but to speak. But as long as she chose to remain silent, she would teach her the sound of music. After that, it would be left to the good spirits of the earth, water, air, fire and the sky, those deities of hers that were like her daily companions.

Thus, Kalpana was re-educated twice over. The first was at school, but this time, listening without making any comments or whispering to her friends. It was an exercise in control, a form of control that even adults would have struggled to possess. It had an effect on her thinking itself, as she understood one evening, sitting outside their brain temple. She spoke much less within herself. What she told her inner ears was not ceaseless chatter like earlier, but more carefully chosen words. It was as if words had become her internal currency and thinking ended up costing as little as possible. She also learnt another great lesson: that much of speaking was outside one's control. She had begun to understand—even if she would not have been able to formulate it in these terms—that speech was not really under the control of the person who spoke.

It was Deeksha who, curled up next to her one night, voiced the thought that lay vaguely at the back of Kalpana's mind. 'You seem so happy not talking now. I am afraid that when you want to speak, you will not be able to do so.' Kalpana smiled.

Encouraged, Deeksha added, 'So you better speak to me, or you will become truly dumb.'

Kalpana and Deeksha, in their own internal worlds, imagined what it would be like to be totally without speech. The thought inspired Deeksha so much that she picked up her new slate and wrote: *I will also stop speaking like you.*

For a moment, a short fleeting moment, Kalpana panicked. Deeksha was capable of anything. She wrote back on the slate in big letters: *NO.*

Deeksha shook her head. She rubbed out the '*NO*' and wrote: *From today.*

Panic-stricken, Kalpana grabbed Deeksha to shake some sense into her, as if trying to shake the words out of her.

Deeksha laughed and whispered loudly, 'Never, Akka. Never will I keep quiet. I cannot be like you.'

ALMOST EVERYONE HAD FORGOTTEN ABOUT THE TIME Kalpana had gone missing, and the mystery associated with those three days. Seeing Kalpana's open face, full of life and of questions, they had ceased to remember an already forgotten incident.

Kalpana soon recognised that learning in school without speaking made the experience of learning quite different. Her teachers' words entered her at a slower speed. They were clearer and uncluttered without her own words colliding with them. Surprisingly, she found that she had begun to listen more carefully, and had even discovered a remarkable piece of information while in her English class.

The English teacher was earnest like the other teachers, but she also had a higher standing among her colleagues. She had, unlike many others in the school, finished an MA in Udupi. She was not just a teacher of English but could also speak in English if needed. So it was that at every government function, the English teacher would say something in English to the audience. Incidentally, she had also married into a richer family in the village, as if that was almost to be expected because she was an English teacher.

In class that day, Kalpana had slowly gone into a zone while listening to her teacher read out some English poems. She soon found herself listening to the words themselves and not the voice of the teacher. In the cavernous silence in her mind, each of these words sparkled like a crystal. She not only heard the word, but also heard various other sounds present in the word. That night, when she tried to communicate this experience to Deeksha, she remembered their cousin Suresha. When he ate a jackfruit, he would not just say it was good. He would smack his lips, twirl his tongue, take a deep breath, and explain what kinds of smells and tastes were present in the fruit. When he got carried away by Kalpana and Deeksha's open-eyed interest, he would say, 'I can even tell you the kind of soil the tree grew in.'

For Kalpana, that day, language became like the jackfruit. She was no longer listening to the sound of the word, but was experiencing its various 'smells' and 'tastes', those swirls of the tongue that created sounds and even—this, much later—the inner clicks of the mind as it created the words. Her body became an ear, able to detect vibrations in words, the reverberations of the syllables. She was so immersed in experiencing the sounds that she did not remember the words or their meanings.

Since there was so much to tell Deeksha, that sultry night, Kalpana wrote down her thoughts on words. Deeksha read this but couldn't understand how Kalpana could forget the meaning and instead focus on the sounds and smells—how absurd!—of the words.

She said, 'Words don't smell. Only we do! And there is no word without meaning. When you hear a word, its meaning is also there.'

Kalpana wrote in reply: *So when you hear a word, you also hear its meaning?*

'Yes.'

So when you hear the word 'hot', you also hear its meaning?

'Yes.'

Can you tell me what it means?

Deeksha thought quickly. 'Hot means sweaty.'

So when you hear the word hot, you also hear sweaty, since you say the meaning is heard along with the word?

Deeksha was flummoxed. 'No, you don't hear somebody saying sweaty, but the moment you hear the word "hot", you think of sweaty.'

Kalpana wiped the slate and wrote her words with a renewed energy. *So the meaning comes to you after you hear the word?*

Deeksha was confused. 'Yes. No.' Irritated, she said, 'You are so difficult, Akka. You confuse everything. You will be a bad teacher.'

They lay down in silence, waiting for soundless sleep to creep into them. Deeksha turned over and pinched her sister. Kalpana had progressed so much in her control that she did not let even a little sound escape her. She just swatted away Deeksha's hand.

Deeksha said, 'See, this is how it is. First you felt the pinch, and then you felt the pain. But pinching and pain go together.'

Deeksha jumped up on her mat for her denouement. 'This is how hot and sweaty are.'

Kalpana turned away, smiling, marvelling once more at her little sister.

THE SECOND RE-EDUCATION FOR KALPANA WAS THROUGH Gangamma and the singing lessons. It was clear that her experience of sounds at school was influenced by her singing lessons. For Gangamma was not just another music teacher. She was, firstly, not a teacher at all, and had never taught anyone systematically. And, as she would often say, mostly to herself, no music teacher had ever taught singing to a girl who refused to speak.

The first few days, Gangamma did not teach them anything other than to make sounds they liked. Deeksha and Kumari enjoyed this part immensely—where else would an adult allow them the freedom to bark like a dog, cluck like a chicken, roar like an imagined tiger and snore like their parents? Kalpana silently watched the girls create these sounds while waiting for what Gangamma really wanted to teach them.

The second set of lessons was about imagined sounds, those they had never heard before. But with every sound that Deeksha and Kumari made, Gangamma showed them that they were only copying known sounds. Kalpana tried to imagine creating sounds for herself, sounds she had never heard. When the children went back home after these classes, they would try to make all kinds of sounds. Gangamma told them to listen carefully—the night was full of so many unheard sounds. The mountains grunted, the leaves whispered, the rain grumbled, and the wings of birds created a shockwave of sounds. 'Listen to all these,' said Gangamma. 'Listen to the silence of the night.'

So Deeksha and Kalpana discovered a new routine after everybody else had gone to sleep. They would sit in absolute silence, trying to listen to the sounds of the night. When it rained, they heard the drumming of the hurrying drops, and when it stopped, they would hear the single note of a drop of water falling slowly from the roof to the ground. When the crickets started their cacophony, they could feel the sound of these creatures as a solid wall. The sound was uniform, extending as a wall in front of them and impossible to break through. But the more they heard the unwavering whine of the crickets, the more accurately they could make out slight differences in the sounds. In the midst of the maddening, constant frequency, they began to hear other sounds. The little rustle of lizard's feet and the intake of breath from Ajji, chopped into little syncopated beats by the ceiling fan.

They heard, too, the dogs barking and the sounds from the forest, the signs of the busy, living world of the night. But most of all, Kalpana heard her favourite sounds, sounds she had never heard before: the clouds tickling each other, the rubbing sounds of the wind brushing against the trees, the swish of the tired wings of birds and the constant grumbling of the mountains. She could sit on her mat like a monk and feel all the night sounds rushing into her, each one greeted like a new friend.

Kalpana wanted to record these sounds so that Deeksha could sing them for their music teacher. She tried writing descriptions of the sounds, but when Deeksha read them, she couldn't reproduce any of them. Kalpana felt reassured by this exercise, for it proved to her once more that language could never describe musical sounds.

It was an odd sound that finally broke through the dam of resistance in Kalpana, at least partially. The sisters were so involved in their nightly exploration of sounds that, very often, they would fall asleep even while straining to catch new sounds. The nights had become a completely new universe for them. Where, earlier, it used to be a time for sleep, now the night had become a lively world that they looked forward to. One night, both of them had fallen asleep listening to the unending rain that created a monotonous tip-tap around their ears. Suddenly, Kalpana woke up as if stung by a particularly sharp sound. The rain had stopped, the crickets were not as loud, and even the fans had stopped rotating because of a power cut. Kalpana had a memory of the sound that had woken her up. She strained to catch it, and a few minutes later, she heard it again. It was hesitant, as if unsure whether or not to knock on her ears, unsure whether it would be welcomed or not. But that sound woke a memory in Kalpana so strong that she heard the sound as if it had been produced right next to her.

It was the sound of a bus horn, a sound alien to the million other sounds of nature around her. It was not the clear sound of the horn either; it was the sound that is produced only in the deepest part of the night, on rainy, misty, winding mountainous roads. It was a sound of hope, despair and warning, a sound that carried the effort made by the bus in climbing the mountain. This particular sound was accompanied by two headlights that curved and curled around the ghat roads, bounced off boulders on the mountain, rushed through the dense trees and scattered the startled creatures of the night. It reached her, as clear and distinct as if it had found its home and the very reason for its existence.

The sound released a torrent of other sounds within her. She immediately and clearly recalled how she had found her way out of the forest after those three frightening days. This sound had been her light, had shown her the path to the road on which she had been found. The prayers Ajji had said came rushing back to her, the words that she had so carelessly strewn to the wind. She remembered, as if it was all happening right in front of her, the crystal-clear notes in those words that beckoned her and led her to follow them, follow their dancing forms. She, who would have been more aware and conscious of her surroundings, only saw the words, saw them run playfully, dancing ahead of her. That night, she saw all the events unfolding clearly and she could not hold back her own sounds. She closed her mouth tightly, but they began to leak out, tiny little sounds, and then louder whimpers. If Deeksha had not woken, seen her sister whimpering and immediately held her, Kalpana would have spoken. She would have shouted, and nobody could have stopped her. The moment Deeksha held her, Kalpana relaxed. Her whimpers became the voice of the night, and it sounded like she was whispering to the clouds, the mountains, lizards, insects, snakes and, yes, tigers. Deeksha had never heard Kalpana's voice sound so clear, so musical, so magical. But Kalpana did not give in to the urge to speak. Instead, from that day on, all she did was sing, creating musical sounds that nobody but she could hear.

THE BRAIN TEMPLE WAS BECOMING FAMOUS. WHAT WAS A meeting place for the three girls soon attracted more girls once Kalpana started going to school. It began innocently enough one evening, when a group of girls from Kalpana's class saw the three girls sitting outside their shrine. They came over and joined them. Deeksha and Kumari excitedly showed them the idol, the small shoots that were slowly growing around it and the compound made of numbers scratched around the shrine. Deeksha said that she knew ants, bees and grasshoppers came to pray to the brain. One of the girls asked, 'So what? They can now do multiplication and division?'

She looked at Deeksha so seriously when she asked this question that Deeksha blurted out, 'Yes, of course they can.' Kumari jumped to Deeksha's defence by saying how she had seen ants cut a leaf into tiny bits and how each ant took a certain number of pieces to build their nest.

'I think they broke it equally for all of them. They know division,' she said confidently.

The girls were impressed and gazed solemnly at the ants scurrying all around them. Soon, this, and other stories said and unsaid, spread. The shrine became known as the place to get god's blessing to pass mathematics exams. A few more girls came by, and the open space surrounding the shrine became a playground where the girls would play throwball and 'running and catching'. When, one evening, a group of four boys swaggered in, the three girls decided that it was too much. They told the boys that it was a girls-only temple and no boys were allowed. The boys, affronted, refused to move. Deeksha and Kumari fought with them, but the boys threatened to bring more of their friends. One of them made the mistake of trying to poke at the idol of the brain with a stick. Kalpana, who had stayed silent till then, suddenly let out a shrieking note from deep within her.

To add to the sudden fear in the boys, Deeksha said, 'My sister is the priest of this temple. I don't know what she will do next. Better leave now or you will fail in all your classes.'

The boys did not come back and neither did too many girls after that. But there were always a handful of girls who would hang around the Brain and it became known as 'that girl place'.

GANGAMMA WAS IN FOR A SURPRISE. TWO DAYS AFTER sounds had finally dribbled out of Kalpana, the girls went for their evening music class. The three girls sat on the porch of her house, while Gangamma occupied a cane chair, looking down at them. Before she could say anything, Deeksha put her hand up and said, 'Akka finally spoke yesterday.' Gangamma was shocked and looked at Kalpana in surprise. Kalpana shook her head.

Deeksha continued, 'No, not speak like we do. She made a sound. An angry sound. We can say she sang, and we all heard her.'

Kumari clapped delightedly. 'Now we know her mouth is working fine.'

Gangamma looked at Kalpana and Kalpana looked back at her. Gangamma said, 'So, Kalpana, can I also hear the sound you made?'

Kalpana remained quiet. Deeksha tried to prod her, but Kalpana did not react.

Deeksha said, 'What I am saying is that Akka can speak if she wants to.'

Gangamma knew that. 'But why should she want to talk?'

'To speak to us. To speak to me.'

'Why should she speak to you?'

Deeksha was silent. Kumari held her hand. Deeksha made up her mind and said, 'Because she is my sister and sisters speak to each other.'

'That is not a good reason, Deeksha,' Gangamma gently replied.

'If she doesn't speak, I won't know what she is thinking.'

'Why do you want to know what she is thinking?'

'Because she is my ...' Deeksha saw Kumari shaking her head. 'Because ... because it is good for her. Yes. If she doesn't speak, we won't know what she wants, and so it is not good for her.'

'But she has been fine without speaking all this while.'

Deeksha was stumped. She and Kumari looked at each other and then at Kalpana.

Kumari said, 'I speak because I want to speak. I can't keep silent.'

Gangamma smiled. 'So, if Kalpana is silent, it means she does not want to speak. So let her do what she wants.'

Deeksha felt let down. Didn't her sister want to talk to her? She turned to Kalpana and asked in a low voice filled with the dread of rejection, 'Akka, you don't want to speak to me?'

Kalpana did not know what to say. Listening to Gangamma, she felt like she was being accepted as an adult. What a serious discussion they were having about her! But then there was Deeksha with her innocent, hurt eyes, looking up to her. Kalpana was exasperated and looked to Gangamma to speak for her.

'No, Deeksha,' Gangamma promptly replied. 'She wants to talk to you. But there is a reason she is not speaking now.'

Deeksha felt even more let down by Kalpana since she was letting their teacher speak on her behalf. She said, 'Then ask her what is the reason. Is there a reason at all? You please ask her.' She looked at Kalpana defiantly.

Gangamma asked Deeksha, 'Do you know the reason?'

'Yes, I do. On the day Akka went missing, Ajji was saying prayers and Akka asked her where her prayers go. So Ajji told her to follow them and see where they go. So Akka ran behind the words, wanting to see where they went.'

Gangamma was astounded, and it showed on her face. 'What? That is the reason for her not talking?' This information agitated her so much that she got up and started pacing the porch.

'No, that is not the full reason. Akka believes that language is a lie, so she will not speak any language.'

Gangamma was surprised again. She could not have imagined such a reason.

Looking at Kalpana, she asked, 'So you think language is a lie?' Kalpana nodded. 'Even if it is all a lie, why did you stop speaking?'

How could Kalpana tell her? That if she began, she would never stop speaking. Earlier, it was her head that had seemed so full of unspoken words. Now the words occupied even her stomach. It felt big and full and tense all the time. She was not really sure why she had stopped speaking—was it only because she was lost in the forest for three days? She had thought it was because she felt betrayed by the gods behind whom she ran, full of trust. And betrayed when the gods vanished, just like words, when she most needed them. But lately, she had been thinking that her decision not to speak was perhaps a way of hiding how frightened she had felt in the forest. How dirty she had become. How not a single word within her had enabled her to find a way out of the forest. How she had recognised the complete futility of language when she spent three days with millions of creatures who did not speak like she did. Was that when she realised the complete falsity of language?

But she couldn't explain any of this without speaking.

Kalpana pulled out her music notebook. Like the other two girls, she too had a notebook and a new pencil. But she had not written anything in it. Now, she opened the book and started writing. She had thought about this moment. Now, it was time.

I followed the prayer. I followed the sounds of Ganesha. I did not see where I was going. I could only see and hear very clear sounds all around me. I ran behind them so happily. And then I was in the forest. The rain came and I got lost. Three nights I stayed there, and then I found the road. I thought I would die in the forest. I called out to Ganesha all the time. Nobody came to help me. Ganesha is a lie. His name is also a lie. The words led nowhere. They lead nowhere.

Gangamma read this once, then reread it twice more. She could not believe that this little girl had written these words. Deeksha put out her hand to see what Kalpana had written. Kalpana grabbed the book from Gangamma and put it in her bag. They all sat silently, none of them knowing what to say.

Then Kumari, who had been thinking intently about something, said, 'Ajji, isn't writing the same as speaking?'

Deeksha giggled. 'No, Kumari. Writing is to use pencil and paper, and speaking only the mouth.'

Kumari added, 'And the brain.' She turned back to Gangamma. 'Ajji, I am saying writing is the same as speaking because Kalpana talked to you now when you read what she wrote. Instead of hearing her, you just read what she spoke.' She stopped, confused about what she was trying to say.

Gangamma had no idea how to answer these kids. For a fleeting moment, she thought how interesting it would have been to be a teacher in a school.

Kalpana was angry with Kumari for reducing her writing to speech. Annoyed, she tore up the sheet on which she had written and put the little torn pieces into her bag.

Gangamma turned to Deeksha. 'I asked you why she should want to speak. Why do any of us want to speak?'

All three looked puzzled. So she added, 'If you want to learn singing, you have to answer this question.'

The girls remained silent. 'Okay, let me ask this another way. Why do you want to sing?'

Kumari put her hand up and immediately pulled it down. 'I want to sing because I like it.'

'You like it like you like a sweet?'

'Yes, but it is also different.' She looked at Deeksha, who nodded encouragingly. 'It is better than a sweet. I feel very happy when I sing.'

Kalpana opened her notebook and started writing.

'Why are you happy when you sing?'

'I don't know. I feel happy.'

Kalpana had written: *Happy that others are listening to you?*

Kumari understood this question. 'No, no. I sing when I am alone, and I am happy then. If my mother or father are listening to me, I get worried and not that happy.'

Gangamma had an insight. She turned to Deeksha and said, 'Kumari has said something important. Can you tell me what it was?'

Deeksha looked at Kumari, who shook her head. Deeksha was also not clear what she should say. She began, 'She said she is happy when she sings.'

'And …?'

Kalpana stared at Deeksha, as if she too were asking this question aloud.

Deeksha thought, but nothing came to her. She looked around for answers in the yard surrounding the house. She got up and fidgeted.

Gangamma said, 'What else did Kumari say?'

'She is happy and … yes, she likes to sing when nobody is listening to her.'

Gangamma prodded her with a look. 'So what can you say?'

Deeksha walked up and down the porch, and suddenly, she understood. She shouted and ran down from the porch to the gate and back.

'I know, Ajji, I know,' she squealed. 'I know. We sing only for ourselves. But speaking is not like that. Only a mad man talks to himself.'

Kumari jumped up in delight, waving her tiny hands. 'Correct, correct,' she said. 'Only a mad man talks to himself.'

Gangamma smiled and said, 'But singing we do for ourselves. Even if nobody listens to us.'

Kalpana wrote furiously: *If I keep singing by myself, they will call me mad.*

Gangamma calmed the three of them and made them sit. 'Maybe somebody is always listening to you. If you make a sound, do you think somebody will always hear it?'

In a small voice, Kumari said, 'God?' Kalpana glared at her.

Gangamma pointed to a small path in the garden, along which water flowed to various trees and plants. 'I pour water here'—she pointed—'and then the water flows. Water does not flow to feed the trees. It just flows, and whichever trees and plants need water, they take it.'

Deeksha and Kumari nodded as if they understood perfectly.

Gangamma continued, 'When we sing, every note is heard by others. Sound is like water. It just flows. The dogs hear my songs, the peacock dances to it, and even the leaves of the plants wake up when I sing. I give my sounds to the world, and that is why I sing.'

Deeksha said solemnly, 'While it is only for other people that we speak.'

Kumari added softly, 'I speak to the dogs and chickens also.' When they all turned to look at her in surprise, she bravely added, 'They speak to me also—that is what I think sometimes.'

All four of them sat silently, listening to their own thoughts. Nothing was clear to any of them, but they felt as if they were together, with one purpose. As if these singing lessons would show them something, anything. They sat till it began to get dark and they could hear the bells around the cows entering the neighbour's house. They sat till Mother came to Gangamma's house, worried that the girls had not yet reached home. She saw the four of them sitting in silence instead of singing, with two dogs lying equally silently amidst them.

As they left, Gangamma realised what she had to teach them. Something very different. She would tell them something about sounds that she had never talked about. She would teach them the very magic of singing, for these were not ordinary girls.

THE FIRST CONFLICT BETWEEN GANGAMMA AND KALPANA took place after a few classes. The classes that were about producing different kinds of sounds were fun and the three children enjoyed them. The problem arose when Gangamma said that she would teach them a short song. She told them that when she began to learn singing, the first song taught to her by her father was a short prayer for their local spirits. The prayer asked for blessings before the performance. Gangamma first sang the song, then she asked the girls to repeat each line after her. Kalpana sat quietly, and Gangamma realised what the problem was.

'This is not the same as speaking, Kalpana. This is a song.'

Kalpana wrote angrily: *These are words. I won't say them.*

'No, they are not words. They are a song. They are music.' Gangamma tried to explain what she had said. 'Kalpana, we speak to tell something to somebody. But this is a song. We are not speaking to anybody.'

Deeksha nodded. 'Even though it is all in Kannada.'

Kalpana wrote: *You are speaking to god.*

Reading that, Kumari piped up, 'No, we are singing to god.'

Kalpana scribbled faster: *No, it is the same as speaking because you are asking god to protect you.*

Gangamma clapped her hands to get their attention. She said, 'I will say the word "mara".' The girls instinctively looked at the tree nearby. 'When I said this word, all of you knew what I meant.' They nodded. 'Now I am going to sing it,' she declared.

Gangamma sang the word. It sounded nothing like the spoken word. It did not even seem to be produced from her mouth, but from the depths of her body. Even when she had pronounced the word in full, it was not the same as the word for tree. None of the girls even thought of looking at the tree. They remained silent for a time after Gangamma finished singing the word. Deeksha whispered in awe, 'That did not even sound like your voice, Ajji. How did you produce that sound?'

Gangamma smiled. She was aware of the impact of her 'song'. She, like many other singers she knew, those singers who went from place to place singing and collecting money and food, could sing long songs made up of just a few words.

She turned to Kalpana and said, 'So, when I sing the word "Devi", I am not saying her name. This devi is not the one in your temple but the ruling spirit of our family. She protects us. When I sing her name, I am calling out to her. I am shouting out for her. I am singing for her.'

Kumari looked at Gangamma innocently. In the fervour of the moment, Gangamma looked more imposing than usual. 'So, does Devi hear you when you call out to her?'

Gangamma pulled Kumari up. She asked her to walk towards the gate. She called out, 'Kumari.'

Kumari turned back and asked, 'Yes, Ajji?'

Gangamma said, 'Walk outside the gate. Go out a little bit.' She called out her name again and asked whether Kumari could hear her.

Kumari's voice reached them loud and clear, even though they could not see her. 'Yes, Ajji.'

Gangamma called her back. The girls felt like they had all conducted an experiment together.

Gangamma asked, 'So, what did you learn from this?'

Kumari said, 'I could hear your voice clearly.'

Deeksha added, 'Your voice was loud.'

Kalpana wrote: *Even when we couldn't see you, we heard you.*

Gangamma patted Kalpana and told them how words could connect those who could not see each other. 'So, when I call out to my Devi, even if none of us can see her, she can hear me.'

Deeksha and Kumari were charged up. This was the closest encounter with Devi they had had in their lives. They had visited many kinds of Devi temples, hundreds of them strewn all over the region they lived in, but the Devi was always something impersonal and sometimes frightening for them. Here was a Devi whom their music teacher called out to!

Kalpana was visibly annoyed. She wrote in big letters: *How do you even know that there is a Devi who listens to you? Where is she? Have you ever seen her? Does she wear a red saree?*

The three of them sat patiently while Kalpana wrote. Deeksha couldn't help saying, 'Akka, speaking is faster than writing.'

Emboldened, Kumari added, 'It is much easier also.' Struck by a question, she asked Gangamma, 'Why do we write? Why can't we all just speak? Even in school we have to do only writing. We have to write all our exams, and I have to buy proper pencils, and then my fingers start hurting.'

When Kalpana finished, Gangamma read what she had written. Deeksha asked her, 'What is she saying now? Show, show.'

Gangamma said, 'She asks how I know that there is a Devi. Have I seen her?'

Deeksha asked, 'Yes, Ajji, have you seen her?'

'I may have, but why should we believe only those things that we can see?' She paused and looked at the eager little faces looking back at her. 'I want all of you to listen silently to the many sounds around us now.'

After a few minutes of listening, she asked, 'Can you tell me what you heard? Did you hear a musical sound?'

Together, Deeksha and Kumari said that they had heard a bird.

'How do you know that it was a bird? Did you see it?'

'Oh, I know without a doubt,' Deeksha said.

Kumari added, 'You can go behind your house and check.'

Gangamma smiled. She had never imagined that children could be so quick in their responses. And so confident!

'So you know there is a bird just by hearing its sound, right?'

They nodded. Deeksha added, 'I don't see thunder. I hear it, and I know it is there in the clouds.'

Kumari chanted, as if the two of them were singing a song, 'I don't see the principal, but I can hear her from another room when she shouts at students.'

'In the dark night, I know there are lizards running around even if I don't see them.'

Kumari jumped up in excitement. 'I can hear so many crickets, but I haven't seen even one so far!'

They turned towards Kalpana. She was glaring at them, as if they had joined sides against her. But she thought for a moment and then smiled. She wrote: *Listen carefully.*

The two girls screwed up their eyes in concentration. After a few moments, Kalpana tapped them on their backs. They opened their eyes. Kalpana wrote: *Did you hear a sound like the wind?*

They nodded, somewhat unsure.

Kalpana wrote some more. *That is the elephant that is flying behind the house and over the mountain.*

And she laughed, little sounds that struggled to escape her mouth.

Kumari felt chastised. Deeksha looked at her and said, 'Don't make fun of us, Akka. There are no elephants that can fly.'

That is what I am saying.

She rubbed out 'saying' and replaced it with 'writing'. And wrote further: *There is no Devi. Devi is like this flying elephant.*

She looked at Gangamma, suddenly worried that she would get angry.

Or Ganesha, she added.

Gangamma read this in silence. She thought about what she wanted to say. Then she said that it was time to end the class, but left them with these words: 'When I speak, there is a meaning behind the words. But when I sing, you will feel the trees, the birds, the wind, the butterflies. When I sing the words, I remove their meaning. When I sing, I am only giving you the pure sound with no meaning.'

Gangamma stopped. She was unsure whether she had expressed herself correctly. The children looked blankly at her. Gangamma had never before articulated music in this manner, not even to herself. Where did these ideas come from?

She got up and told the children to leave. It looked like it would rain soon. As they left, she gave them an exercise to do before the next class. 'Choose one word you like. Try to hear it in all possible ways. Feel how it sounds. Forget its meaning.'

They nodded, but still looked blank.

To Kalpana, she added, 'Singing shows what is inside you and not the objects outside you. Think about that.'

Mother was patiently waiting at the end of the road with two other middle-aged women, who had been telling her how surprised they were. They had never thought of Gangamma as someone who would teach children. It made her oddities more acceptable.

WHETHER THEY LEARNT ANYTHING ABOUT MUSIC OR NOT, Deeksha and Kumari learnt something new. When they started paying attention to the sound of the words and not to their meaning, they began to note how the same word sounded different when different people uttered it. It was Kumari who said to Deeksha that she now understood how her name sounded different when uttered by each of her family members. Deeksha happily added that her name sounded different when her mother was angry with her and when she called her to eat. The two girls also decided to inform Gangamma of another finding of theirs: words sounded different when they were uttered by a smiling person, a scowling person, an angry person, a calm person. They agreed that sounds could also be heard as happy, sad or angry. Deeksha concluded this observation with a flourish: 'And boring also, like when teachers say them in class.'

Deeksha was worried that Kalpana would go back to her complete silence. She, like everybody else, was waiting for the day when Kalpana would start speaking normally. She wanted so much to talk to Kalpana. It was tiring, this game of keeping quiet, reading Kalpana's writing and interpreting Kalpana's facial gestures. Speaking made life much easier. She didn't know what else to do to get Kalpana to speak. Even going to school hadn't really helped her speak. She would sit in class and write in her notebooks, but nothing had triggered her to start speaking. Not even a visit to the principal's room one day. Nor her stern lecture to Kalpana about growing up without being able to speak. Nothing the principal said seemed to have an effect on the girl. Not even when the principal ended her tirade by saying, 'Nobody will marry you if you continue to be like this.' After Kalpana left, with not a single expression on her face, the principal began to wonder whether Kalpana was actually dumb or whether she was 'all right in the head'—her words to the peon.

So Deeksha was worried. One morning, when she got up, she saw that Kalpana was already up and sitting on her mat. Deeksha had woken with a clear thought in her head. She said, 'Akka, remember what Gangamma Ajji said. Singing is about you, not about others. So singing cannot be a lie. Otherwise it will mean that you are a lie. And you are not a lie.'

KALPANA WAS SITTING IN THE MATHEMATICS CLASS, listening to the teacher drone on about fractions. She was disturbed and distracted. What Deeksha had told her that morning had stayed with her. She was becoming aware that she was perhaps wrong in thinking that language was all about the outside world. Gangamma's view that singing was about her internal self and not about the outside world made sense to her. She hadn't understood it fully when Gangamma had declared it in her booming voice, but when Deeksha had told her that singing was not a lie, Kalpana had begun to recognise that there was a difference between music and the language she spoke. She had not understood this either, but was stuck on what Deeksha had said: 'You are not a lie.'

Kalpana started doodling in her notebook, the teacher, the students and the classroom all forgotten. The doodles were a confused expression of her thoughts surrounding the question of whether she was a lie or not. Suddenly, the squeaky voice of the teacher entered her thoughts. Kalpana became aware that she was in the mathematics class. She also realised that the teacher was looking at her and so were all the students. Had she fallen asleep? She looked at the board. There was a big fraction written on it: 56,100/255.

'Can you do this division?' The teacher seemed to ask this question of the class, but she was looking at Kalpana.

Without thinking, without even recognising what she was doing, still caught in a miasma of doubt about lies, Kalpana said spontaneously, '220.' The teacher checked the answer against the notes in her hand.

Then she truly understood what had happened. Kalpana had spoken, although it was just a number that she had called out.

The children too suddenly realised this, and they started clapping, some for the answer and some for the first sound that they had heard from Kalpana after she had come back to class.

The teacher rushed to her and took hold of her hands. 'You spoke,' she said with great delight.

Kalpana stared at her, feeling betrayed by her own self.

The teacher was excited. 'It means that your speech is fine. Tell me something. Say something to the class.'

Kalpana was silent.

'Tell me your name.'

Kalpana just stared at her.

The teacher was totally deflated. She had felt so joyous. 'You can't speak?' she asked.

Kalpana shook her head.

'But you spoke now—you said the correct answer.'

Kalpana nodded in affirmation.

'So you *can* speak.'

Kalpana shook her head in the negative. But the teacher would not give up so easily.

'Can you say out loud the answer now?'

Kalpana was silent.

In an inspired attempt, the teacher asked, 'Can you recite all the numbers till hundred?'

Kalpana stayed quiet. The children started murmuring, and the teacher ran out of patience and time. The class bell rang, and Kalpana only succeeded in getting more glances and whispers directed at her.

But she was greatly shaken by this episode. She had failed at keeping quiet. But not entirely, since she had not spoken a word of language but had only uttered a number. Numbers were not language, she decided. They also did not lie. They were like her. This insight gave her tremendous joy. 220 was always 220. It did not become, one hot day, 125 or any other number. Kalpana was so excited by this idea that she wrote it down. While writing, she suddenly remembered, a little guiltily, the brain temple of which she was the priest. She had neglected the shrine in the time she spent at school and in her music classes. But now, in the aftermath of her utterance in the class, she had an inspiration. She decided to organise a festival at the temple. Already they had enough girls who were regulars there. More than the shrine, it was the pleasure of being away from their homes that drew these girls together. Deeksha had suggested that instead of playing in the area around the shrine, they could read a book or maybe hold a class. Kumari said that since it was the brain temple, they needed a book fit for the brain. Deeksha and Kumari had immediately said, 'Maths book,' and looked at Kalpana. Kalpana knew that if she were speaking, she would have taken a class in mathematics outside the shrine.

Sitting under a tree at lunchtime, waiting for Deeksha to come, she planned the festival. It would be a music festival, but all the songs would contain only numbers. They would sing mathematics, and they would put bright lights around the brain—not like in the temples of gods, which used only oil lamps. She decided that if the adults wanted to sing songs about their gods, then the children would sing songs about little numbers, big numbers, prime numbers, decimals, fractions. There were so many gods in mathematics for them to sing about!

Deeksha hurried over to where Kalpana was sitting. She said excitedly, 'Your whole class heard you. Let me also hear it. What was the number?' Kalpana shook her head.

Kumari came over and slumped next to Kalpana. 'Everybody is talking about you.'

Deeksha asked, 'What are they saying?'

'About Akka speaking in class.'

'Akka, what did you really say in class?'

Kalpana shook her head. She was finding all this attention too tiring, especially when she had more important things to do. First, she had to figure out how she was going to tell Deeksha about her plan for the festival.

THE DEEPAVALI FESTIVAL WAS APPROACHING. EVERY YEAR it was celebrated with a series of music and dance performances, all of them centred around the Devi temple. Ajji had great plans for this year's festival. As a way of thanking the Devi for bringing Kalpana back, she had asked her son to sponsor one evening's food for all the devotees. She had also promised the Devi a special garland made from a rare flower that only bloomed around this time. She had asked Siddaiah to get a bunch of these flowers from the market in Udupi. As if flowers from Udupi would have the sanctity of the temple there. It was very difficult to knit these delicate flowers into a garland, but that was the least Ajji felt she could do for the gods for having brought Kalpana back to them.

For a few weeks before the festival, all anyone could talk about were the many activities that were being planned. Kalpana heard about them at school, on the streets and in her house. Even her usually quiet father was animated about Deepavali that year. Her mother had promised to make special sweets for the two girls. She had also promised eighteen gods that she would visit their temples with the two girls. Thankfully, these temples were distributed around their village and she planned to complete the pilgrimage in three days.

Deepavali also gave Kalpana the perfect occasion to plan her own music festival. It would not be as grand as the celebration at the temples, but she would convince her mother to give them some money for the lights and maybe some sweets for the girls. She was thinking of perhaps inviting some adults too. Not for a moment did the three girls think of how others would view their brain god.

When Kalpana wrote down her idea for Deeksha to read, Deeksha was excited. She immediately responded by saying that their festival should have Gangamma Ajji's performance. Kalpana nodded but was doubtful whether Gangamma would agree. She was also worried whether Gangamma would agree to sing about mathematical numbers instead of her own Devi.

Deeksha said, 'We can have a function to make you a priest. We can put a garland around your neck and then fall at your feet.'

Kalpana laughed soundlessly, imagining herself as a mini version of a goddess.

'Imagine,' Deeksha said, 'you will be the first woman priest here.' She thought for a few minutes and then added, 'Why do even women gods have male priests, Akka?'

Kalpana did not know nor care about priests and temples.

Deeksha thought some more. 'But our temple is very special.' Suddenly, she was struck by a doubt. Was their god male or female? She asked Kalpana, 'The brain is not male or female? Or is it? Is there a female brain and a male brain?'

Kalpana once again marvelled at the way Deeksha thought. She had no idea how to answer her.

She wrote: *Ask the science teacher tomorrow.*

GANGAMMA WAS VERY HAPPY TO HEAR THE RESULTS OF THE exercise she had given the girls. Both Deeksha and Kumari told her excitedly about how their names sounded so different when different people called out to them. They told her about how they thought some words were angry words, some were happy words, some sad words, some boring words. Kumari added that when she focused only on the sound of the word without worrying about its meaning, she could feel the sound in her ear canal.

'The word was like a trickle of flowing water in my ear, moving slowly inside me.'

Deeksha went one step further. 'When I focused only on the sound, I began to see the word in front of me.'

Kumari started giggling. 'How is that possible, Ajji? That is so funny—seeing a word.'

Kalpana looked very annoyed.

Gangamma was astounded by the experiences of the two girls. She asked Deeksha, 'Did somebody tell you about seeing the word?'

Deeksha was aghast. 'No, Ajji, I was doing what you said. I was listening to the sound of my ajji talking to my mother. First, I couldn't do it, since I was understanding what she was saying.' But soon, Deeksha went into a zone where Ajji's words became sounds that did not have the accompanying qualities of her hoarse voice or their meaning. At that moment, words appeared in front of her in a row, slowly moving. Deeksha felt drowsy. She shook her head and lost that vision.

Gangamma said, 'Deeksha, what you said about seeing words is very important, especially for singing. Many singers like me feel the same.' She turned to Kalpana. 'Write down what I am going to say now. You said the Devi is a lie and that we cannot see her. When I sing about my Devi, I am not calling out to her or pointing her to you. I am singing because I am searching for her through that sound. I keep trying various sounds when I sing that word or when I sing about her. I am not singing to tell you how the Devi looks. I am singing to try and see the Devi through these sounds. It is like the Devi is made up of all these musical sounds, and when I am truly and deeply immersed in singing, I can see her in the same way that Deeksha saw the words.'

Kalpana furiously wrote down what Gangamma said and showed it to her. Gangamma read it and said, 'Good. You have understood what I said. Now you can also write this: words may lie but music does not.' Kalpana happily wrote it down.

Gangamma continued, 'So, Kalpana, did you also try experimenting with sounds like these girls?'

Kalpana had not. She had been dismissive about the exercise and ignored Deeksha when she tried to show her how the same word sounded different when Mother, Father and Ajji uttered it. But she could not tell Gangamma that, nor did she want to tell her that she had done the exercise. Then she would herself become a lie, she thought.

So she shook her head. Her morose face said all that needed to be said.

'That is fine,' Gangamma said. 'Try it and tell me next time.'

Kalpana nodded and then wrote in her book: *220*.

Gangamma looked at it, puzzled. Seeing her expression, Deeksha leaned over and peered at the book.

'Is that the number you said in class?' she asked Kalpana.

Kalpana nodded. Deeksha told Gangamma about the mathematics class and what she had heard from the other students. 'She spoke that number clearly.'

Gangamma asked Kalpana to repeat the number.

Kalpana was embarrassed. She shook her head and then wrote: *All of you read out that number.*

Gangamma read it first, her voice ringing and clear. Deeksha also pronounced it correctly. Kumari read it but stumbled on a syllable in between.

Kalpana wrote: *Is 220 a word?*

The girls thought hard and Deeksha said, 'Yes. It looks like one.'

'But,' Kumari added, 'when you say it, it is a very long word.'

Deeksha nodded. 'Yes, it is actually like a sentence!' The two girls clapped their hands in delight.

Kalpana was happy to hear this. She knew numbers were different. And now the girls had said it themselves: numbers were sentences hiding as words.

Deeksha asked Gangamma, 'Ajji, will different people speak this word differently?'

Animated, Kalpana wrote: *No, the number cannot be changed. It is the same. There is no angry 220, sad 220, no loud number or soft number.*

Kumari jumped up, her polio-affected leg wobbling. 'Numbers are only numbers.' She didn't even know what she was trying to say.

Numbers are not words or even sounds. They are completely true.

Kalpana stopped. She wanted to write so much more, but she didn't know how.

Gangamma asked Kalpana, 'So there is no music with numbers?'

Kumari squeaked, 'Devi is not a number.'

As if these were the final words on the subject, Kalpana wrote: *There is music. You can sing with numbers. But that is different from singing with words.*

This was the cue, although unplanned. Deeksha stood up and solemnly announced to Gangamma, 'Akka wants to have a music festival for Deepavali, where all the songs will only have numbers and not words. She wants you to be the first singer.'

Gangamma broke into loud laughter. Singing numbers—for a person who brought the image of god before her eyes through her songs! She laughed uncontrollably.

Kalpana stopped her by showing her what she had written: *Maybe you can show us how to see numbers through singing just like you see your Devi through your songs.*

Gangamma had no answer to that. She stared at Kalpana, and all three girls thought she was angry. Deeksha plucked the notebook from Kalpana and read what she had written. Puzzled, she said, 'Yes, it is true, isn't it, Ajji? We do not see numbers just like we do not see the Devi.'

Kumari nodded. To her, mathematics was always true. Her teacher repeated this in almost every class. Whenever she solved a problem on the board and whenever a student gave a wrong answer, the teacher would say, 'Remember and never forget. There is only one answer in mathematics. That is the truth.' Kumari and her classmates had never understood the teacher. But now, Kumari had a glimmer of insight. If one could see numbers, they must be true. And you could see numbers by singing them like a song.

Kumari felt like she had been liberated. She wanted to run around Gangamma's compound, around the trees. She got up involuntarily, felt the heaviness of her polio leg, and sat down.

Gangamma was once again moved. She had never imagined that teaching could be so rewarding. New ideas were being formed right before her eyes. It was almost as if thinking was a form of singing, and grasping this thought moved her deeply.

As they left, she gave them another exercise. She told them to find the one sound that was special to them. 'It should be like your name. When you hear it, you should feel like you are hearing your name. It is a sound that calls out to you. Hearing it, you should think, "That is me. That is my sound. That is my voice."'

Kumari immediately said, 'When somebody calls "Kumari", I know it is me.'

Gangamma clarified, 'No, not your name. Like your name, is there one sound that you think is you?'

The girls looked nonplussed.

Gangamma thought of a better way to explain this. 'What is your favourite colour? You have favourite colours, right?' They all nodded. 'Like that, do you have a favourite sound? Even if you do not have one now, go and listen to all the sounds and choose your favourite one.'

MOTHER HAD DISCOVERED THE BOTTLE THAT DEEKSHA HAD kept in the corner of the kitchen. It looked empty, but there was something like moss at the bottom. Deeksha had stuck a piece of paper on it that read: 'School work'. So Mother called Deeksha and asked her why the empty bottle was still in the kitchen. Deeksha told her it was something her teacher had asked her to do.

Deeksha showed Kalpana the bottle and said that her words were indeed becoming plants. Kalpana wrote: *Take it to school. Look at it under the microscope.*

Kalpana was fascinated with the microscope. One day, their science teacher had brought a small plastic one to class. She took a piece of dried leaf, placed it below the lens, and asked the students to peer through it. It was great fun for all the students, and Kalpana, in particular, enjoyed seeing shapes and forms she had not seen before. Things look bigger when seen through the lens, the teacher repeatedly said, but that there were countless things around her that she could not see was a revelation for Kalpana. It was also the right time for her to have encountered the microscope, after her experience of not speaking, and having started singing classes. She was more attuned to the unseen world, and when she first saw the new forms, she felt a deep sense of satisfaction that the world had indeed conformed to her expectations.

She wrote: *Ask the science teacher your question about the brain, whether it is female or male.*

At school, Kalpana was already famous, more so because she was seen as an oddity. This was taken to the realm of the absurd when a team from the government department in Bengaluru visited the school. The principal summoned Kalpana to her room and introduced her to the three officials: two pompous men and a portly lady. She told them how the school took care of their students even when they had serious undiagnosed problems. One of the men immediately said, 'Hope it is not something infectious. You have to be careful letting such cases into the school.' He looked at the other two officials; it seemed as if his comment was more for their benefit. But the visit was good for the principal. It marked out her school as doing something special, and when they spoke about it, it would not be as yet another lost school in yet another anonymous village. It would be the school where there was an extremely intelligent girl who had mysteriously lost her voice, and (this the principal had stressed) a girl who would only utter numbers. All the attention had increased Kalpana's fame or notoriety, depending on one's point of view.

In a small way, Deeksha also began to share Kalpana's notoriety. Now there were two crazy girls in the school—

moreover, they were sisters! Her exploits in Upadhya's class had been exaggeratedly told to the teachers and some senior students. The fact that she, Kumari and Kalpana were together all the time put her in the company of two 'odd' girls, one who walked with a limp and the other who never spoke. But Deeksha's fame at school went up another level after her run-in with the science teacher.

One day, just as she did in Upadhya's class, Deeksha jumped up with her hand in the air as soon as the science teacher came into the room. But the teacher was in no mood to indulge Deeksha and told her to sit down. Later, as the class was winding down and after she had dictated the notes she had wanted to, the teacher—more as a distraction for the tired class—called on Deeksha to ask her question. The question had been festering in Deeksha's mind, and she had been fidgeting throughout the class.

When asked, she got up slowly. 'Miss, we know there are males and females, right?' Some students started sniggering. Just the words male and female would get them to start giggling.

The teacher looked at Deeksha, waiting for the class bell to ring. She didn't like the first question and kept quiet.

'Miss, we also know that all of us have a brain, correct?'

Still the teacher remained noncommittal.

'My question, miss, is whether our brains are also male or female. What I am asking is whether my brain is female since I am female.'

Some students started laughing, even though they had not understood the question. Deeksha turned to look at the bench behind her and pointed to a short, scrawny boy trying to shrink farther down the bench. 'Miss, is his brain male?'

The whole class burst into laughter. Just the act of pointing at the boy was cause enough for hilarity. Deeksha, hearing all the laughter, smiled, although she had little idea why she did so. Furious, the teacher walked up to Deeksha and dragged her to the front of the classroom.

'This is a joke, is it?' She pulled Deeksha's right ear and then gave her a knock on her head with her knuckles. 'You are so smart now, is it?'

Deeksha turned to her and said in a small voice, 'No, miss, I really want to know. A teacher told me one day that I think like a girl. I saw the poster on the school wall on which it said that it is the brain that thinks. So I thought my brain is what makes me a girl.'

There was a shocked silence after she finished. The teacher was embarrassed and didn't know what to say. As for the children, they were trained never to talk about what made them boys or girls. Perhaps Deeksha was not really talking about the brain but about some other organs? Unspeakable organs?

Kumari stood up to support her dear friend. 'Miss, if I am a girl, then I should have a girl brain, no?' She sat down, having done her duty.

The teacher pulled Deeksha's ear again. She announced to the class that all brains were the same. She made the mistake of clarifying her point by saying that the difference between a boy and a girl was not in the brain.

A boy in the back, hiding behind his friends, suddenly discovered a voice that he would never find again in his life, and shouted, 'So where is the difference?'

Again, the class broke into embarrassed laughter. The teacher pinched Deeksha's arm and told her, 'You are as mad as your sister.'

Deeksha pulled her arm away forcefully and declared, 'My sister is not mad.'

A bunch of girls, led by Kumari, ran towards Deeksha as the bell rang and the teacher stalked away from the class.

THAT NIGHT, AFTER ALL THE LIGHTS HAD BEEN TURNED OFF, Deeksha and Kalpana sat in their tiny room, leaning against the wall. Surprisingly, the sky was entirely free of clouds, and through the tiny window they could see it, a vast, dark sky with innumerable stars. Deeksha recounted all that had happened in class, how the students had laughed and what the teacher had said.

Kalpana nodded in understanding and wrote: *Male and female are just words. So they are also lies.*

Deeksha said, 'I told them that, Akka. So many people tell us that we behave like girls. And our science teacher also said that the brain is the cause of our behaviour.'

Kalpana wrote: *You are right. They can't understand you.*

Deeksha continued, 'So, I said, if my brain makes me behave like a girl and a boy's brain makes him behave like a boy, then my brain is a girl-brain and the boy's brain is a boy-brain.'

Kalpana clapped and hugged her sister. She wrote: *You are very clever.*

Deeksha looked sadly at Kalpana after she read this and said, 'Not as clever as you, Akka.' At the same time, she remembered her teacher's comment about Kalpana being mad.

They sat in silence till Deeksha said, 'Is our brain god male or female?'

Kalpana wrote in big letters: *Girl-brain.*

Deeksha finished what Kalpana would have said: 'With a girl-priest.'

As Deeksha fell asleep, she thought of all the things she would have to take for the brain god. Now that they had decided that she was a girl, she decided to take her coloured hairbands, some coconut oil, and maybe a comb too. She fell asleep with a smile on her lips.

THE RAINS WERE BECOMING MORE SPORADIC AFTER TWO months of sustained rainfall. That Sunday, when Kalpana and Deeksha went to their temple in the morning, it was cool and cloudy. Thanks to the rain, a lush growth surrounded the temple. To Deeksha, it seemed as if the stone shrine had grown a little bigger. It was beginning to look like a tiny dark cave, due to the thick grass around it. Deeksha went to pull the grass out with her hand, but Kalpana stopped her. She took a stick from the ground and beat the grass with it. She poked it into the shrine and found that the ground there was still soft. She wanted to be sure that there were no snakes. After all, this region was the kingdom of cobras and king cobras. Almost every family in the village worshipped these snakes.

When they were sure that the shrine was empty of unwanted creatures, Kalpana and Deeksha began pulling out the grass and weeds. The idol was looking mossy and 'tired', according to Deeksha. Kalpana sent Deeksha home to bring a cloth for wiping the idol. When Deeksha ran back with the cloth, Ajji followed her at a little distance and stood watching the two girls under the tree.

Kalpana wiped the idol clean. She then anointed it with the turmeric and kumkum they had brought with them. Deeksha took out the hairbands, a small plastic bottle of coconut oil that they used daily on their hair, a comb and a couple of hairpins. She gave these to Kalpana, who looked at this odd collection, not knowing what to do with them.

Deeksha looked at her face and said, 'Our god is a girl, correct?'

Nodding, Kalpana placed all the items in front of the idol.

Deeksha said, 'We need a lamp.' Kalpana nodded again, though she had wanted electric lights to be strung around the temple. To surprise Deeksha, she had brought a small flashlight from the storeroom. It was supposed to be used when the power went off at night, but everyone seemed to be quite used to the power cuts and the darkness that followed, so they rarely used the flashlight.

She turned on the torch and angled it towards the idol. Deeksha clapped. 'It looks so beautiful now.'

Kalpana decided that a string of lights inside and outside the shrine would make it look really beautiful. She looked around, but could find no way to get electricity to the shrine. She decided to get her father to buy six small torchlights to be used during their festival.

The girls cleaned up the area around the shrine.

'It will be nice to have loudspeakers so we can play some music for our god,' said Deeksha.

In response, Kalpana collected a few thick sticks and planted them around the shrine. She gestured to Deeksha to get some more cloth for cleaning.

Deeksha ran home and came back with a small bunch of torn, faded pieces of cloth. Her mother followed her this time to the door, and she and Ajji stood staring at the two girls.

Kalpana tore some of the pieces into strips and tied them to the sticks. The place was instantly transformed. It was like a mini temple fit only for children.

Soon, a couple of girls walking along the village road saw the two girls and ran to the temple. In an hour or so, a bunch of girls, including Kumari, had congregated there.

Mother and Ajji walked out of the house to see what the girls were doing. As they came closer, a couple of girls ran to them and said, 'Come, come see our new temple.' Mother was shocked to hear this. She had not ever imagined that the girls were building a 'temple'. They had never shown any interest in pictures of gods or in the prayers of the elders at home.

Kalpana saw them and nudged Deeksha, who ran to them and said, 'You cannot enter. This place is only for girls.'

Ajji tried to peer around her. Deeksha pushed both of them away and told the two girls who were standing nearby, 'Don't let everybody come here. This is not for grown-ups.'

Eventually, Mother and Ajji stood at a little distance from the shrine. The sticks had now been adorned with coloured 'flags' made from old pieces of cloth. They watched the twinkling light inside the shrine illuminate the black stone, which, to the two women, looked like the top of a head.

Ajji told Mother, 'See how the light is white and twinkling. China-made torch.'

Mother shouted out, 'Deeksha, make sure you bring the torch back home.'

Deeksha ran to her, embarrassed. 'Amma, you go home now.' She paused and added, 'But it would have been better if you, as older people, had brought some sweets for our god.'

Ajji and Mother had begun to walk away, but then, Ajji turned and went back to Deeksha to ask, 'What god is that?'

'You wouldn't know, Ajji,' Deeksha said. 'It is a special god for all of us girls. We created this god,' she added proudly.

Ajji couldn't keep quiet. 'Oh, you have a name for your god?' She shouted out to Mother, 'Now the children are creating their own gods.'

Hearing that, Mother hurried over to them. 'You cannot create your own gods,' she whispered, worried that the news might spread in the village.

By now, a bunch of girls stood near Deeksha. She would not back down. 'Why can't we create our own god?' she demanded.

Mother tried to pull Deeksha away from her friends. If any of this talk went back to the families of the other girls, who knew what would happen!

Deeksha stood her ground. 'Why can't we have our own gods? Who gave you all the gods in our temples?'

Kalpana had hurried over by then, and heard Deeksha's questions. She would have intervened, but she saw that Ajji was getting angry. So she went and stood next to Deeksha and held her by the wrist.

Ajji said, 'You cannot ask such questions. We do not create gods. They are already around us.'

Deeksha looked around, a tiny figure in front of the adults, and said something she would regret later. 'Where around?' She looked in all four directions and declared, 'I don't see any gods here.' Turning to the other girls, she asked, 'Do any of you see any gods here?'

There was a shocked silence. Ajji slapped Deeksha, saying, 'You talk too much.' Mother dragged Deeksha away, and Ajji told Kalpana, 'You don't talk at all, and she is all the time talking. This is all your fault.'

Kalpana came close to losing her fight with words then. A torrent of words rushed to her tongue and would have tumbled out with terrible consequences. She turned her face away, saw the twinkling brain, and immediately calmed down.

Mother called over her shoulder to the other girls, 'Go home. Go and play some simple game. Temples and gods are for your elders to worry about.' She tried to smile as she said this, hoping that they would not remember and transmit what Deeksha had said.

Kalpana picked up the torch and the other girls silently left the area. Deeksha was still resisting her mother's attempts to drag her away.

Kalpana could hear Deeksha saying, 'Our god is not like yours. You will see.' Kalpana walked slowly behind the three of them. She could see her father now, standing at the doorstep and looking at them. For a fleeting moment, she thought that maybe he would understand. But then she realised that she would not be able to talk to him, to explain to him. She felt an inexorable sadness, an intense feeling of loneliness.

IT WAS THEIR FATHER, HOWEVER, WHO TURNED OUT TO be the unexpected saviour. When the procession of four entered the house, he took one look at Deeksha and saw that she had been crying. Even without his asking, his wife told him, almost whispering, 'You have no idea what these girls are doing.'

They all seemed to be waiting for his response. So he said, 'What?'

'These two girls are saying that they have created their own temple with their own god! Can you imagine if others hear about this? Already, who knows what they think of ...'

Father started laughing, and laughed so much that his wife ran to get him a glass of water.

'Their own god!' he spluttered. 'What a great idea! Even our swamijis haven't discovered this trick.'

Deeksha and Kalpana looked at him in great surprise. They would never have anticipated this response.

'This is the next great business. Our people have been making money in the name of all our gods, but none of them have thought of what my two girls have.'

He started laughing loudly again. Deeksha was suddenly not sure what her father was laughing about. She said, 'We are not making money. We didn't think it was a god actually. We only wanted to build a temple for the brain.'

'For what?' Father's voice was almost a shrill scream. It had been a long time since he had laughed like this. 'A brain is your god?' The way he said it, Mother also started smiling. She was fine with it if it was all merely a game for the children. But with gods and temples, one never knew, and this she knew for sure.

Ajji was not so sanguine. She told her son, 'You are their father, you should be telling them that they cannot create their own gods. Gods are not playthings for them to do whatever they want.'

Mother nodded hesitantly.

Seeing them, Father quietened down. He looked at the wide-open eyes of his two daughters. He suddenly remembered how little he saw of them, and how little he knew of what they thought and did. Looking at them, he decided that he would not let them down. So he found a middle path.

He told his mother, 'Hinduism has a core principle that god exists in everything.' He turned to his daughters. 'You must know the story of Prahalada.' Deeksha and Kalpana looked at him as if they did not know the story, although they had heard it enough times. 'Prahalada's father was very angry that his son was praying all the time to Vishnu. So, in a fit of rage, he asked him where his beloved god was hiding. Prahalada told him that god resides in everything; there is no place where he is not present.'

Ajji showed her dissatisfaction with this tame rendition. Father turned to Mother and said, 'I think Prahalada was not older than Kalpana when this happened. Maybe the same age!' He looked around the room as if he had discovered a great secret—about Prahalada or about Kalpana, he wasn't sure.

Mother smiled. She told Deeksha, 'I hope you understand what your father is saying. Our gods are present even in your idol of the brain. All our gods are already in your idol, so they are the true gods in your temple.' She was happy that her problem had been resolved so easily. Her husband did manage to surprise her now and then.

Deeksha asked, 'Are you saying that Ganesha and Hanuman are *living* in our idol of the brain?'

Mother nodded. 'That is for sure. God is in everything.'

Kalpana was furious. She threw down the bag she was holding, and shaking her head vehemently, ran to her mat and lay on it. She started crying. Deeksha ran behind her and tried to console her. Her mother too called out to her, not knowing what had happened. They had all seemed so happy and smiling for a moment! Father felt let down; he had been enjoying this interaction with his daughters. Pity it was so brief and so catastrophic. He thought that maybe Kalpana was having a 'mental issue' and thought of the 'mental doctor' again.

Kalpana sat up, picked up her notebook and wrote: *Ganesha is not in our temple. Our brain has no gods in it. This is all a lie.* She underlined the word 'lie' till it looked like an apartment building with a sculpture on top.

Mother was distraught when she read what Kalpana had written. Father was puzzled. He had hoped that Kalpana was getting back to normal. Only Ajji understood.

But still, the mood that had kept Kalpana's father in good spirits had not completely drained out of him. Seeing his wife so worried, he quipped, 'I thought Kalpana was like Prahalada, but it looks like she is actually more like his demon-father.' He couldn't stop laughing loudly at his own wit.

Deeksha had the last word. She went to her father and said, 'Kalpana is feeling very sad now. She had wanted to celebrate Deepavali in our temple. But you have made fun of it. The only thing you can do now if you don't want us to feel sad is give us money for lights and buy sweets for all the children.'

Father stared at her. She had never spoken so many words addressed only to him. He was already seeing his daughters differently. He nodded and said, 'I will make all the arrangements,' thinking that this was one more part of the complex game of playing gods and humans, or, equivalently, fathers and daughters.

IN THE MIDST OF ALL THESE HAPPENINGS, THE THREE GIRLS had to do the exercise given by Gangamma. They had no idea how to go about it. Deeksha and Kumari discussed it on their way back from school. They decided that the best way to find out what they liked was to listen to all the sounds they could hear.

Kumari said, 'It is like going to the grocery shop and tasting all the chocolates in the glass jars. How much fun it would be to taste all those different sweets one after another.'

Deeksha added, 'If we do that, we will only get a stomach ache.'

Kumari replied, 'If we listen to all the sounds, we will get an earache!'

Deeksha had never experienced an earache before, but stomach aches were more frequent than she liked. She was on a roll. 'Imagine a shop full of glass jars, each of them filled with our favourite sounds.'

'But,' Kumari said, 'if we look at all the sweets, we can see that they have different colours and shapes. We can then choose what we like. But if you look at a glass jar with all the sounds, there is nothing that we can see. So how will we choose?'

Deeksha nodded. 'Yes, how will we know there are sounds inside the jar?' The two girls looked at Kalpana, who looked away. She was curious to see where their thinking would end.

'We can shake the jar. We might hear them.'

'Or we can open the cap, but then the sound might run away.' Deeksha darted away from Kalpana, saying, 'I am the sound running away. Come and catch me and put me back in the jar.'

Kalpana was inspired by these ideas. When she went home, the first thing she did was take out her notebook and write, *If we can taste sounds, then listening to them can give us a stomach ache. Do sounds have colours and tastes?*

She closed her eyes and tried to hear the sounds around her. When she closed her eyes, it was all black. She heard sounds, but there were no colours on the blank, black wall that she saw with her closed eyes. She sat quietly for a long time. Voices drifted in and out. She could hear a sudden twitter of birds, a stray bark, the sound of a motorbike. Then she heard the wind, the rustle of the fan in the hall, a faint snatch of radio music. As she sat with her eyes closed, colours slowly drifted in and began to bounce around in the blackness. She had no control of the colours, they came and went as they wished. And when the sound of the whistle of the cooker came from the kitchen, she smelt the raw jackfruit that was being cooked in it. As she focused on the smell, she could feel the taste of the jackfruit. Shocked, she opened her eyes. She then wrote, memorialising her experience: *Sounds have colours and tastes, but only after I asked the question. I don't understand.*

Deeksha had no idea how to go about choosing her favourite sound. Her mind was too active and thinking of a hundred things at the same time. She liked so many sounds that she had trouble choosing her favourite. She tried reproducing some of the sounds to see if she liked making them. But she was quite inept at replicating them. She told Kumari about her problem and tried to imitate the sound of a bird she had heard. She couldn't create even a bad imitation of that sound. Hearing her, Kumari started giggling, and those sounds fell like a thousand beads on Deeksha, rolled off her, bounced on the ground and ran away in all directions, giggling even louder. Deeksha was mesmerised by that sound—no, not just the sound, but the way in which she heard the sound. She had giggled along with Kumari countless times, but she had never heard the sounds of the giggles with such clarity. Spontaneously, she pulled out her water bottle, poured out the little bit of water that was left in it, and kept the mouth of the bottle in front of Kumari's surprised mouth. The last of Kumari's giggles fell into the bottle, and Deeksha closed the lid of the bottle tightly. 'This is my favourite sound. I will give Gangamma Ajji this bottle,' she said.

Kumari chose her favourite sound by accident. She was lying in bed, trying to fall asleep while thinking about the events of the evening. Her mother had heard the news about Gangamma teaching music to the three children. One of her neighbours had told her that she had seen Kumari going along with the two girls to Gangamma's house. Kumari's mother had asked her about it, and without thinking, Kumari said that she was not learning music but sometimes went with Deeksha to her music class. Her mother was dissatisfied, but before she could say anything, Kumari added that the classes were very interesting and maybe she should also learn music. Her mother was surprised, since music was not really of interest to anybody in their house. If she asked her husband, she was sure he would say that it was all the effect of her school. She told Kumari that it was not a good idea to learn music and that she should focus on her studies. Anyway, they could not afford to pay money for a music class.

Kumari tried once again. 'I really love music,' she said. 'I like it more than anything else.' When this plea seemed to be failing, Kumari played her trump card. Looking down at her polio leg, she said, 'I can't play like other children. At least music is something that I can do.' Her mother went into the kitchen without answering her. Later, at night, when Kumari was lying on her mat, her mother told her, 'You go to a few classes and then we will see. But I don't have money. Tell the teacher I will give her a hen.' She caressed Kumari's head and added, 'Don't tell this to your father.'

Kumari was delighted. She felt as if she had been released, not from something, but towards something. Lying in bed, she started concentrating on the many sounds she heard. Her father's voice from outside the house speaking on the phone. Her mother's movements on her bed as she tossed about. And then the million sounds from outside: the sudden rustling of the hens' feathers, dogs whining and barking, trees talking to each other and, as always, the sound of the mountains around her. These sounds entered her house like uncontrolled children, but what seemed amazing to Kumari was that they did not collide with and distort one another. She could hear each one of them clearly, as if they had come as individuals to greet her. Listening to them so closely, she felt drawn to all the sounds and could not choose between them. In this heightened sense of hearing, she began to fall asleep, when she heard a far-off song from a temple hidden somewhere in the mountains.

With the festival fast approaching, many villages had started organising all-night music and theatre performances. On certain clear nights, the sound of these performances would be carried across miles. Kumari was just entering her sleep state when the clear notes of a song came hurriedly through the open windows. It was a sound that had been scrubbed clean on its way by the trees and shrubs and butterflies whose wings gently pushed it along. It was a sound as sharp as a thin needle, but filled with music.

Kumari fell into the lap of that sound and had her first experience of a true, clear note. It sounded like the sound Gangamma had made during class, a sound so ringing and sharp that it made the hair on her arms tremble. Kumari immediately knew that this was the sound she wanted, the sound that she identified with. She desperately wanted to remember it, wanted to get up and try making that sound. But she couldn't get up from the state she was in. She felt tied to the bed. Panicked, she tried to reproduce the sound. She couldn't. But when she relaxed, she could feel the sound she created flow with the sound she heard. She heard these two sounds as one, as a resonating tune reverberating through the length of her body. She could almost see herself as a cylinder, with this pure sound flowing from one point to another. She fell asleep with the sound entering every part of her body, and she slept with the knowledge that she would never forget this sound, which was hers alone.

Kalpana's choice was perhaps somewhat predictable. She too thought about what her favourite sound was. She, unlike the other two, was more experienced, since her capacity for carefully listening to sounds had greatly increased after she stopped speaking. She was aware of sounds that she had never recognised before but which were all around her. And when she sat in her heightened state, listening to the layers and layers of sound, she was in a different world. It was a world where she was both blind and dumb. Each one of these sounds was like a person, somebody who spoke to her. She remembered her insight that numbers were like sentences. In this mood of discerning sounds, she realised that single sounds were compressed stories of many sounds. But this sensitivity to sounds was also a barrier for her. Once she realised that every sound hid many deeper layers of other sounds, she could not choose only one among them. She struggled with this dilemma for a few days. Then the day before her music class, she found the answer. She finally discovered her favourite sound. Thinking about what Gangamma would say about it made her smile.

THAT SUNDAY MORNING, WHEN THE THREE OF THEM LEFT for their music class, Deeksha insisted that they take a quick detour to the village temple. She wanted to get some information on how to make Kalpana the priest of their own temple.

There were not many people in the temple at that time. Most would come around forenoon when the main prayers were conducted. Kalpana wanted to stand outside the temple, but Deeksha and Kumari made her sit in a corner while they went to meet the priest. They waited for the priest to finish his prayers, and finding that he was still busy, they went and sat near Kalpana. They found the priest's wife sitting close by with a mound of jasmine flowers in front of her. She was stringing them into a garland.

She was surprised to see them. 'What, the three of you in the morning? This is a surprise.' She looked around for their parents or Ajji, and then looked at Kalpana sharply. 'Have you started speaking?'

Deeksha answered, 'No, she still cannot speak.'

'You should have come to the temple earlier. Anyway, it is not too late. Your ajji has organised a prayer for her during the festival.'

Kalpana felt a flutter in her body when she heard this. If she started speaking after this prayer, then everyone would praise Ganesha and Ajji for giving back her speech!

Deeksha jumped in. 'But Akka is learning to sing.'

Kumari was impatient to leave for their class. Pointing to the priest, she asked, 'What puja is he doing?'

'He is saying prayers.'

'What is he saying in the prayers?'

The priest's wife laughed. 'There are so many prayers. Now he is probably chanting all the qualities of the god.'

Deeksha was surprised. She had thought prayers were all about asking god for something. 'Qualities like what?'

'Like god's beauty, strength, kindness ...'

'That is what prayers are about?' Kumari was also puzzled.

'One of the prayers. There are so many.' She looked at the three of them. 'You should come to a prayer class. We teach these prayers to children. You bring your friends and come here, and I will teach you some prayers.'

Kumari was confused. She asked softly, 'Why is he telling god that he is beautiful and strong? God knows that, correct?'

Kalpana nodded vigorously. Deeksha added, 'Yes, why is he saying that to god then?'

The priest's wife was amused. 'Prayers praise god, but it's not for wanting something that you say prayers. Haven't you ever told your mother that she is a good cook or a good mother?'

They nodded, unsure and hesitant. They couldn't immediately recollect when they had said this, but it was something they might have done.

'Does your mother not know she is a good cook? She does. You are only appreciating her. Similarly, we appreciate god.'

Kumari was still unsure. 'But you can also ask god for something, no? To get good marks?'

The girls laughed. So did the priest's wife. 'Of course you can. And then you come and thank him. Thank him for being so good and kind to you. Some prayers do that.'

Deeksha asked, 'You tell god how good he is so that other people can know?'

Kalpana pinched her. She pointed to the Devi's shrine. Deeksha didn't understand at first, but seeing the Devi, resplendent in her attire, she nodded her head. 'Sorry, god is also a she.'

The other two girls nodded, but the priest's wife was silent. She was puzzled at their interest.

'Why are you so interested now in prayers?'

Deeksha looked at the priest and said, 'We were just talking about how difficult it is to be a priest. And now you are saying that a priest needs to know many prayers!'

'Yes, but it is not just the prayers. You have to have years of training to be a priest. You have to understand the shastras, learn all the rituals of worship. It is not easy. And after all that, you get no money. It is not an easy job.'

Kumari said innocently, 'Then the priest should ask god for more money.'

Kalpana would have smiled had she not seen the expression on the face of the priest's wife. The woman said angrily, 'Are you making fun of him?' But looking at Kumari's face, she recognised that it was a child's question. 'It is because of our prayers that we have this life. Otherwise it would have been worse,' she said curtly.

As they walked to Gangamma's house, Deeksha decided that Kalpana could not undergo so much training to become a priest. She told Kalpana, 'I don't know if there are prayers for the brain. If prayers tell us about the good qualities of the brain, we can ourselves create a prayer, right?'

Kumari nodded. 'Our science book has all the qualities of the brain.'

Deeksha agreed. 'Maybe the science book is a book of prayers!'

The three girls walked to their class, unusually silent and reflective. Before they reached Gangamma's house, Deeksha had a sudden illumination. 'I think that Kalpana has already got the training to be a priest for the brain. Going to school is the training. So now she can be the priest for our brain god, just like the temple priest.'

Kalpana and Kumari nodded, happy that another problem had been solved.

GANGAMMA WAS WAITING FOR THEM. SHE WAS PACING up and down in her compound. She heard the girls before they reached the house. They seemed to be in a good mood! She would have chastised them for making her wait, but Deeksha spoke before she had a chance.

'Ajji, we have done the exercise you gave us.'

The three girls arranged themselves before her. Gangamma sat on her cane chair.

Deeksha put her hand up. 'I will go first,' she said, making her command sound like a suggestion. Gangamma agreed, as it was exactly what she wanted. Deeksha was the least musical among the three, and Kalpana she wanted for the last.

'You asked me to choose my favourite sound,' Deeksha announced, looking at Kumari and then at her bag. 'I have brought the sound for you.' She removed the water bottle from her bag.

Gangamma looked at the bottle. She thought that perhaps Deeksha's favourite sound was a sound the bottle made when it was struck.

Then Deeksha did the unexpected. She turned the bottle up and down. She rotated it in her hand. Kumari couldn't stop giggling. Kalpana looked on silently.

Deeksha shook the bottle and held it near Gangamma's left ear. 'Can you hear the sound?' she asked.

'The bottle is empty, Deeksha. How can you hear anything?'

Deeksha shook it some more. 'Can you hear it now?'

'No. What have you put inside?' Gangamma peered into the bottle, expecting to see seeds or stones. It was empty.

Then Deeksha made a show of opening the cap slowly. 'Ajji, now listen very carefully. When I open the cap, you should hear a sound.'

Kumari was jumping up and down jerkily with excitement.

Gangamma stopped her. 'Deeksha, have you put an insect in the bottle?' she asked, not wanting any tiny creatures entering her ear.

'No, no,' Deeksha said, and Kumari started laughing loudly. This was so much more fun than she had thought it would be.

Warily, Gangamma watched as Deeksha opened the bottle cap and placed the mouth of the bottle against her ear. There was only the deep sound of the air in the bottle.

'Did you hear any sound?'

'No,' said Gangamma, wondering what the girls had done.

Kumari couldn't contain herself. 'Deeksha collected the sound of my laughter and locked it in the bottle.'

'So, when I opened the cap, you should have heard her laughter,' Deeksha said accusingly. 'Are you sure you didn't hear anything?'

Gangamma was about to say that sound could not be bottled like water, but then she paused. She had always known that when she sang, she picked out the notes and sounds from within her. Many times, she had surprised herself by singing something she had not sung, or even practised, before. When she was in the flow, she felt that all she had to do was vocalise the sound that rushed out from inside her body. Perhaps she herself was like a bottle, which looked empty but was filled with hundreds of nomadic sounds. She looked at Deeksha with affection for having catalysed this thought.

'I heard the sound, Deeksha. I heard it. I had to listen carefully.'

Kalpana was watching Gangamma and didn't trust her answer. She took her book and wrote: *You could have heard Kumari from your other ear and not from the bottle.*

Gangamma patted Kalpana's arm. 'I know what I hear through my right and left ears.'

She turned to Kumari for her sound.

Kumari sat down properly with her leg tucked sideways under her. She adjusted her top and placed her hands on her thighs.

Deeksha clapped. 'She is going to sing a song.'

Gangamma intervened. 'No song. No singing. Only your favourite sound. I hope you will not give me an empty bottle, like Deeksha.' Glancing at Kalpana, she added, 'I also hope you are not going to draw your favourite sound. From you, I want to hear it.'

That made Kumari more nervous. She sat straight and looked at Gangamma. She tried to utter the sound that she had taken within her, that had nestled with her as she slept. She could hear it clearly inside her. The trick was to get it out. She tried to produce that sound just like she uttered a word.

What came out of her mouth was nothing like the note resonating inside her.

Gangamma understood what she was doing. 'Kumari, forget all of us. Forget me. You don't have to make that sound. Just let it come out of you.'

Kumari took a deep breath and closed her eyes and mouth. She forgot everyone around her. She heard the wind in the jackfruit tree, but that too was soon shut out. She desperately wanted to get the proper sound. She wanted to impress Gangamma. Somehow, this felt like the final test. She sat in silence and lost count of time as she went searching inside herself for her favourite sound. She could hear it within her, but she needed the skill to pluck it out and release it.

When that happened, it was unexpected. Unexpected for Kumari, and for Gangamma and the two sisters. Kumari had no control over the sound that escaped her. It was a sound of such purity that to Gangamma it felt like a stream of extremely cold water had fallen on her face. Deeksha and Kalpana were shocked at the sound that emanated from Kumari. It was not the giggly voice of their friend. The sound went on and on, one unwavering note.

Gangamma felt tears in her eyes. They were not tears of joy or sorrow. It was just what true music did to her. It entered her eyes, her brain, and tickled the tears hiding inside her. She dabbed at her eyes while Kalpana and Deeksha looked transfixed at Kumari, who looked like a tree trunk attached to the ground.

Kumari closed her mouth and slowly opened her eyes. She looked at Gangamma and saw her eyes. She immediately understood. Gangamma pulled her close and blessed her with a hug.

Deeksha said, 'Listening to her, I thought it was just like the sound that Ajji gave us in our first class.' Looking at Gangamma, she added, 'Kumari will sing like you when she grows up.'

Kumari smiled with great happiness. She didn't know how to remain silent in the afterglow of her performance. Shyly, she looked at Gangamma and said, 'My mother said she will give you a hen for teaching me music.'

Kalpana, secretly affected by Kumari's singing, held her arm tightly, as if by pressing her arm she was saying that she, like Deeksha, was her soul sister who shared the same sounds.

Gangamma took a break. She told the girls to walk around her garden. She needed time to digest her own experience with Deeksha and Kumari. She also knew that it was going to be an extremely important exercise with Kalpana. Her response would be crucial to the possibility of her speaking soon. She went into the house and took three balls of a sweet made of coconut and jaggery. These would be both reward and incentive.

The girls came back, and there was silence for a few minutes as they ate the sweet. It stuck to their palates, and all three girls focused on eating. Gangamma wanted Kalpana to be fully composed before she asked her for her favourite sound.

When the three girls stopped munching, Deeksha and Kumari looked at Kalpana expectantly. Kalpana opened her notebook but did not write anything in it.

Gangamma prodded her. 'It is fine. You can sing your sound or write it if you like.' Even as she said this, Gangamma wondered how Kalpana would be able to write a sound, especially since they had not learnt even the basic notes yet. Gangamma's approach to singing was as unorthodox as her life. She did not believe that music began with the basic seven notes, svaras, or the hidden srutis. For her, music was a continuous expression and not described through discrete notes.

Kalpana stared at the notebook and then closed it. She shut her eyes and sat upright. Deeksha was sure that she was going to make a most exciting sound.

Kalpana sat in silence. Not a part of her moved. Her whole body was calmness personified. She sat still like that for a minute or two. Then, she opened her eyes and smiled at Gangamma.

Gangamma smiled back. 'That is your favourite sound?'

Kalpana nodded.

Deeksha said, 'No, no, she did not create any sound.'

Gangamma told her, 'Yes, she did, and that is her favourite sound.'

Deeksha would not let it go. 'No, she did not say anything. She was fully silent.' Seeing Gangamma smile at her, Deeksha understood. 'Silence is her favourite sound?'

Kalpana nodded. She had thought that this would be a good challenge for Gangamma and was surprised at her response. Kalpana had slowly become aware that her favourite sound truly was silence. It was remarkable how, after having stopped speaking, she had begun to hear less and less of other people's voices. Initially, the voices had crowded together, and the frustration of not being able to speak had made her mind, filled with her own voice, talk incessantly to itself. But over time, she had reduced the internal chatter. After starting the singing lessons, she had discovered long stretches of silence within herself. And, in the nights when she sat up trying to listen to the sounds around her that she had never heard before, she discovered the power and the sound of silence.

When she began this exercise for Gangamma, Kalpana had realised that her capacity to distinguish the qualities of one sound from another had grown. She found many sounds she liked, particularly the delayed raindrop falling on the ground, the sudden flight of the wind through the trees, the first stirring of the crickets as they got ready to sing, the far-off sound of a single bell. But when she had to choose her favourite one, she could not decide. Till she understood that all the sounds she liked had a special relation to silence. The sound of a water drop falling on the ground was magnified by the silence between the drops. It was the sound of the bell in the background of the massive, dark silence of the night that appealed to her. When Kalpana inferred that the common element in all the sounds that she liked was the silent presence of silence itself, she had felt a rare sense of joy. She knew then that it was her experience of silence that had sustained her own silence for long.

Gangamma understood her. Understood her perfectly. And she too was pleased, as it gave her an entry to prod Kalpana further.

Kumari looked at Gangamma and said, 'But how is silence a sound?'

Deeksha concurred. She felt let down. She had thought Kalpana would make a sound and perhaps sing a whole song. She had been sure of it. But now Kalpana had played a mean trick. 'That is cheating, no, Ajji?' she asked.

Kalpana glared at Deeksha. She hated nothing more than being called a cheater.

Gangamma said, 'No, it is not cheating. Yes, silence is a sound. How is it a sound? Come close and I will tell you.' Gangamma's voice automatically dropped a notch. It was as if silence could be spoken of only by being silent, and since that was not possible, it could only be spoken of by becoming aware of silence.

When the girls bunched together near her feet, Gangamma placed her right palm on Kalpana's head. Her head was hot, and her thick hair was slightly sweaty. Gangamma pushed her fingers into Kalpana's hair and felt her scalp. She closed her eyes and sat like that for some time.

Deeksha and Kumari did not know what to say or do. Kalpana, initially surprised, felt her eyes close. Within a span of seconds, she stopped hearing any sound and just felt Gangamma's warm palm like a blessing hovering over her head.

After some time, Gangamma removed her hand and opened her eyes. She turned to Deeksha. 'Do you know what I was doing?'

Deeksha said, 'I don't know. My mother puts her palm on my forehead to see if I have a fever. So maybe you were checking for a fever in Akka's head.' She felt pleased with her answer.

'No, I was not doing that. I was listening to what Kalpana was telling me.'

Kumari laughed. 'Akka has a mouth on her head?' She paused and looked around, and then said innocently, 'Or you have ears in your palm.'

Kumari and Deeksha shrieked in pure joy. Deeksha added, 'We haven't been able to listen to Akka all these days because her hair is covering the sound from the mouth on top of her head.'

Even Kalpana smiled at that vision. Deeksha put her palm on Kalpana's head and Kumari followed.

'Oh, she is speaking a lot. We can hear,' shouted Deeksha.

This was how the girls tried to give voice to Kalpana. Gangamma told them how sounds were produced and what they meant. It was a lesson that had been drilled into her by her father, who, without having read the texts on music, had learnt from various oral sources the foundations of the music that he practised. It was the music of the soul, he used to tell Gangamma, who did not then understand what he meant by the soul. It was the same music that thousands of singers over the last two millennia had sung all over India. Long before some musicians started saying it, he had already told Gangamma: music has no religion. Singers from all religions were in a common search, he had told her repeatedly, a common search for the voice of the soul, for the voice of gods within each one of us.

To do that, they had to understand the nature of sound. And what Gangamma had learnt from her father could only be understood through extensive practice. She was ready now to tell these girls what her father had said and what she had experienced so deeply.

GANGAMMA HAD FORGOTTEN ONE OF THE MOST electrifying experiences she had had as a singer. She had forgotten it because it was too painful to keep in her memory.

It occurred one night during a performance at a village fair. She was accompanying her father along with two percussionists. Most people had left, and only a small group sat around them. Her father had stopped for a moment and talked to the small audience. Almost all of them were daily labourers who seemed to find a great solace in her father's singing.

The music they created in the next two hours, after the break, was something that they would never be able to reproduce. How it came about was a mystery to her. It was as if, during the performance, something had altered drastically. Her father later told her that whatever happened was only because of the labouring, dead-tired bodies around him.

At some point during the performance, as the music resounded through this small group of listeners, Gangamma started noticing something odd in her surroundings. As she listened to her father singing, she thought she saw patterns forming all around her. Patterns on the grass near her feet, among the little pebbles and the gravel, in the air around her. Her first thought was that the music was producing shapes around her, as well as forms in the space around that small group. She saw these forms move and change in response to the music. As the songs changed, so did the forms.

At first, Gangamma thought that she was dreaming. Or worse, hallucinating with her eyes wide open. But looking at her father and the percussionists, as well as the people around her, she realised that it was something that all of them were experiencing. Everyone was looking at the empty spaces around them as if they could see something or someone there.

She might have remembered this event as being magical if not for her father's words afterwards. When the performance ended, her father and the accompanying percussionists were more tired than usual, but they also seemed more exhilarated.

No one in the small audience moved from their places. They all sat in silence together for at least half an hour before, one by one, reluctantly, they got up to leave. They said nothing; neither did they leave any money for the performers as they left.

Gangamma remembered sitting there after everybody had gone. She told her father, hesitantly, that she had seen shapes as he sang. He had looked at her grimly and said that she should forget what she had seen and never talk about it. She didn't, except once, to ask her mother about what her father had done.

It was her mother who told her that music could have an effect on matter and produce shapes. Music is like sculpting, she told Gangamma, and sounds are used to produce these forms. The world, she said over and over again, is created through sound. But she also added that Gangamma should never talk about it. It could be perceived as the power of evil, she said. There were tantrics who used these powers in wrong ways, and that was the reason her father did not want her to talk about what had happened that night.

Gangamma didn't understand these ideas but let them slowly drip into her being through her performances. She was never again able to see those forms, although a few times in her singing career she had felt that she was close to discovering this power.

The only thing her father had said, as if in atonement for having frightened her that day, was this: *All the sound we create is incomplete and is always accompanied by unheard sounds. So the sounds we make run outside us, searching for these unheard sounds that will complete them.*

This was the lesson she shared with the three girls.

It was Kalpana who understood her almost instantaneously. Gangamma could see it in the way Kalpana's face lit up and in her smile, as if a light had come on behind her face.

Gangamma was as surprised by Kalpana's response as she was by her own capacity to teach something. Was teaching just this, the power of making these girls think what they had not before?

The four of them sat in silence, trying to understand what she had said. Deeksha and Kumari were becoming hyper-excited by all that they were learning. So much, so soon, and so difficult! How could there be unheard sounds? They didn't even know what questions to ask. Gangamma and Kalpana sat back contentedly, as if they had discovered a place of rest. Deeksha, still animated, said accusingly to Gangamma, 'I still don't understand what you are saying, and Akka is looking like she has understood everything!'

Gangamma did not want to explain further. She did not know what to say; nevertheless, she spoke. 'What it means is that all sound is incomplete. Every sound is an attempt to say something, but the sound is never enough. So every sound is always a search. Searching for something. Searching all the time. To become a musician, you have to learn how to listen to the unheard sound.'

After a few minutes, when it was time for the girls to leave, Gangamma leaned back and took a deep breath. A sharp sound emerged, a sound that gradually rose in pitch and volume. The girls were mesmerised.

Gangamma stopped and asked, 'Where is this sound produced from? I want you to think about where the sound you make is actually coming from. Which part of the body? Or is it from your mind?' She stopped. Teaching was tiring.

She asked the girls to come closer to her. She leaned forward and whispered, 'Sound is all around you. When I sing, I am only plucking the many sounds that are already around me.' Looking at Deeksha's eager face, she added, 'Yes, like the fruits on the tree.'

'I am not the one who produces the sound,' she continued. 'I am not the singer. It is the sound all around me that comes out through my mouth. Now go and think about what I have said.'

The three girls walked back silently, slowly, too slowly. Gangamma too was silent after they left. She sat on the porch with her eyes closed, searching for those sounds that would agree to enter her or were ripe enough for her to pluck.

WAS THERE SOUND ALL AROUND THEM? COULD THEY PLUCK these sounds surrounding them? Kalpana was deep in thought as they walked back. The other girls were also silent, each thinking of questions without wanting to get answers. For them the questions made so much sense by themselves and actually seemed to be answers in the guise of questions.

As they approached her house, Kumari stopped under a large tree. She pointed to the space around her, pirouetting awkwardly on her feet. 'There is nothing here. Nothing that we can see,' she said. 'Except that it is all filled with sound. How is that possible?'

'Gangamma Ajji has become crazy,' Deeksha said, giggling. 'Where are the sounds around us that we can pluck? Like fruits, she says.' Kumari and Deeksha started laughing.

Kumari mimed plucking a sound from the air around her and swallowing it. She made a noise that sounded like a musical note. 'See, I caught this sound from the air and now I can sing it.'

Hearing the girls, Kumari's mother peeped out of her house and saw them under the tree. She called out to her daughter. Kumari turned to the others and said, 'See, my mother is calling, I have to go now.'

Deeksha stopped her. 'Your mother only called out your name. Why do you say that she is calling you to go home?'

Kalpana, who was still deep in thought, was awoken by this utterance. She looked at Deeksha and wanted to say, *Yes, how did you know? Where were those words that you heard in the sound of your name? Where was that sound hidden?* Words frothed on her tongue, but she would not speak, and a wad of saliva formed on her tongue. She spat it out.

Deeksha looked at her in disgust. 'Chee, Akka, what are you doing?' Turning to Kumari, she added, 'It seems as if you heard words that your mother didn't say. Words that the two of us didn't hear. So maybe those words are in the air around us.'

Kumari looked at her solemnly. 'Yes, Gangamma Ajji was right. There is so much sound all around us that we do not hear.' She limped away, lost in thought, and even forgot to turn back to wave at Deeksha when she reached the door of her house.

Kalpana wanted to say so much, but she knew that even in her silence she had been saying something all this while. When they reached the house, she ran in, past Ajji and her mother. She went to the storeroom and picked up her notebook. She took out her pencil and started writing.

My silence is filled with words. If you know how to pluck them from my silence, then you can hear me speak.

She wrote these lines three times and underlined each one. She took the book into the hall and showed it to her mother. Her mother stared at the words, trying to make sense of them. Her worry about Kalpana increased.

Ajji plucked the book from her and read what Kalpana had written. She mumbled, 'Girls these days don't know what to say and what not to say.'

Deeksha grabbed the book from her and read Kalpana's words. She told her mother, 'See how correctly Akka writes. All of you think she is not speaking, but it is only that you are not hearing her. What if you are all deaf and Akka is speaking properly?'

'Don't be a fool, Deeksha,' said Ajji. 'You are going to become like her.'

'Why not, Ajji?' Deeksha asked, not willing to yield. 'I want to be like her. I can hear her. What she is saying is like the sounds made by hundreds of butterflies around her head. You should try listening to them, and then you would be able to hear what she is saying.'

Mother's worry about Kalpana was now transferred to Deeksha. Would she also become like her sister?

Seeing their confusion, Kalpana took Deeksha's hand and took her inside their room, as if they had enough to say in silence between the two of them.

MOTHER WAS VERY WORRIED ABOUT DEEKSHA, AND Kalpana's influence on her. That night, she did not let her husband watch TV. She wanted to tell him about the 'nonsense' that Deeksha had said, but was sure that he would not listen to her. So she sat in the hall and hoped that Ajji would add her voice to hers. Just as the news was about to begin its flashing headlines, she got up, turned off the TV, and said, 'I want you to think about your daughters.' Father was surprised that she had turned off the TV. Ajji looked at him as if she was surprised too.

'What is there to think about my daughters?' he asked.

'You know what Deeksha told us today?' she said, hoping to draw Ajji into it. 'She said that Kalpana is actually speaking, the problem is that we are not listening.'

Father was still looking at the blank screen. 'You shouldn't take what she says seriously. Haven't you heard her crazy ideas all these years? You should have just told her that we don't hear Kalpana since she is not speaking loud enough.' He started laughing loudly, as if his jokes were always at the surface of any comment he uttered. 'Get her to speak into a mic and carry a loudspeaker with her. Haven't you seen those sellers who come in autos, carrying a loudspeaker to amplify their voice? Maybe we should get her one.'

Ajji was more than irritated. She did not understand her son at all. His father had never been like this. He had not been overly concerned about how their son was growing up, but he had never laughed as if he was scared of talking about anything. She couldn't resist adding, 'As usual, she hasn't told you everything. Deeksha said that only *we* can't hear Kalpana, but she can hear her all right. I am wondering who among these two is mad.'

Mother would not allow Ajji to form a bond with her son. 'Please don't call the girls mad. They are just young girls who ... who sometimes say things they don't understand.'

Ajji would not let it go. 'Deeksha wants to be like her sister, she says. Can you believe that? Don't you want to talk to her?' She knew her son would not listen to her, the words were more for her daughter-in-law's benefit.

Father said, 'Put on the TV. The news is not as exciting as my daughters, but I need to know what is happening in the world. I have to deal with it every day. The two of you can deal with the fantasies of these girls.'

He had done his job and given more than his fair share of advice—that too, after a hard day's work.

Mother walked away murmuring, 'Don't blame me if Deeksha also becomes like her sister.'

Ajji went back to muttering her prayers, Father looked unseeingly at the TV and its meaningless breaking news, and Mother went and banged a few vessels in the kitchen. Deeksha and Kalpana sat in their room, staring out of the window into the growing darkness and listening to the inevitable sound of the inevitable rain.

'I AM NOT THE SINGER. IT IS THE SOUND ALL AROUND ME that comes out through my mouth!'

How many times had Deeksha repeated those lines! She whispered them to herself, she giggled the words into Kumari's ears, and she used them like thorns to poke her sister. When Kalpana got irritated, she would say, 'I am not the speaker. I am not making these words. It is the sound all around me.' She danced and skipped around Kalpana as she said this, like the words that so ephemerally entered and exited Kalpana's ears.

The only way Kalpana could stop Deeksha was by writing: *If you are not the singer or the speaker, then who is singing and speaking? If you say that it is the sound around you, which sound decides to enter your mouth?*

She stared at what she had written and then added: *How do these words enter you? Through your nose? Or when you are snoring?*

She wanted to laugh, but she was frowning when she passed the sheet to her sister.

Deeksha fell silent on reading these questions. But Kalpana wouldn't let her get away so easily. She had been really irritated by Deeksha's prancing body and dancing words. As Deeksha began to fall asleep on her mat, Kalpana wrote: *It is a ghost who is speaking for you. The ghost is inside you.*

She nudged Deeksha and made her read these lines. Deeksha laughed as she read them and curled back to sleep. When sudden showers lit up the drums of the sky, she slid closer to Kalpana and held her tightly.

Kumari was the one who understood these questions best. The next day, as they were walking to school, she mimed plucking something from the air. Deeksha looked at her attempts to jump and asked her, 'Why are you suddenly jumping around like this?'

Kumari laughed. 'I am trying to see if I can catch the sounds around me, the sounds that are making me speak. I can see these sounds; they are like the lemons on the tree in my compound. Have you seen the lemons hanging all over the tree? All you have to do is pluck them. I think sounds are also like that, don't you think? They have to be ripe before they can be plucked!'

Deeksha looked at Kumari in surprise—how did she think of these things?

Gangamma's words were like a virus. They entered the three girls and infected them. They could not listen to any sound without trying to search for the unheard ones. And once they started the search, they began to realise that it would not be too difficult to discover the vast world of unheard sounds.

By the time they walked from school to Kumari's house, Kumari had summarised what they had understood. 'Sounds are like fruits in the trees around us. When we sing, we pluck these sounds. Singing is like farming.'

Deeksha added, 'It is also like plucking flowers. My ajji goes around trying to see if she can pluck flowers from any plant growing in the village!'

Kumari giggled. 'Your ajji is a singer.'

'But fruits and flowers are not sounds.'

Kumari and Deeksha sat outside the gate of Kumari's house. They sat in silence and listened. And they plucked the sounds they could hear. It grew dark, and the tinkle of countless sounds slowly became the twinkle of many yellow lights hidden among the trees and mountains.

THE CHARACTER OF SILENCE HAD CHANGED FOR ALL THREE of them. Once they started listening to the sounds hidden in the silence, the need to talk became less. The three girls would sit in silence in their brain temple, staring at the shrine, the trees, the stray cows and the wandering, sometimes buzzing, sounds around them. It was as if they did not want to speak at all or, as

Deeksha once observed, 'It is like we are talking to each other in silence.'

Kumari responded sombrely, 'I can hear your silence clearly.' She stopped to think about what she had intuitively said. She was becoming aware that she often said things she didn't fully understand.

Kalpana stared at the two of them, willing them to listen to what she had to say through her silence. They continued to sit in silence, and as they got up to leave on hearing Kalpana's mother, Kumari added, 'Like we sing together, we sit in silence together.'

Deeksha wanted to say something, but contented herself with holding Kumari's hand. As they watched Kumari limping away to her house, she said, 'Akka, I can hear the silence much better than the words people say. I can see at last why you don't want to speak.'

THIS AWARENESS OF SILENCE HAD A DIRECT CONSEQUENCE. Upadhya was very upset. His two brightest students had suddenly become quiet in class. They seemed to have no questions, and there were no sudden, sparkling smiles or giggles. The whole class had become silent, or so it seemed to him. He tried to ask Kumari and Deeksha some questions, to see if they would talk. But they would answer like the other children, in monosyllables, as if it was a duty they had to perform, or just stare back at him silently.

One day, he couldn't stop himself. After another tiring class where he felt the students steadily losing interest in what he had to say, he called Deeksha and Kumari over. They stood in front of his chair and he looked them directly in the eye.

'What is wrong with the two of you?' he asked, trying not to sound like he was scolding them.

Deeksha was so surprised, her mouth fell open. 'Wrong? No, Sir, we are fine. No problem at all.' Kumari nodded vigorously.

'You are both so silent. What happened? Any problem at home?' Then he remembered. 'Any problem with your sister?'

'No, Sir. We are all fine. Sister is also fine.'

Upadhya would not relent. 'But why have you become so silent?'

They kept quiet. They didn't know how to answer him. They knew—from their immersion in silence—that even answers had to be plucked from the air. Unless they could pluck the words, they had no answer. How could they explain this to him?

Kumari bravely tried to say something. 'We think silence is also a language. So when we are quiet, we are actually talking.'

Deeksha nodded, finding some words to say. 'In silence, we listen to many more sounds. Even your voice seems as if it is coming from a far-off place.'

Deeksha and Kumari looked at each other, struggling to finish. Finally, Kumari said, 'It is so peaceful listening to silence.'

Upadhya was struck more by their seriousness than by what they had said. Silence was not what he wanted as a teacher. He said, 'You were asking so many interesting questions. If you become silent, who will ask them? If you don't speak, the other students will go to sleep.'

The girls giggled on hearing this. Finally, Upadhya did what he had actually set out to do, to tell them what they should do in his class. 'All this silence is okay. But too much silence is bad. You will become like Kalpana. You will forget how to speak. And then what will you do? You will have to bark to get your food, like a dog does. So, start talking and start asking questions in my class. You can be silent at home or even in the other classes.'

There was much that Deeksha and Kumari would have liked to tell him. Instead, they stared at him with big, round eyes.

That silent image stayed with him. In the staff room, Upadhya went to the science teacher and asked her whether girls suddenly stop speaking. He was being delicate, but his colleague understood him very well.

'At this age, Sir,' she replied, 'girls undergo many changes. Anything is possible.'

She uttered the last sentence in a manner that suggested to Upadhya that he should not be surprised if girls of that age transformed into creatures that only myths could possibly create.

THE THREE GIRLS WERE ITCHING TO TALK TO GANGAMMA. But she had gone out of town for a festival in a neighbouring village. The day she came back, they were at her doorstep. Gangamma was not planning on having a class that day, but seeing the eager faces in front of her, she decided to talk to them.

Deeksha sat close to Gangamma and held her hand. Gangamma tried to pull her hand away, but Deeksha would not let go. 'We can hear silence,' she declared.

Kumari, not wanting to be left behind, added, 'And we can hear the sounds all around us, sounds that others do not hear!'

Deeksha giggled. 'Kumari says that singers are farmers!' Seeing Gangamma's puzzled frown, she clarified, 'We pluck sounds like farmers pluck fruits and flowers.'

Kalpana was inspired to write in her notebook: *Like farmers, we also grow sounds, new sounds.* She underlined 'grow' three times.

Deeksha and Kumari grabbed the note from Kalpana and read the line aloud. Kumari clapped delightedly. 'Yes, we grow new sounds. Like we grow rice.'

Gangamma thought of the paddy fields now filled with water. How long it took for the rice to grow! How much work to get little grains of rice from the land! She smiled. She didn't have to speak; her very presence seemed to trigger the girls.

Once they started thinking thus, they could not be stopped.

In a singsong voice, Deeksha said, 'We grow sounds, we pluck them when they are ready, and then ...' She looked at Kumari expectantly.

Kumari stared at her, trying to hear what Deeksha had not yet voiced. 'And then ... and then ...'

Both of them said at the same time: 'Then we cook them. Hot, hot.'

Gangamma wanted to be like these two girls, to jump up, dance around and clap her hands. And then seriously say, *This is what singing is. Hot rice and fish curry to be had in the rains.* But she couldn't do that, of course. So she merely said, 'That is a very good idea. We create songs like we create food. Food makes us happy and satisfied. So does music. Like we taste food, we also taste music.'

As the four of them sat, a great sense of peace settled on them. They were not even hearing each other in their silence. All the sounds that had shyly hidden themselves when they were talking came out and hesitantly announced themselves. Sounds they had never heard, never thought of, flowed into the four of them, and in that silence, they came the closest to a state of being that Gangamma would have called bliss.

For Kalpana, the last few days had been a revelation. She thought that they were all leading to a final answer for her. It seemed that it was only a matter of time before something momentous happened. But that would not be possible until her question was answered.

In that blissful silence, she wrote her question, the sound of the pencil on the paper sounding like a truck growling through a slushy field.

I still don't understand. Where did all the sounds around us come from? Who is creating them?

The two girls and Gangamma read this one by one. Gangamma kept quiet.

Kumari was brave enough to say what Deeksha also thought. 'God?'

Kalpana shook her head. *No, animals and trees and wind,* she wrote. She looked around her, searching for inspiration. She scribbled furiously: *Even the sky. God does not create sound.*

They lapsed into silence again. Gangamma felt lethargic, not ready to even go to the kitchen to see what she should prepare for dinner.

Deeksha, unable to keep quiet, muttered, 'Maybe god is sound.'

Kumari laughed. Deeksha joined her. They both thought they were laughing at the absurdity of what Deeksha had said.

But on this occasion, Gangamma finally did what she had been wanting to do. She stood, pushing herself up with her forearms. 'Deeksha is right,' she said, beaming at the girls. 'God is sound.'

Kalpana wrote: *Then why are you calling out to your Devi? Is Devi the sound of your god?*

Gangamma paused before replying to Kalpana's question. 'No, the sound of Devi is a sound that goes in search of god. I am not calling out to god when I utter her name. I am only using that sound to search for her. Like when I call your name, I am searching for you.'

Kalpana stopped her and wrote: *When you call me, it is because I am there in front of you. You call me and I come to you. But god does not come when you call. Or when you pray.*

She showed this to Gangamma as a statement and not as a question. She was becoming aware that it was impossible to keep doubting. Everybody misunderstood her doubts, as if she had these questions just to fight with others. She knew something that none of the others knew. She knew the lie of calling out to the gods—especially while in a dark forest, lost and all alone. She was also beginning to realise that she would eventually give in and start talking. It was impossible and so tiring to fight everybody all the time. To be different. How easy it would be to open her mouth and let the world out in a rush of air. How liberating that would be!

She opened her mouth unconsciously but Gangamma, looking at her, shook her head as if she knew what Kalpana might do. Kalpana watched Gangamma's head—which seemed bigger than usual—and closed her mouth.

The moment passed and Kalpana remained quiet, unsure when she would speak again.

Gangamma looked at what Kalpana had written. About god not coming when called. She knew that unless this question was answered, Kalpana would never speak nor sing. The more she stared at the question, the more confused she became. Did her Devi come to her when she called out to her? When she sang to her?

As the girls left, Gangamma resolved to answer Kalpana, whatever the answer may be. She remembered, too, why Kalpana had gone missing. Impulsively, she decided to sing at their brain temple. People might laugh at an adult playing childish games, but then, those people had always laughed at and whispered about her.

THERE WAS ONLY A WEEK LEFT FOR THE BRAIN FESTIVAL. What had started off as an ambitious celebration, one to rival the Deepavali celebrations of the main village temple, had been reduced to a single performance by Gangamma. The girls were not sure that even this would take place, since Gangamma had laughingly said that there was no way she would sing only numbers.

THAT YEAR, THE FESTIVAL IN THE VILLAGE WAS SHAPING up to be something special. Father had decided to buy clothes for the family from the nearby city. The school was energised for another reason—a rumour. Nobody knew how the rumour had started: that Kalpana was going to speak immediately after Deepavali. It was so newsworthy that nobody cared where it had come from. There was a sense of anticipation, which spread from the school to the village. It seemed as if everybody in the village knew that Kalpana would speak the day after Deepavali. The teachers talked amongst themselves and the little children took turns giggling, as if the secrets they held could be told to others through their giggles. Even the principal smiled, not once but twice, at Kalpana, when she saw her in school, something she had never done before and never repeated for any other student.

Like most rumours, this one too was soon caught in its own knots. It was said that Kalpana would speak after Deepavali but *only* if nobody asked her about it. No one knew who had created the rule, but they followed it silently. Kalpana herself didn't understand the increased attention, but the science teacher asked Deeksha whether Kalpana really would speak soon. By the next day, Deeksha had heard many rumours about the rumour. She described all of them in great detail to Kalpana that night, laughing every few minutes, amazed at the imagination of the children around her.

Upadhya started a speculation within the rumour. He wanted to say something to Deeksha, to show solidarity with her. But he didn't want to whisper what the others would have. He thought he was being true to his status as a venerable teacher when he said, 'Deeksha, I wonder what your sister's first words will be.' This was overheard by Deeksha's classmates, and by the next day, everyone was looking at Kalpana in expectation, not of her speaking but of the first word she would utter.

Three days before the festival, Deeksha told Kumari, as they sat watching the chickens in Kumari's garden, 'They are all talking as if Kalpana is going to be reborn after Deepavali.'

Kumari felt tired looking at the energetic hens running around aimlessly. She said, without really thinking about it, 'Then she will be the first person in the world who is born speaking.'

When Deeksha told Kalpana about this comment that night, as they rolled uneasily on their mats, waiting for a breeze or a sudden torrent of rain, vaguely excited about the festival, Kalpana laughed soundlessly. She knew well that she would not speak, come what may. She began to look forward to disappointing all those waiting faces in the village.

The rumours rolled in fast to their abode. When Kalpana's mother went to the grocery shop, the man there kept beaming and nodding his head as if encouraging her. Mother was puzzled, especially when he added, 'Good news, good news. We are all very happy.'

She had smiled back at him as if she knew what he was talking about. She didn't understand until Ajji pulled her out of the house and dramatically whispered to her, 'Kalpana will speak after Deepavali, it seems. Everybody in the village knows about this. Except us. Never mind. My prayers have been answered.'

That evening, when the two girls came back from school, Mother had prepared a jaggery sweet. Ajji smiled at Kalpana. She tried to pat her on the head, but Kalpana pushed her hand away. When the girls were inside their room, Deeksha gleefully whispered, 'So these people also know about it.' When Father heard about it after getting home, he came to Kalpana, looked at her benignly, and rubbed his stomach in great satisfaction.

Later that night, Deeksha, hoping against hope, tried one more time. 'You're sure you won't change your mind? Everybody is expecting you to speak. Look how happy you will make all of them.'

Kalpana pulled Deeksha's ears. *Not you too,* she scribbled, underlining the words over and over again.

TWO NIGHTS BEFORE THE FESTIVAL, THE THREE GIRLS HAD a class with Gangamma. The rumour had found its tortured way to the music teacher, as was to be expected. Gangamma had smiled on hearing that Kalpana would speak, knowing only too well that it would not happen. Or, at least, not in the way the village thought it would. But she was confident that some resolution would occur. She knew that much depended on her and her answer to the one question that had precipitated all these events. For three days before the class, she had struggled to find some way to tell Kalpana about language, music, and the gods. Kalpana's questions had challenged her, made her ask questions of herself that she had never asked before. When she sang, she felt the truth; she felt the true sense of the real. But in answering Kalpana's questions, she had realised that she was not using the word 'Devi' to call out to her or to point to her. It was something else, and it was only in the restless night preceding that class that she discovered what she would say to Kalpana.

The girls had been busy arranging Gangamma's concert at their brain temple. Deeksha and Kumari asked as many students as they could to attend their celebration. Kalpana suggested to Deeksha that they specially invite the science teacher but no other adults. *She will like the brain god,* she had scribbled on the slate, and Deeksha had doubtfully nodded. The three of them went to their temple and cleaned the shrine. More moss had grown, and the brain idol now resembled a living, pulsating green brain.

Deeksha hesitantly asked Kalpana, 'If plants have brains, will they be green like this?'

Kumari hopped and giggled. 'Green brains for plants,' she shyly said, 'and black brain for me.'

Hearing the three of them laugh, the squirrels, ants and earthworms came hurrying towards them. The trees rustled, and a sudden gust of wind swept away the leaves they had piled near the shrine.

They decided that Gangamma would sit in front of the shrine. They would put flowers on the idol and have a small garland for Gangamma. Deeksha said that it would be so much nicer to distribute the sweets after the music. Kalpana nodded. She would find a way to use her silence and get her mother to make some jaggery balls for all the children who came to their event.

They had only one momentary doubt: whether any students would come at all. Deeksha felt that at least ten of her classmates would come. Kumari looked doubtful, but Kalpana mimed thirty with her hands. Kumari was overjoyed, as if all thirty children had already come to listen to Gangamma.

So, when they went to Gangamma's class, they had much to tell her. About her performance, about the children who would come for it, and about the science teacher who would finally get to see the brain god after years of teaching children about the brain! Gangamma listened to all of this silently. Although she had promised to sing for them, even she wasn't sure she had meant it seriously. Singing for a bunch of children and that too, in some crazy temple the girls had built!

Deeksha was worried when she saw the expression on Gangamma's face. She had seen that expression too often on her mother's face when she refused to do something Deeksha had demanded.

'Ajji, you will really like our temple now. We have cleaned it. Kalpana is our pujari and will do puja to our brain.'

Kumari chimed in, 'Ajji, our brain god is green. What do you think the colour of my brain is?'

In reply, Gangamma only said, 'Everybody in the village believes Kalpana will speak after Deepavali. Is that so, Kalpana?'

Deeksha giggled. 'She will answer you only after Deepavali.'

Kalpana shook her head. Although irritated that others seemed to have decided when she would speak, she was also a little pleased that she was so much in their thoughts.

Gangamma said, 'It doesn't matter. After what I tell you today, you can decide. I have finally understood what to tell you.'

She began by saying that they would not learn any singing that day. She asked them to sit close around her.

Then she addressed Deeksha and Kumari. 'Kalpana is a special girl. She is doing what even strong adults cannot do. She stopped speaking even though she can speak. None of us can do this. It needs great strength to control your tongue. There are times when I do not want to respond to what somebody has said, but I fail. I cannot keep quiet. Even when I do not want to say something, my mouth speaks on its own.'

Kumari and Deeksha nodded eagerly. 'Yes, yes, it is like that for us also,' Deeksha added.

Gangamma said, 'See, you are not able to stop speaking even now. And look at Kalpana. You think she doesn't want to speak? You think words are not bubbling inside her, waiting to explode out of her? That they are not hurting her because she is not letting them come out?'

All three of them looked solemnly at Kalpana. She smiled at them, though she felt tears creeping into her eyes.

Gangamma said, 'It needs a kind of strength that none of us have.' She paused, and then said a bit louder, 'Only gods possess that strength.'

Deeksha bowed to Kalpana like she would before the gods in the temple. Kumari did the same.

Gangamma continued, 'But why did Kalpana keep quiet? She told us it was because she found language to be a lie. How did language lie to her? Only the four of us know. She was lost in the forest and she called out to the gods to help her. The gods who all of us say are all around us. Lost for three days, during the hot days and rainy nights, she called out to Ganesha, to Devi, to hundreds of gods. But nobody came to help her. She felt betrayed, not just by the gods, but also by our language that gives names to these gods.'

She paused. All three girls were listening raptly, though Kalpana was looking down at the ground.

'Any other girl would have been happy to come back. Would have told us the story of what happened. But Kalpana is special. She is not like us. She is a searcher. A true seeker. She is searching for what all of us take for granted. That is why you came to me. If Kalpana had not stopped talking, you wouldn't have come to me. Firstly, you would not have wanted to learn singing. And if by any chance you wanted to, you could not have come to me. I am not like the other women in the village.'

Deeksha took Gangamma's hand in hers. Seeing that, Kumari held her other hand. Deeksha said, 'Ajji, you are also special. Like Kalpana.'

Kumari added, 'We are so glad we came to you. We should thank Kalpana for not speaking.'

Looking at Kalpana, Gangamma said, 'When your mother came to me, she said she was hoping that you would begin singing. Actually, she was not expecting you to sing. She was only hoping that you would at least make some sounds. And while the two of you did, Kalpana kept silent. But I know she sang inside her. If I listened carefully, I could hear her.'

Kalpana looked at Gangamma in surprise and with a slight sense of betrayal. 'It didn't matter if she did not speak for us to hear,' Gangamma continued. 'Watching her, I began to understand what my father had taught me about music. How the sound we make is only one part of the full sound around us and inside us. I understood that Kalpana was not being silent. She was speaking, but not with words for our ears. Even knowing that, I wanted her to speak. I thought I could make her speak. But I failed. And I am happy I failed. Because Kalpana is not an ordinary girl. Until her question about god is answered, she will not speak.'

She stopped. Deeksha put her hand up. Kalpana pushed it down. Gangamma looked at Deeksha, who said, 'Ajji, now she has got so used to not speaking, she will not speak again. I think she will soon forget how to speak and won't be able to, even if she wants to.'

Kalpana lightly tapped her on the head.

Gangamma took hold of Kalpana's hand. 'But her questions bothered me. Kalpana was right, but also wrong in what she said. I didn't know how to answer her. I too had become like everybody else in accepting what was told to me. For the last month or more, I have been thinking about language and music. Does language really lie?'

Before Kumari or Deeksha could say anything, she quickly continued, 'It lies, and it also speaks the truth. But Kalpana's question was about calling out to the gods. It was about prayers to gods. If there are no gods, then who are we praying to? What are we doing when we call out to the gods? And if the gods *are* there, where are they? These were the difficult questions that Kalpana forced us to think about.

'So I thought about the word "mara" and the meaning of that word. I was thinking of a tree when I used that word. I started thinking whether the words for gods and my songs to gods were like "mara". Did they point to something?

'I got the answer only two nights ago. It was always within me, but I had stopped listening to it. Lying on my bed, looking out of the window at the dark skies, I heard the answer clearly in my head. Now I think I can at least give you a simple answer, but it is for all of you to understand it in your own way.'

Gangamma took a sip of water from the small earthen pot near her and continued, 'Why do I sing to the gods? Why do I call out to them in my songs? Music is different from our ordinary language. When you say "mara", I know that you mean a tree. But when you say "Devi", I do not know what you really mean. It is not because we do not see Devi like we see a tree. It is only because when I call out to the gods, the word I use, the sound I make, is a way of searching for god.'

She stopped suddenly. It had taken a lot out of her to come to this point. She had never been good at explaining things, and never to children. She felt exhausted. When she saw three blank faces in front of her, she felt that she should not have spoken.

Then Kalpana nodded. Staring into Gangamma's eyes, she nodded again. Deeksha and Kumari continued to look at Gangamma, their mouths slightly open.

Gangamma tried again. 'When I want to dig in my garden, I use a spade, right?' Deeksha and Kalpana nodded. 'When I use a spade, I am using it to create a hole in the ground. I use tools like spades to do something. There is no hole when I begin. The spade creates the hole. The spade creates the reality of the hole.

'When I sing, when I call out to my Devi, I am using those sounds and words like a spade. I am using them to do something. I am using them to search for the gods. The word is a way of searching for god. Since I don't see my Devi or touch her, I go searching for her. Where is she hidden? For me, Devi is a sound. She is hidden in the music I sing. When I sing about her, I am not describing her but using these sounds to search for her.'

Kumari said softly, 'The music class was better. I am not understanding this at all.' Deeksha also looked worried.

Gangamma said firmly, 'This class is meant for Kalpana. It is she who must understand. When she called out to Ganesha, it does not mean that Ganesha was around, waiting to come to her assistance. Through those sounds, she was trying to find a path to reach Ganesha. Sometimes the effort doesn't succeed. But sometimes it leads to him. We can only keep trying to search, constantly.'

Gangamma paused. There was little more she could say, except for these final words: 'God is a sound hidden within other sounds. How do you search for a sound hidden among other sounds? How do you search for a treasure hidden in the ground? You keep trying, searching. All music is a search. When we utter a sentence, when we speak, we are stating something, but music is not like that. You are not stating anything when you sing.'

She closed her mouth exaggeratedly, as if communicating to the girls that she had had enough of speaking. For a moment, she felt like Kalpana—not wanting to speak any more. Language is worse than a lie, she thought. Language is the destruction of music, a way to destroy truth through words, sentences and meaning. She felt deflated.

Kalpana jumped up and did what Kumari usually did: she started clapping. Deeksha and Kumari too joined in, not knowing what they were clapping for.

Gangamma smiled and asked Deeksha, 'So you understood what I said?'

Deeksha replied, 'Yes, we have to keep listening to sounds, and god is hidden somewhere in those sounds.'

Kumari would not be left behind. 'So we have to keep exploring every sound we hear. Because Devi could be hiding inside one of those sounds.'

Gangamma hugged the two girls and looked at Kalpana. 'Does this answer your question?'

Kalpana nodded, and added a smile.

'Will you speak after Deepavali?'

Kalpana stared back impassively.

All four of them sat quietly. The sun was setting, a few timid lights were struggling to come on, the faraway peaks were bidding goodbye to one another for the day and the birds had stopped singing in the trees.

In that silence, Kumari asked hesitantly, 'Why does god want to hide inside sounds? Why does god want to hide at all? Why is Ganesha not in front of me, like the tree?' She was not asking this of anyone in particular, her words an offering to the trees, birds and insects around her.

That night, Kalpana scribbled in her notebook: *What if you discover that the hidden person is actually not a god? Then what will you do, do, do ...*

The three girls had to find another way to understand what Gangamma had said. They each thought about what they had heard as they fell asleep listening to the countless hidden sounds in the night-silence surrounding them.

THE NEXT MORNING, A DAY BEFORE THE FESTIVAL AND THE performance by Gangamma, the three of them met at the brain temple. Each had brought something from home: objects to decorate, to clean and to adorn. Kumari had told her mother, and only her mother, about their temple. When her mother looked worried at her use of the word 'temple', Kumari went back to her safety net. 'This is schoolwork, something our teacher asked us to do. She calls it a "project".'

The word 'project' was alien to the Kannada Kumari's mother knew. She had no idea what it meant, but her daughter seemed to be using English words so effortlessly. She felt proud of her and said that she would come with her to the temple and listen to their music teacher.

Ajji had seemed her usual suspicious self when Kalpana and Deeksha left the house with their hands full of things, and some stuffed in a cloth bag. The girls didn't ask her to come to the concert. They knew that Gangamma's voice would reach the threshold of their house, where Ajji sat muttering her prayers, as if she was scolding the mountains.

They cleaned the shrine and swept away the leaves on the ground where they would sit. Kalpana wanted Gangamma to sit on a raised platform, but they could only find a broken log nearby. The three of them dragged and rolled the log over, wiped it clean and put some flowers around it. Kumari looked at it with a worried frown. She asked, 'Can Gangamma Ajji sit on it? She might fall.'

Deeksha giggled. 'And roll away like the log.'

Kumari added, 'Roll away like the sound she makes.'

But they did not let that worry stop their preparation. Their temple and the ground around it were now ready for the next day. Many children would come, they would listen to their music teacher and eat the sweet jaggery balls that Kalpana's mother had prepared. Kalpana knew that they would all stare at her after the event, wondering when she would start speaking.

They sat under the tree, wanting to enjoy the sight of their shrine and the clean ground. The sun shone, and countless ants, beetles and other tiny insects, seen and unseen, went here and there, as if they were the girls' friends. And when three dogs came jogging and sat lazily on the ground, resting their faces on the earth, there was total peace. The three girls spontaneously held each other's hands and sat in silence.

Kumari broke the silence. She said, 'I was thinking so much about what Gangamma Ajji said yesterday. I didn't understand much, but ...'

Deeksha nodded. 'I was telling Akka the same thing. How are words a tool for searching for the gods?'

She remembered what Kalpana had tried to teach her through drawing. They had sat together at night, in the surprising presence of the moonlight that shone through the window. Kalpana had refused to have the light on while she drew on the slate with white chalk. It was as if she was trying to say that not only are sounds hidden here and there, but also light, which lay hidden inside pieces of chalk.

She had drawn an arrow from the word 'mara' to a tree, to suggest that the word attached itself to the tree that it stood for. Then she wrote the word 'Ganesha' and drew an arrow. She looked at it for a moment and then drew a question mark at the end of the arrow.

Deeksha said, 'Yes, I see now. We hear the word "Devi", but our eyes keep searching for the Devi.'

Kalpana had understood what Gangamma was trying to say. She clearly understood that words, many words, had no place to stop, no end, no resting place. Words for gods went travelling in perpetual search of something, without even knowing if that thing was there. Gangamma was trying to communicate only this: god is not an individual but a process, a constant search through sounds. Kalpana realised she would have to find a way to enter the world of sounds that she had run away from.

THE DAY OF THE FESTIVAL DAWNED BRIGHT AND SUNNY. Not a single cloud in the sky. It was a day that would have made even the dogs stretch and walk on two legs, their forelegs paddling in the air. The morning had announced its arrival, while the sky was still dark, through the loud music from the village temple. As the sun rose, stray sounds of crackers started echoing around the mountains, like bonsai bombs going off deep inside the forest.

Ajji was up and bathed by the time Deeksha dragged herself up. Then, remembering that it was Deepavali, she jumped up and shook Kalpana awake. Every year, for the festival, they would wear new clothes, have a feast, and in the evening, go to the village grounds for a yakshagana performance. This year would be even more special. They had their own temple festival to start the day with.

By ten, attired in their still starchy dresses, the two girls stood outside their shrine. They had eaten idlis for breakfast and their mouths were filled with a sticky sweet. They had brought fresh flowers, which they distributed on and around their idol. Deeksha had wanted Kalpana to wear something on her dress to indicate her role as a priest. Kalpana vehemently shook her head in refusal. She had decided that she would not do anything that would draw attention to herself. The only exception that she allowed herself was to wear flowers in her hair. Her mother had said, 'You look so pretty,' her voice communicating her hope that Kalpana would speak the following day. Earlier, Deeksha had said that before Gangamma sang, they should say something about their temple. Kalpana had responded by scribbling, *You and Kumari can do it.*

Kumari came soon after, almost running when she saw the two girls. She too was dressed in new clothes. Her mother had pinned a rose, one that had surprisingly flowered that morning in their backyard, in her oiled hair. Kumari walked with waves of perfume leading the way, the silken smell of rose mixed with that of fresh coconut oil. She too had brought a special gift for their idol: a few cashews.

She said apologetically, 'My father had got some from the factory, and my mother gave me a few to eat because it is the festival today. But I want to give them to our brain god.' She placed the cashews before the mossy green-and-grey idol. Deeksha looked at the nuts, wondering if she could eat a couple. Kalpana smiled and picked up the cashews, leaving only one on the ground. She distributed the remaining among the three of them.

The first girls came by half past ten. They all looked as if they had been washed by the skies and dried by the golden sun. They were slightly self-conscious as they were all wearing new dresses. There were many envious glances at each other's dresses, but nobody said anything. They looked at the ground and at the log where Gangamma would sit.

Deeksha announced in what she thought was an official voice, 'You will sit in front of the temple. Our singer will sit on the log.'

The girls, almost as one, refused. They would not sit on the ground in their new clothes. While they were still arguing, Kalpana saw Gangamma at a distance. The three girls moved quickly towards her. From another part of the ground, Kumari's mother was also approaching. Surprisingly, the science teacher was with her. Kumari ran towards them.

When Gangamma came closer to the group of girls, they fell silent. Deeksha was excited to have the adults visiting their temple. She showed the three women the idol of the brain and bravely said, avoiding Kumari's mother's eyes, 'This is our new god, the brain god. She is a female god. And she will only have a female priest.' She pointed to Kalpana with a flourish.

If the other girls had any doubts about the two sisters being mentally sound, they vanished. Kalpana as a priest! A couple of them giggled, and Kumari stared at them.

Kumari's mother was extremely surprised. She had never thought that the school would allow students to build a temple, and that too for a brain! She had heard of special efforts to teach science and thought perhaps this was one such. The science teacher was equally nonplussed. But the two women couldn't help but admire the shrine, the flowers, and the neatness of it all. It was not difficult for them to imagine this as a temple, even though they would never be able to see Kalpana as a priest.

Kalpana's mother had by then walked over. Ajji sat near the main door of the house, staring at the crowd under the tree.

There were now more than twenty children standing around. The girls were ready to start the programme.

Deeksha stood in front of the crowd and said, 'Today we are celebrating Deepavali in our own temple. This is a temple meant for girls and it is the temple of the brain. The brain,' she said, looking at the science teacher, 'is what makes us good students, as our teacher taught us, and so we have built a temple for it.'

A few girls clapped hesitantly at first, but on seeing Gangamma's smile, all of them clapped vigorously.

Deeksha continued, 'Every temple has a special programme for Deepavali. So we too wanted to have one. We asked our music teacher to sing for us today.' She looked shyly at Gangamma.

Again, the girls clapped. Gangamma placed her hand on Deeksha's head and smiled at all of them. There were girls in that crowd who would avoid looking at her on the street. She turned to Deeksha and asked, 'Should I stand and sing? Should they stand and listen?'

Kumari stepped forward and pointed to the log. 'That is our stage, Ajji.' Gangamma looked at the log and the wide-eyed group of girls staring at her in expectation. Nothing would make her sit on that piece of rotting wood.

She pushed the log aside and sat on the ground. All the girls in their new dresses stared down at her.

Gangamma had little patience. 'All of you sit in front of me,' she said loudly. The girls scrambled to find a place to sit. The teacher and the two mothers sat behind the girls.

Gangamma sat in silence, staring at them. A cow came ambling towards the shrine and Kalpana chased it away. Some adults could be seen standing on the main road, looking curiously at the crowd of children.

Gangamma was true to her word. She did not sing the songs she usually did. She started her performance by talking. Kalpana, Deeksha and Kumari sat right in front of her.

Gangamma began, 'These three girls have created this temple for the brain. When I heard about it, I thought, why a temple for the brain? All of us have brains. So why build a temple for it? I am too old to understand these little girls, but I slowly learnt that the brain is like a god and is present in each one of us. It is inside, hidden, but we know it is there. Initially, I was also not happy when they called it a temple. I thought they should have called it a school. But then I thought again, and I knew that they were right—our temples should have been schools, to teach all of us, without prejudice, to become better human beings.'

The students stared back at her silently. They knew that schools were not the same as temples.

Gangamma, oblivious to how she had become yet another teacher, continued, 'The girls wanted me to sing something special, something befitting the brain. They did not want me to sing the songs I usually do. They asked me to sing using numbers and not words. How can we sing numbers? I did not know how to do it, but then I realised that numbers are also words. The more I thought about numbers, the easier I found it to sing them. These three girls have been my teachers.'

Two of the girls from Deeksha's class started giggling, imagining Deeksha as a teacher.

Gangamma sang. She began with the first word: 'one'. 'Ondhu' in Kannada. She sang the word, stretched, bent, contorted, bounced, fragmented it and brought it back into one. The girls were transfixed and forgot that the song was only about a number.

Listening to Gangamma, Kumari once again promised herself that she would become a singer and nothing but that. Deeksha, sitting and holding hands with Kumari, decided that whatever happened, she would help make Kumari a singer like Gangamma. Kalpana sat in peace, feeling a sense of happiness that had long eluded her. The intense conflict within her, the words wanting to burst out of her, seemed to have subsided. Listening to Gangamma, watching the little lamps flicker in front of the brain idol, sensing all the girls behind her, she decided that even if she wouldn't speak, she would try singing. Gangamma had changed the very sound of ondhu, and to Kalpana, the many sounds she created out of this word seemed to have so many different meanings. It catalysed within her images of a river, of mountains, and of a rope stretched from one mountain to another. A single word, when sung, could do so much! She was truly surprised. She felt a sudden need to hold the other two girls. It was as if the song was creating vibrations in her body that could only be stilled by the vibrating bodies of Deeksha and Kumari.

After the song on ondhu, Gangamma sang a song about the brain. She had composed what she thought was a funny little song on the prowess of the brain. She sang it like a lullaby, with a lot of nonsensical words thrown in between. The girls laughed, visualising her description of the brain as an old woman, a rubber ball, a schoolteacher, a bus driver and so on. The girls were very impressed—the brain was indeed a god! That image was reinforced when they all got a delicious sweet at the end of the performance.

Some of the girls, not sure of what they should do, went around the shrine three times. Some others bowed before it before they dispersed. The two mothers walked towards Kalpana's house. The science teacher told them how impressed she was with their idea and said that she would discuss the brain in the next class.

Gangamma stood with the three girls around her, each holding on to the other like they were one circular organism. Gangamma did not need to be told what they felt. She could see it on their faces.

Kumari declared in front of the shrine, 'I want to sing like you, Ajji. I will come and learn every day from you.'

Gangamma laughed and said, 'No, no, not every day. I will become very tired answering all your questions.'

Gangamma was to go to the neighbouring village for lunch. Before leaving, she said, 'I really like your god. But remember, singing is as hard as learning about numbers. I will see you in class the day after tomorrow.'

She walked away slowly, the three girls staring at her oscillating back, leaving behind multiple imprints of the sound of ondhu on the mud, sand, rocks and trees around the shrine. Even the ants, beetles and other insects were anointed with the aural lines of ondhu, like the three lines on the squirrel's back.

THERE WAS A GREAT SENSE OF EXPECTATION IN THE village about the yakshagana performance in the evening. Most yakshagana troupes did not perform during the rainy season, but this troupe had made an exception for Deepavali. The performers would normally go on for hours into the night, but because of the rains, the organisers had decided to start at seven and end around ten. There would be a puja in the temple before the performance started.

The ground adjoining the village temple was cleaned up. The performers were preparing themselves, painting their faces, putting on their costumes, and warming their voices and bodies. There was a steady stream of people. They would go to the shrine, offer their worship, and then move to the ground. There were rows of chairs, and lights strung on poles placed a few metres apart.

Kumari came to Deeksha's house, accompanied by her mother. The two girls set off with their mothers for the performance. Kalpana decided to stay back. She wanted to avoid being stared at and could not bear the unspoken expectation of friends and strangers. She would listen to the songs from her room. She had always enjoyed listening to the sounds that gently flowed in the night from many distant places. Little villages that were just yellow pinpricks in the mountains would send waves of music in the silence of the night. Unfortunately, Ajji too had decided she wouldn't go. She settled down in the doorway, staring in the direction of the temple, in a posture that suggested she could make out the individual dialogues of the actors on the stage. She sat like a guard, as if Kalpana was waiting to run away into the night.

There was another reason Kalpana did not go. She felt a great change in herself after Gangamma's performance. She recognised that she had come to a defining point in her refusal to speak. Her anger against language had subsided and she herself was not clear why she should not speak again. But she was sure that she would not speak the next day. She would not give the village gossips that satisfaction. She decided that the first sounds she made would be in Gangamma's class. That would be her payment to her teacher, to the person who had changed the lives of the three girls.

Deeksha and Kumari sat together with a couple of girls from their class. Deeksha's father sat with a group of men, while the two mothers sat with other women in a circle. The performance started, the night grew darker, more dogs and cows came to watch, sniff and munch, and the music and dialogue came out blaring and jarring from the speakers. Bored, Kumari and Deeksha moved towards the line of vendors, with their little carts, who had set up shop behind the audience. Deeksha took some money from her father and went to the old, creaky popcorn machine on a cart powered by a smelly, noisy generator.

Kumari and Deeksha bought two packets of popcorn, hot, and burnt in parts. They sat behind the chairs, away from the noise of the popcorn machine, in silent bliss, munching their popcorn. They looked at the sky, and even as they watched, black clouds rolled in urgently from the brooding mountains. The stage was very brightly lit and a scene in the story was being enacted with great energy. The two of them felt a wonderful sense of freedom, being out of the house so late at night and sitting by themselves.

Deeksha's mother came in search of them to take them back to the house. She wanted to go back home. Half her mind had been on Kalpana and on having left her back in the house. She could also not stop thinking of the possibility that Kalpana would begin speaking the next day. The women with whom she sat had been so excited by this 'news' and spoke as if it had already happened. Listening to them, Kalpana's mother had a sudden doubt, one that began gnawing inside her stomach, making her feel as if her stomach was full of bile. What if Kalpana did not speak the next day? She did not even want to think of it. She would rather be told that Kalpana would remain dumb than to live in constant hope that she would speak someday.

Deeksha and Kumari were so enjoying sitting by themselves under the night sky that they told her they would return later with Deeksha's father, who was watching the show intently with his group of friends. Mother looked at the growing clouds and told them to reach home before the rain began. She went up to her husband and reminded him not to forget to bring the girls back when he left. He waved out his answer to her without missing a beat of the action.

When she reached home, she found Ajji sitting across the doorstep. As she went nearer, Ajji said, 'Why didn't you stay for the end?' Mother muttered that she was tired and went inside. Kalpana was lying on her mat and scribbling in her notebook. She saw her mother peep into her room, but ignored her. Not knowing what else to say, Mother said, 'Deeksha will come later with your father. I am going to sleep.'

SOMETIME AFTER NINE, WHEN THERE WAS STILL SOME time for the show to finish, Deeksha and Kumari went towards another cart that was selling cut cucumbers spiced with salt and chilli powder. They bought one small cucumber each and moved away from the bright carts. On the stage, the main actor who was playing the role of the god Rama was miming a song. The singer sat behind the actors, and his already powerful voice was amplified by the mic. Deeksha and Kumari moved towards the edge of the crowd and stood near a speaker at the back of the grounds. Suddenly, the song caught their attention and Kumari said excitedly, 'See, that is the note that Gangamma Ajji tells us to get. He is singing like her.'

The two of them moved closer to the speaker, as if the sounds were being produced by the black box. The sounds from it reverberated around them, and they immersed themselves in it. When it became too loud to bear, they moved away, but the thousands of notes and sounds buzzed inside their ears, filled their mouths and noses and heads. They giggled, and as they walked away, the first sound of far-off thunder greeted them. Deeksha looked up, as if she was seeking out the place where the sound of thunder was created, and said, 'Look, can you hear that other note, the flat sound, as if two things are being slapped against each other?'

Kumari acted as if she were jumping up to reach the clouds and added with a giggle, 'Now see me catch that sound of a little girl whose voice is present in the middle of the thunder.'

So saying, she ran into the surrounding bushes, and Deeksha followed her, shouting, 'And hear the song in the wind blowing through the tree.'

But Kumari had moved towards another tree. Pointing to the hidden birds in the darkness, she squealed, 'And the birds that sing better than you and me. They should be Gangamma Ajji's students instead of us.'

Even before the first rain of the night came down, the two girls were enveloped by sounds that reverberated and filled them from all sides. From left and right, up and below, from the clouds, from the hot, molten rocks deep down in the earth, from leaves that had been woken up from their sleep, and birds who suddenly discovered their lost voices to sing for these two little children. The night became a bright world filled with numerous tinkling sounds that merged with the delighted laughter of Deeksha and Kumari. They rushed in search of these new sounds, which appeared and disappeared before their eyes. And in this bright, burning cacophony of sounds, they heard a note, a single, clear voice that called out to them like a steady lamp in a world of darkness. Delighted, they rushed towards the sound, Deeksha leading the way, trampling through bushes and pushing aside branches, and Kumari limping and skipping bravely behind her. They had no sense of time in a world where each sound was nothing but a sound of time, and when they reached the spring of that one clear sound, they felt that they had at last experienced the true meaning of music.

It was at that moment that the whole mass of heavy clouds stretching from one mountain range to another collapsed under its own weight. It was not just another spell of rain, another monsoon shower, but a ferocious bolt of sound and rushing water, as if the night sky was a dam that had suddenly broken. All the sounds around Deeksha and Kumari vanished in the ferocity of the rain. The water woke them from their dream world, and it was just a matter of seconds before they realised that they were in the middle of darkness, where the shapes of the trees looked like creatures in a comic book. They rushed to stand under a broad tree and held each other's hand tightly.

The show was coming to its climax, to the final scene where Ravana is killed by Rama. Deeksha's father and his friends would have watched till the end even if they had to sit through the rain, which was threatening to fall anytime now. He looked around for the two girls and did not see them. So he got up and went around the patient crowd which continued to sit, knowing well that the rain was just waiting to drench them in a matter of minutes. By the time he moved towards the back of the audience, heavy drops of rain were falling, and he saw that some women and children had taken shelter inside the temple already. He looked around and still could not see the two girls. He went back to his friends, relieved that the girls had either gone home or were inside the temple already. The climax of the performance coincided with the ferocious sound of the rain. Father and his friends were completely drenched, but felt that the rain was befitting of the performance. They agreed that it was one of the best shows they had seen. On his way out, Father peeped into the temple, but did not see the girls. He walked home, singing in the rain, feeling like a teenager, thinking of the days when he and his friends used to follow the famous yakshagana troupes like they followed the progress of the rain across the different regions. Rain, he knew well, was not just regeneration—it was birth and rebirth at the same time.

He reached home soaked and found the door shut but unlocked. His mother was asleep in her corner. He went directly to the bathroom, washed himself and entered the bedroom with a towel wrapped around his waist. He was still whistling, although very softly, the last song he had heard. The climactic, resonant song of Rama defining the nature of truth and morality. How charged up he was after listening to it! He changed and lay down on the cot next to his wife. The current was off, the rain was hammering down on the house, and he truly felt at peace.

He dozed off till a particularly loud thunderbolt woke him. He looked out of the window. His wife too woke up. She saw her husband and said, 'Hope you dropped Kumari home before the rain.'

He just looked at her, thinking she was mumbling something. Then her question struck him. 'No, I thought she came with you and Deeksha.'

Mother sat up instantly. 'Didn't Deeksha come with you?'

He got up immediately and went to the adjoining room, where the girls slept. He thought he saw two shapes lying on the mat, but when he went into the room, he found only Kalpana. Mother came in, carrying a torch. In a panic, she swung the light across the room, as if Deeksha could be sleeping under the window or the almirah.

Kalpana woke and looked up groggily to see her parents towering over her. 'Where is Deeksha?' her mother asked, her voice on the verge of breaking. Kalpana looked at Deeksha's mat and saw that it was empty. Before she could respond, Father ran out of the room with Mother following him. Kalpana heard him ask Ajji about Deeksha and could imagine her answer. Mother and Father ran out of the house without an umbrella and with only the torch for assistance.

The temple was closed, but two of the actors were in the temple hall. They had packed their gear and were waiting for the rain to subside before they drove away. They saw a man rush into the temple, a woman following him. When they heard that they were looking for two children, they joined them in the search around the temple. The ground was wet and slushy, and the chairs were scattered about in a disorderly manner. There was not a single light, or person, to be seen. Not another person to hear their loud shouts. The darkness of the surroundings was punctuated by the constant roar of water falling and flowing.

Mother started crying, and then wailing. Father took her into the temple and pulled out his wet phone to call his friends. He told his wife that perhaps Deeksha was staying at Kumari's house. Then he got his wife to sit on the motorbike belonging to the actors and took her home. Ajji took one look at her and started wailing. Kalpana came running out and Father told her quite calmly, 'Take care of your mother. Deeksha is not in the temple.'

He raced the bike to Kumari's house. The place was completely dark. When he banged on the door, Kumari's father appeared. 'Deeksha here?' Father asked. The other man stared at him mutely. His wife came out and, hearing the question, told her husband, 'He is Deeksha's father.' And to him, she said, 'No, we thought Kumari was staying with Deeksha at your house tonight because it got so late.'

Kumari's father burst out in anger. 'These girls, all the time playing their games.' And then the enormity of what had happened hit them both. He asked Deeksha's father, 'The girls are not at your house?' Father shook his head. Kumari's father, with growing anger, shouted at his wife, 'I told you not to let her do what she wants.' To Deeksha's father, he said, 'They must be caught in the rain and standing under some shelter somewhere. We will find them soon.' He changed into shorts, joined Deeksha's father on the bike, and they roared away towards the temple.

DEEKSHA AND KUMARI WERE STANDING UNDER THE TREE, fully wet, but feeling warm and muggy. They were both in a state of excitement. The night had not yet become fearful. They were still in the aftermath of their experience with the sounds. Their eyes and minds had opened to such an extent that they were looking all around them with interest and wonder. It was their first time in a forbidden world—in the dark night, alone, and among trees so dense that it seemed there were thick walls just some distance away. As soon as they felt the rain decreasing, they started walking back in the direction they thought they had come from.

They knew they were lost after more than half an hour of walking. The rain hadn't reduced, and they were not only getting tired but also beginning to hear sounds that did not sound like music. Kumari's legs were feeling sore and she wanted to sit. They searched for a stone under a tree, on which to sit. They found a stout log and settled down on it. A few minutes later, a sudden rush of water came surging down the path. The log started bobbing, and the girls panicked, trying to hold on to it. It started moving slowly downstream, as if the meandering mud paths had become yet another aimless riverine. Abruptly, a powerful flow of water came rushing down the path, and before they knew it, they were swept along with the log, deeper into the forest. After some time, the log came to rest on the ground, and the rain abated. They let go of the log, totally wet, and walked to a tree nearby to sit under it. The forest seemed to be filled with a hazy light. The first dawn of fear came when they heard the howling of an animal, even as the rain trickled down to just occasional drops of water. That single sound made them imagine animals and snakes around them. Kumari started crying. Deeksha sat down next to her, put her arm around her shoulders, and said, 'Don't worry.' She was silent for a moment and then said confidently, 'Don't worry. Kalpana will find us.'

KALPANA WAS CLEAR ABOUT HER COURSE OF ACTION. FATHER had come racing home on the motorbike with Kumari's father. He had told them they were going to search for the girls and left. But, by then, Kalpana knew that Deeksha and Kumari were lost in the forest. She very clearly knew that they had got lost just like her, running behind words and sounds. She also thought she could guess where they might be. She did not want them to undergo what she had, lost in the forest for three days in the rain. Her mother was in a state of shock and Ajji had gone back to her prayers, staring out of the main door. Kalpana went to the storeroom and picked up her school bag. She removed the notebooks from it, went to the kitchen and filled two bottles of water, and put them in her bag. She emptied all the sweet jaggery balls her mother had made for the festival into a plastic bag and dumped that into the bag too. In a tin drum, partly hidden on the kitchen shelf, there was a biscuit packet, biscuits that were given out like rations to the two girls and to Ajji. She dropped that too into her school bag and went back to her room. She picked up two raincoats made from sheets of plastic. In her mother's room, she stood on a stool and grabbed another similar raincoat, which belonged to her mother. She then went to her mother, who was lying on the bed. Mother's crying was more pitiful now. 'Not them also,' she kept moaning.

Kalpana held her tightly. She put her mouth close to her ear and whispered clearly, 'Don't worry. I will bring them back. I know where they will be, even if they are lost.' Her words felt odd to her own ears. It sounded like somebody else's voice. She felt very calm. She wanted to tell her mother more. Much more. That she knew the forest, and the forest must now be scared of her.

Mother was so shocked to hear the forgotten voice of Kalpana that she sat up and said loudly, 'You can speak. You can speak.'

Kalpana pushed her back down. 'Now, please be calm. I will get them back. Don't worry.' She smiled as if she knew the exact course of the future. In the darkness, she looked like yet another smiling idol.

Before Mother could say anything, she put on the raincoat, ran to the hall, and slipped on her canvas school shoes from the corner shoe rack. Before Ajji could turn from her vigilance directed to the mountains, she had slipped lightly past her and into the rain. She heard Ajji shout her name.

She stopped. She turned back and looked at Ajji. How frail she looked, standing in the rain, getting wet and staring into the unforgiving darkness all around her. She turned away and was about to run, but changed her mind and ran back to Ajji.

She stood in front of her and smiled. She spoke clearly, as if she had never stopped speaking. 'Ajji, I know where words go. I followed your prayers and I know where they went. I know where your gods hide. Don't worry, I will get the the girls back.' She reached out, touched Ajji's withered hands and ran away before Ajji could utter a sound.

Kalpana did not go to the temple. If, as she thought, Deeksha and Kumari had followed the sounds and words and gone into the forest, there were only certain paths that they could have taken. She closed her eyes, standing in the rain, at the edge of her village, a tiny figure dwarfed not just by the silhouetted mountains but also by the sheets of rain all around, and thought of the moment when she had run into the forest. Of the words of the prayers that she followed, words like butterflies fluttering around her, which had led her into the forest. She imagined herself on that day and saw clearly where she should enter the forest from. She composed herself, looked bravely into the dark forest through the pounding rain and stepped on to the path that she knew would lead to Deeksha and Kumari.

She walked for a few minutes, feeling a sudden sense of liberation. All the fear that had consumed her in the forest had vanished. She walked some distance. The rain had lessened, and even in the darkness she could begin to see shapes. She saw a small mound and climbed on it. She stood on top and shouted as loudly as she could: 'Deeksha! Kumari!' The rain seemed to quieten down, as if letting Kalpana's words resonate without any obstacles.

Kalpana shouted, 'I am here. I am Kalpana. I will find you. Do not be scared. Do not be scared.'

In the sudden stillness, she shouted again, 'There is nothing to fear. Listen to all the sounds. Listen to them and sing what we learnt in class. No animal will come near you. Listen to the words from the trees, the rain, the birds and the snakes. They are talking to you. They want to talk to you. They only want you to listen to them. Listen and sing. Nothing will happen to you.'

So saying, she scrambled down the mound and ran inside the dark forest, along paths she created with the lightness of her feet. Every few minutes, she would shout the names of Deeksha and Kumari, and sing all the songs she had wanted to but hadn't in Gangamma's class. She made up for all the music lessons, her bottled-up comments in school to her teachers, the principal and other students, and ran joyously, with abandon, skipping and shouting through the forest.

BEFORE DAWN, THERE WAS A CROWD ON THE GHAT ROAD. This was where Kalpana had come out of the forest the first time she had gone missing. Through the night, the news had spread in the village. Now it was three girls who were missing. Stories of Kalpana speaking had also spread, and each time somebody recounted it, the story had magnified. Kumari's mother was in shock, and her father still angry. He was sure that the girls were just lost or playing a game of hide-and-seek. Deeksha's mother was broken, although she held on to the hope that she had felt when Kalpana spoke to her. Her husband was totally lost, seemingly most upset by Kalpana's decision to speak. He had imagined all kinds of problems and solutions, but it seemed as if Kalpana had wilfully put them through all that suffering. He couldn't understand why his own child would do that, and that feeling created a terrible void within him. It was worse than any betrayal he had felt before. Ajji refused to enter the house and stood waiting on the main road. Nobody could force her to go back home.

Early next morning, seeing that Ajji was not going to move, Babu and his friends put up a bamboo shelter under which she could sit. They quickly constructed a thatched roof, and Ajji sat inside, waiting and watching for the three girls to get off a bus or emerge from the forest, waving to her.

Kumari's father led a group of people into the surrounding forest area near the temple grounds. They were hearty men carrying sickles and knives, and walked around shouting the girls' names.

Kalpana's father did the same with another group of young men in a different spot.

Everyone knew it was just a matter of time. *Unlike the previous instance,* each of them thought.

Dawn broke and the sun rose in all its cheery vigour. Roosters woke their voices lazily. Siddaiah stood around with a few young friends, staring at the muggy forest and periodically calling out the girls' names.

By afternoon, they were talking about the days to come. They started talking about 'the last time', when Kalpana was lost for three days. Slowly, they began to feel that they would have to wait for three days, as if the girls were part of some cosmic pattern. They decided to take turns standing by the highway till the girls came out of the forest.

The two fathers had no luck either. They did go quite some distance through the slush and the broken and rotting trees, but they had no way of knowing where to even go. They made noises that would have driven tigers away, but not a squeak from the girls did they hear in return.

The school principal came along with her peon trailing behind. She visited both the houses and left traces of her disappointment with the girls. 'In spite of all that I tried to do,' she told the two silent, scared and grieving mothers.

Gangamma came back to her house from the neighbouring village. She had heard the news in the morning and had rushed back. She went straight to Kalpana's house. Kalpana's mother started sobbing when she saw her and went on saying, 'Kalpana spoke to me before she left in search of the other two.'

Gangamma held her tightly and whispered repeatedly, 'I know these girls. Nothing can harm them. They are braver and better than all of us.'

Gangamma then went to Kumari's house. Kumari's father was sitting outside with a few men. She went in and met Kumari's mother, who was sitting on the floor, inside the hall, surrounded by women. She went and sat next to her. Kumari's mother reached out to touch her. Gangamma told the crowd of women, 'Kumari is not an ordinary girl. None of those three girls is ordinary. They will come back. You will see.' All of them stared passively back at her.

The third day was a day of great expectations. The temple had organised a special puja. School had not yet started, given the magnitude of the disappearance. Children hung around outside their houses, all of them scanning the horizon for the three girls.

Men went in batches into the jungle and came back with not a clue.

Siddaiah and his friends waited with a bigger crowd on the third night. When dawn broke, they were ready. Ready to shout and cheer. The batteries in their phones were all charged and ready to spread the message immediately.

Ajji sat in her makeshift shelter in the sun and the rain. She refused to leave or eat anything till the girls came back. People who saw her said, 'She is ready to die. She is just waiting for the girls to come back.'

Gangamma spent all her time in her backyard overlooking the edge of the jungle. In the evening, she stood there and sang to the forest. She sang for hours in the darkness, hoping her songs were a rope by which the girls would find their way back. She sang with hope, with fear, and with growing desperation.

They all waited, watched and hoped.

Sunny days became rainy nights and rainy days became sultry nights. Policemen went in and forest guards came out. And still there was no sight of the three girls.

No sight of three little girls walking majestically down the main road of the village, a limping, polio-afflicted girl in the middle. The three of them, walking to a rhythm, listening to music that only they can hear, smiling so brightly that the sun pushes aside the clouds in envy, for a chance to be reflected off their faces.

No sight of three brave little girls, who had vanquished tigers and king cobras, who had swept aside rotting trees and insidious creepers, majestically stepping out from the foliage with a song on their lips and pure notes of unheard sounds rising from their souls.

They all sat and waited. And waited.